QU
OF THE DAY

QUESTION OF THE DAY:
THE ANDRE POLK
MEMORIAL ANTHOLOGY

EDITED BY

J. J. CLAYBORN
& T. L. EVANS

Question of the Day: The Andre Polk Memorial Anthology
Copyright 2015-2017, Various Authors
Cover Design: Josh Hayes
Cover Image Credit: Josh Hayes, Copyright Josh Hayes, 2017
Published by Clayborn Press, Phoenix, AZ
IBSN: 978- 1549741364

Printed in the United States of America.
10 9 8 7 6 5 4 3 2 1

This Edition published in September, 2017 by Clayborn Press, LLC

CLAYbORN
pRESS

Special thanks to:

All of the authors who have donated their works in Andre's memory. Andre may be gone from this world in the flesh, but his legacy lives on in each of us.

Dedication

This book is dedicated to the memory of our friend and colleague, Andre Polk, whose time came too quickly. Each and every one of us who contributed work to this volume knew Andre through a Facebook writer's group, *Space Opera: Writers*.

Andre was a bright person, in every sense of the word. He was intelligent; he was fun; he always made the group a more interesting place. Very often he would ask the group at large a "question of the day". Sometimes these questions would pertain to the technical mechanics of the trade-craft of writing and publishing, but often they were deep philosophical questions that really made you think. Andre excelled at that - making you think - making you question everything you thought you knew. It was one of the qualities that I admired most about him.

In the wake of his passing, the group has not been the same without him. Regrettably, he never had a chance to finish the novel he was writing before he died, but I have no doubt it would have been a fantastic book. He was always one of my favorite writers.

Andre fell ill suddenly and died unexpectedly due to complications of sickle cell disease. His unexpected loss was a shock that rocked our writing community. One minute he was posting from the hospital, then next he was gone. This book is dedicated to his memory. Inside these pages you will find contributions from 20 authors who knew Andre. This is our homage to our friend - our way of saying our goodbyes. All of the authors have donated their work to this book. All of the royalties that would go to the authors, and all of the monies typically collected by the publisher are being donated to Andre's family in his memory.

We sincerely hope that you enjoy reading this collection of stories in his memory. To pay respects we have prefaced each story with a question, a question that the story will seek to answer in the telling.

-J. J. Clayborn, Editor

Andre Polk was arguably, the most influential writer you may never get a chance to read. Throughout this volume, you will see how just a few of the Questions of the Day that he diligently put forward, influenced his friends and colleagues in the Space Opera: Writer's group. There were, however, many more which spanned every topic related to the group, and planted seeds of ideas that continue to grow.

Those questions ranged topics from hard science to philosophy, from general plot and thematic issues to technical topics about the craft of writing, and from how to best reach your audience to the influence technology has on our interactions. Each one was thought provoking and inspirational, yet to me, they were but a small part of what Andre represented to us. Indeed, his questions and his ever-positive attitude built something more out of a mere social media group; it built a community.

Andre had been posting his QOTD's for some time before he really entered my consciousness. Oh, I had read, and thought about, and even answered some of his Questions of the Day, but it was a different post that really made me pay attention to Andre as an individual. You see, up to that point, I was reasonably well published (primarily as both an academic writer and a ghost writer, though I did have one volume of my own out at that time), and while I enjoyed the posts in the Space Opera: Writer's group, I still viewed it as just another Facebook group. Then came Andre's other question, and it struck me like lightning.

Like many of us, Andre was working on a Space Opera novel (not surprisingly, considering the group we are talking about), and his initial vision for his work in progress was a grand scale, multiple perspective piece. As he wrote it, however, he began to fear that his scope was too large, his cast of characters was too big.

So, being Andre, he posted his concerns in the group. The responses were universally sympathetic consisted of a wide range of answers. Some suggested that he should write whatever he pleased, others suggested quick fixes, and still others suggested that a massive revision was needed.

Now, it was clear which answer Andre had wanted to be right. It was the same answer any writer would want: the one that resulted in the least work and kept most to his initial vision. We're only human after all. Yet, as was ever Andre, he did not just accept those responses that best suited the answer he desired. Instead, he sought clarification. He asked more questions.

These were not just simple questions, they were challenging ones. Questions that pushed back, not just at the answers he didn't want, but to all of them. Hard fixes, easy fixes, no fixes: he questioned them all. He sought understanding, not validation. He didn't want an answer that would make his life easier. He wanted an answer that would make his book better.

In the end, he chose the answer that created the hardest fix. He chose to combine characters, melding plot lines to make the story flow better. To make it read well. He sacrificed his "vision" in order to make a better novel, and as he did, he found he built better characters. More complex ones with greater depths, and he reveled in the improvements that his hard work brought. I knew at that moment that this was a writer I wanted to follow. This was a writer I wanted to help in the same way that others had helped me. This young man was smarter and more dedicated than some of the graduate students I had worked with in my years as an academic.

So, I started communicating with him, both in the Space Opera: Writers group and out. I grew to truly admire and enjoy every correspondence we had. More to the point, I grew to respect and admire him, and I learned at least as much from him as he ever learned from me. I knew then that, given half a chance, Andre Polk would be a great writer.

He was not given that half a chance. He died before completing that novel, before I had seen but glimpses of it. I cried. I still cry when I think of it, and not just because of the writing, but because of the man who was becoming a friend.

You see, what most anyone who knew Andre quickly realized was that he had a talent far greater than his writing: he brought people together. In an age where people's first response is to argue, Andre created a community out of a Facebook group. He did not create Space Opera: Writers, nor was he an admin or any sort of power behind the throne. He was just an honest, earnest member. A person who would always supported his friends and colleagues, both with insightful critiques and heartfelt support when one of us posted some personal strife or problem.

He made friends out of us all with his questions, and his ever-effervescent spirit. I cannot say how much I miss him. His every day diligence, his honest and well thought out posts, and, of course, his questions.

I never met Andre, but he inspired me. Not just to be a better writer, but to be a better person.

And to question. To question everything, and to do so with an open heart and open mind.

We miss you Andre. The group is not quite the same without you, but we are struggling to make it so. We are trying, each and every day, to make it something worthy of your memory.

- T. L. Evans, Editor

Andre Polk was among the first people to join *Space Opera: Writers* when the group was founded in 2014. We have added (and "culled") hundreds of members, but nobody has ever quite matched Andre's bursting-at-the-seams positive attitude. His enthusiasm for the craft of writing, his joy at manipulating plot and character, his questions about world-building and physics, were infectious, reminding us constantly with his *Question of the Day* threads why we began writing in the first place. To have Andre taken from us so quickly was bad enough, but it also left a space we will never be able to fill; the one that would have held his first novel. So, we do the only thing we can do, and what we know he would have appreciated: we turned the wildly talented and amazingly varied creative minds from the *Space Opera: Writers* group loose in his honor.

- Scott McGlasson, *Space Opera: Writers* Admin

Table of Contents

To Meet Others

Jeffrey Yorio

The mystery of why people intersect our lives is
unimportant.

You've touched us all, encouraging when we had
doubt.

Showing style, exemplifying grace,

As you sailed into the headwinds of our ultimate
fate.

Beauty abounds, your words, they astound

This family of friends,

Bold and straight forward, never condescending,

The patience of a mentor, the wisdom of a sage

I'm honored and glad to have had

The good fortune to learn from you.

Question of the Day: What would it be like to live as an AI construct?

In the Asking

Nathanial W. Cook

Dylan was the first to awaken. He imagined he yawned, but of course he couldn't really. He hadn't possessed a human body for centuries. Old habits really do take forever to die, he mused. He activated *Quest 48*'s battery of sensors and reached out with his mind.

What was out there, around them? Dylan probed in every direction, with every available spectrum, processing the data that bounced back to him with lightning speed. The result was the same as it had been the last ten dozen times he'd checked.

"Anything?" came a voice not his own. He recognized it in a moment as Nestor's. The flat, unenthusiastic tone with which he'd ask his question led Dylan to assume he already knew the answer.

"Nothing," Dylan said. "Zilch. Zippo. Nada. The opposite of ..."

"I think we get the picture," said another voice - Karin's, this time, the de facto captain of their ship. "Just to verify, you're sure?"

"The nearest stars are hundreds of light years off," Dylan snapped. "There's nothing else. Dark matter. Cold empty nothing. But, hey, feel free to run through the protocols yourself if you want. If there are any tests you can think of to try that I missed, be my guest."

Silence.

"No. I trust you," Karin said after a bit. "We ... we seem to have reached some barren part of space. I don't know. Maybe the universe doesn't go on forever?"

"And yet we're still going," said another member of their crew, Arjun this time. "I hate to be the one to ask, but somebody has to. Why?"

"The mission ..." Karin began.

"... seems like a complete and utter failure," said Nestor. "I mean, we've been keeping on like this for how long?"

"Then you're saying ..."

"I was just throwing it out there, Cap," Arjun said.

"... that we should end it?"

Again, silence.

"All right," said Karin, finally. "Wake them up. Anyone who's still with us. Nestor, you do it."

"Yes, ma'am," Nestor said, and he set about his

task.

He focused his consciousness and projected into the shielded core of the ship, where the mind drives were sequestered. Row after row of little black rectangles, each with a fourteen-digit serial number stenciled on one edge and a tiny light emitter in its upper right corner. Nestor scanned the drives. One hundred in all, most had gone dark and cold by now. Twelve, perhaps fifteen, still glowed with the dull blue light of artificial life.

Rise and shine, he thought, and then initiated Protocol One to bring them out of sleep mode.

The blue lights turned green and began to blink on and off, flickering faster and faster with each passing moment. It was working. The whole crew would be awake and aware soon. Nestor concentrated inwards again and let his essence flow upwards towards the top of the ship.

Once they had all assembled in the Upper Hub. Here, a Leander-Tuss array allowed them all to gather in one place, yet remain distinct from one another, almost like they were flesh-and-blood beings still, sitting around a large room.

"This is everyone? You double checked, just to be sure?" Karin said.

If Nestor has still had eyes, he would have rolled them. Instead, he answered simply, "Yes, ma'am."

Karin took it all in, read the room. "Not even twenty left of our original hundred. It seems morale took a dive a long time ago."

The Hub was dead silent for several long moments.

Finally, Kendrick, one of the newly reawakened

minds, spoke: "I take it from the, hmm, muted atmosphere 'round here that we didn't all get woken up because y'all found a new star system or galactic phenomenon to explore, right?"

"'Fraid not," Karin answered. "We seem to have found ourselves an endless expanse of nothing. A void. No light. No life. No fun."

"Shit," someone said.

"Who did the assessment?" someone else asked.

"Dylan did," the captain said. "And I trust him. But any and every one of you is welcome to run your own tests. Run 'em as many times as you like. I'm sure we'd all love it if one of you showed Dylan was wrong. But ...."

There was a buzzing among the assembled minds as they wondered what to do, what this could mean.

"May I ask a question?" It was Andre who'd spoken up. He was one of the older minds - imprinted long, long ago - but he often seemed younger at heart than the others: an old soul, as some used to say.

"Certainly," Karin said. "Questions are welcome."

"So just to get things clear here," said Andre, "you woke us to consider undergoing Real Death, right? Not just a few of us, though. We're talking about ending the mission?"

"That's right," Karin said. "It's not only up to me, though. Everyone has their say."

"Good," Arjun said. "I'm all for it. Let's end this now. I'm so damned tired of the endless emptiness."

"But why end it?" said Andre. "Why not just go back to sleep. For longer this time. We have to come out of this eventually?"

"You don't know that," Nestor said. "None of us does."

"None of us knows anything. After all these years," Arjun added.

Elena, one of the quieter minds, piped up: "Can't the ones who want out just shut off or whatever? Like with the ones before. We didn't commit mass suicide when they chose Real Death."

"This is different," Karin said. "We have to note in our logs that we've ended the mission. Decided to stop devoting resources towards searching. For posterity - in case anyone recovers our spacecraft someday. They'll know exactly what happened and won't have to try and puzzle it out for themselves."

"And we stop using resources we don't need to maintain the mind drives, sensors, and so on," Dylan added. "We'll basically become just another dead hunk of debris, hurtling through space."

All were silent for a time, and an air of finality seemed to pervade the Hub.

"All right," said Karin. "Are there any further questions? Or should we just have a vote?"

"Let's have the vote," said Nestor.

"No, wait," Andre said. "I have some more questions."

A few groans arose from the assembled, but the captain spoke over them. "Go ahead, Andre."

"Well, I just wonder how you guys can turn your backs on all the possibilities - say there's no more to be explored. Even if there is nothing out there, what about what's in here?"

"Inside the ship?" Arjun said. "I don't know about you, but I've poked around every inch of this rattletrap again and-"

"I mean, us, man. Each other."

"You don't think we know each other after all these years cooped up together?" said Nestor. "Really?"

"Okay, but let me ask you this: What would you want to see outside the ship, if it could be anything you desire? What's the greatest thing you could imagine us coming across? What's the most amazing thing you've ever seen in your life?"

Nobody answered, so Andre continued.

"Do you remember your life before you got imprinted into the mind drive? I do. But I know next to nothing about most of you. Perhaps I once did, but after so long and so much data, I can't recall. And if I did, after we have seen so much, I'd want to know how what we've experienced has changed what we remember and how we view it. Were you married? Did you have a family? What did you like to do? What did you feel was your greatest accomplishment? Did you have a favorite book? Or favorite movie?"

"Is ... is that something retro?" Kendrick asked.

"Maybe to you," Andre said. "But I remember and can tell you all about it. My point is, we have plenty to learn and think about, and sometimes that just keeps you busy, but sometimes it can keep you going and even make you think of some new ideas. Maybe while we're putting our minds together, we'll come out of this void and find something exciting. But, even if not, we can still learn from and maybe even inspire each other. That's my pitch, anyway. I say we don't quit yet."

"Thank you, Andre," Karin said. "If no one else has any questions or comments, I guess we can have our vote."

All agreed, and they proceeded to vote. Karin tallied and shared the results.

"Seven for ending the mission, eleven for continuing on. I guess it's settled then?"

Each crewmember assented in his or her own manner.

"Very well," said the captain. "Back to sleep for me, and I assume many of you. Good night and sweet dreams."

"Cap? I ... I think I'll be staying up a while and talking with Andre," Dylan said. "That is if he doesn't mind?"

"Me too," Kendrick said.

"Sure guys," said Andre, with what felt to their digital sensors like a smile. "I'd like nothing better. C'mon."

And so the *Quest 48* continued sailing through the unknown endless night, searching for knowledge and understanding of another kind.

Question of the day: What do you think cryosleep might be like if we ever get it working?

Hard Cycle

Cheryce Clayton

Too soon.

Adrian struggled to focus through the rhythmic pulses of his sleep pod as it cycled him awake. He didn't hurt; the light was a mild annoyance, and the telltale smell of dead nerve endings echoing burnt hair was missing.

Too soon, was the only thought he could hold onto as the process forced his body awake.

His shortest jump to date was days under a planetary year, and that had woken him with muscle cramps and the smell. It took two weeks from freeze to de-orbit, two months to clear in-system and start to accelerate, and eight to nine months to exit the Oort and start to pick up speed.

Twelve months to one of the Sansheren built weapons station that now encircled Earth system to discourage other aliens from raiding.

This trip was four plus years out and he signed up knowing that wake up would be a bitch in both directions.

Adrian, Telly, and Peter all signed on the blinking line knowing that nine years in dilation would pass while they slept, dropped supplies, and returned. Nine years in dilation and thirty-seven on the ground.

Only, he was waking up, without the normal atrophy and stimulation overload. Too soon.

In-system.

Had to be still in-system.

"Acknowledge," he tried to say to activate his command console, but his throat was still too thick from the sleep pod gases. He coughed, smelled plastic and heat. Pushed against the breaker bar. Heard the faint sound of sirens and shouting voices.

"Acknowledge," he forced out, coughing more than breathing, as he fought the fear that always lived inside him, never left no matter how many times he wrestled it silent.

"Seniority protocol aborted, please designate rank and priority," the computer answered.

And Adrian thought that the gravity spiked, for just a flash, as his entire life sank into his boots with his courage and purpose.

Forty-seven others crewed on the ship and Adrian and his two friends signed on for janitorial, most expendable, almost civilians. With no piece of the cargo investment, no incentive beyond a pay check and time off planet. No rank and no priority.

And then Adrian processed that the computer was asking him.

"Telly," he whispered. "Telly has kids," he said.

Peter was running from a bookie. No worse than Adrian jumping away from Earth and using the sleep cycle for rehab. Commercial rehabs charged twenty percent of a guy's base pay for half a decade to do what a contract jump did while paying you to sleep. Just took a year asleep to clean the opiates out of your brain and reset everything so you wake up clean and sober.

Too soon, Adrian realized again, even as he felt the tremors deep in his muscles.

"Seniority protocol aborted, please designate rank and priority," the computer repeated.

Adrian swallowed air, forced back the cough, and bit his lower lip hard enough to concentrate through the fear.

"Flight crew, Telly Rellena, myself, Peter Groduc," he said.

Forty-eight total crew on the roster and he needed the flight crew to pilot the beast.

The sound melted as the fear faded and Adrian felt himself sinking back into the sleep cycle.

* * *

Too soon.

Adrian struggled to focus through the rhythmic pulses of his sleep pod as it cycled him awake. He didn't hurt, the light was a mild annoyance, and the telltale smell of dead nerve endings echoing burnt hair was missing.

Too soon, was the only thought he could hold onto as the process forced his body awake.

Something was wrong. He struggled against the linger sleep to remember, to think.

Too soon.

He signed up knowing that wake up would be a bitch in both directions. Adrian, Telly, and Peter all signed on the blinking line knowing that nine years in dilation and thirty-seven on the ground would pass in exchange for enough money to not have to worry about money for a long time.

Still in-system. He realized that they had to be still in-system.

"Acknowledge," he whispered as the sounds of sirens and shouting voices crept into his awareness.

He was afraid, felt the fear growing, tried to get his mind running in a productive direction, even as a small part of his awareness screamed that something was wrong.

"Seniority protocol aborted, please designate rank and priority," the computer answered.

Every day dream and hero fantasy pushed against his fear, tried to dictate his response. Told him what to say and do in increasingly unhelpful flashes.

He wanted to scream Shut Up, wanted to shove the breaker bar in front of him and see what was happening outside of the pod, needed to focus.

There were forty-seven crew members above him in seniority and Adrian and his friends sitting low men on the pole.

The totem pole. He felt the fear collide with laughter and fought the panic that pushed at him. He wasn't invested in the mission, didn't have an incentive package. Just another NDN signing on to a scout ship to get first look at a new world.

But the computer was asking him to set the survival priority. Asking a janitor when it should have been asking the captain. Should have had the list carved into its programs back on Earth.

Shouldn't even bother to talk to him.

Telly was running from a woman and her kid, Peter owed some Russians money, and Adrian just wanted a shot at clearing the synthetic opiates from his brain without having to mortgage his future to a commercial rehab.

Cryosleep wasn't stoned, and the fear was eating him alive, building into tremors, and falling into flashes of pain and pressure. Made him feel like his whole world was exploding behind his eyes.

"Seniority protocol aborted, please designate rank and priority," the computer prompted.

Adrian felt a fatalistic calm as he said, "Flight crew, myself, Telly Rellena, Peter Groduc."

Forty-eight total crew on the roster and he needed the flight crew to pilot the beast.

Adrian felt the whispers of fear fade away as the sleep welcomed him back.

* * *

This isn't real, was his first thought as the system cycled him awake.

He couldn't put a finger on why he felt déjà vu,

but it overwhelmed him even as the computer demanded that he set the survival protocols for the ship's crew.

This isn't real, he repeated to himself as he told the computer to save the primary flight crew and then himself and fuck everyone else.

* * *

Each time the computer woke him it got harder to focus, the sleep claimed more of his life, he struggled to remember the last time.

Held onto the thought that things that happened at the edge of sleep rarely made it into long term memory. Fought the fear and panic and held onto the reality that it had happened before.

Tried to keep count, but lost track and restarted, and counted again.

* * *

Again.

Adrian struggled to focus through the rhythmic pulses of his sleep pod as it cycled him awake. He hurt, the light blinded him, and the smell of burnt hair and flesh made him gag against the cough that overwhelmed him.

This isn't real, was the only thought he could hold onto as the process forced his body awake.

But it was, he knew it was real, that the computer was waking him, demanding a survival protocol, and then putting him back to sleep over and over and over again.

Because his fingernails were now long, curled things that tore his suit leg and left crusts of blood where he had tried to clench his hands against the pain that enveloped him.

This trip was four plus years out and he had signed up knowing that wake up would be a bitch in both directions.

But four plus in one sleep was easy, just a day or two of pain on waking and then an honest job to do. Four years in dilation equaled eighteen and a half in real time and Adrian held onto the thought that the constant cycling had aged him, not that he was spending the trip more awake than asleep. Not that he was dying.

Cause that was his fear. That was all he could hold onto.

"Seniority protocol aborted, please designate rank and priority," the computer tortured him.

He had given up on thinking of who should live and who should die and just repeated himself "I want to live," again.

And waited for the sleep cycle to remove the pain for a while.

"Processing," the computer replied.

That was new, Adrian struggled to think even as the cycled pulled him under.

* * *

"I have a live one, Bay 27," a voice whispered passed the muted sounds of his sleep chamber cycling him awake.

And Adrian resisted the urge to stretch while the

pod was actively disengaging from his body.

Too soon, was his first thought, the atrophy and built up pod smells alerting him to something out of the ordinary.

And then the memories flooded him and he struggled to pull free of the pod, hit the breaker bar hard and sat up screaming before he realized it.

The fear and the addiction hit him hard and his whole body convulsed in zero g. with only the still-attached pod tubing holding him in place.

"Live one, Bay 45," a voice shouted and Adrian fought for control even as the room went dark.

* * *

He woke up screaming, every night on the slow trip back to earth.

Alone. In his bunk he woke up screaming, and the freight crew let him have the time he needed to orientate.

To realize that he wasn't on a doomed scout ship, drifting blind, and without enough power to fully initiate the sleep pods.

Wasn't the captive toy of a rogue AI playing Darwin games with the humans it was supposed to protect.

He woke up screaming, had coffee, and then sat, staring out the forward port, and tried to think of what he was going to say to Telly's kid and Peter's parents. Tried to understand why he was still alive when forty-three others were dead and the four other survivors were catatonic.

Question of the Day
* * *

He woke up screaming, again.

Question of the Day: What if interstellar
corporations acted like governments?

Oasis 433

R. T. Romero

Aramon IV, the fourth planet of a merciless red
giant, was an arid world. Without a moon to pull
tide, the planet's water infrequently appeared on the
surface only in scattered, fertile oases.

The leadership of the planet's rebellious settlers
saw no need for Aramon to pay the corporates their
fair share of the planet's profits. They staged an
insurrection planetwide, seizing militia armories in
defiance. It was insane of them to think they could
short-change an interstellar corporation with
impunity.

The assault on Oasis 433 was textbook until a
thunderous detonation bellowed in the staging area.
The platoon supply track had hit a mine, and the

heavy ammo sleds stopped coming.

Delta, the kinetic weapons squad, held the high ground. The lieutenant commed Bravo, Alpha and Charlie squads to pull back to Delta's position and entrench, to await resupply.

The locals had used local materials for building. Making their own adobe, using mud and a locally extruded fiber binding called plasmesh, they avoided expensive shipping costs and tariffs. Their mud brick buildings clustered around the oasis, downhill from Delta's position.

The insurgents began to shift from the defensive into an offensive posture. Delta's two heavy autocannons and four man-portable rockets had been chewing through their buildings, bringing the plasmesh-reinforced adobe down around them.

There were no more rockets, so Corporal Nathan Evens stowed his empty launcher and unlimbered his pulse carbine, intending to settle into the defile of a shallow trench he had hastily dug into the hillside, just beneath Delta's rotary cannon position. He soon saw he had no targets, but the two gunners were exposed and still too busy to entrench.

Nathan was thankful that his photo-ablative armor was light. The joints were well designed and didn't bind when he used his trenching tool to carve his shallow ditch in the dry earth of the ridge. The ground provides better protection than metal against coherent light weapons, with the bonus that nobody had to carry it around. Nathan was smaller than most, but he dug fast and deep. When he finished his own trench, fronted by the dirt he had shaved from the slope, he moved uphill to dig for the heavy ballistics team. They were keeping the locals suppressed. Their heavy armor, powered though it was, impeded their range of motion and ability to dig.

As he shaved dirt, Nathan heard the LT talking fast into the midrange radio arguing for priority, just before the rotary cannon right over Nathan's head ripped off a short burst. It made his ears ring.

The power-armored sergeant who fired cursed under breath. Her voice was female. On her chest piece was stenciled the name 'McKenna'. Shelly McKenna had always laughed with him when he joked, and she seemed to like him. Nathan looked downhill toward her target.

The locals had a dozer blade set onto a wheeled cart, and they were pushing it toward the hill from the battle-scarred adobe settlement. The ground beneath the blade was too soft to ricochet 20mm rounds into the legs of those pushing it, but it was also too soft to support the cart's wheels. They weren't going to get that blade up the hill. Another commander had made a dumb decision trying to make a difference. This time it was the other side.

"Evens!" the LT's voice barked. Nathan's stomach lurched.

"Yo!" he responded, only to wait.

The lieutenant made her decision. "Head back to the support track. There should be some antigrav grips on the track's sidewall. Bring a case of 20mm for McKenna and Bryce. If there's a working munitions sled, bring back some rockets as well." Bryce was the other rotary gunner.

Nathan shifted his trenching tool to his left to half-salute from a crouch, then folded his tool to stow as he moved. He unslung his pulse carbine and ran hunched toward the hill crest, changing the angle of his path as he ran. Coherent light is immediate. You don't have to lead your target, but you do have to sight your weapon. Bots are automated but rare, exclusively Corporate assets.

Once over the crest, Nathan fell into an easy trot through the scrub, back toward a column of smoke that marked the ruined shell of their supply track. Over his helmet's tactical comm he heard the LT order Alpha to focus their attention on the left flank.

The track on the far side of the rise bled oily smoke into the dry breeze. There was a small fire beneath the track's hydraulic sump. The vehicle was canted to the side. A crater on that side was made by an explosion that had dealt a mortal blow. He didn't see any surviving wounded, but there weren't enough bodies visible to account for the whole crew. Nathan briefed the LT as quietly as he could after tonguing up the mike's sensitivity. He muted his helmet when the LT acknowledged.

Sudden movement on the far side of the track prompted Nathan to stop, motionless. A shadow on the ground was of a local insurgent. There was no nearby cover, but Nathan tried to reduce his visual signature by lowering himself to the ground as he moved to the side, pulse rifle ahead of him. From there he could see several locals clothed in dark wraps of fabric, giving them a distinctive outline. They weren't looking toward him, but were focused on something on the ground.

Nathan edged back out of chance view, approaching from behind the cover of the wrecked armored track. He could hear them talking, but he didn't understand a word of it. Suddenly, they sounded celebratory. Someone gave an order.

By that time, Nathan was in a crouch, near the track's rear hatch. He heard quick footfalls: someone was coming up on the right at a trot. Nathan readied his carbine, and as the local entered view, he slammed the stock of his carbine into the man's chest. He had intended to crush the windpipe but missed, instead breaking the man's clavicle with a pop of broken bone. It must have hurt badly, because the insurgent bellowed in pain and dropped his weapon.

All hope of stealth gone, Nathan reversed his weapon and finished the cloaked man with a burst of four pulses. He had to think fast. The enemy had gone silent. Then he heard them moving. If he ducked inside the armored track they could overwhelm him just spraying the interior from both sides of the hatch, so he opted for offense. He spun around the side ready to fire and caught two of them in the open. Their weapons were at the ready. All three fired at the same time, but Nathan's size, for once, was in his favor. He felt a punch in his arm, but both locals went down.

Nathan felt hot blood flowing down his arm. He rounded the back of the track. They had set up the track's mortar. The first guy must have been their spotter.

Nathan glanced down at his arm. The bleeding

was heavy. He needed to apply pressure onto it. His carbine's power indicator still showed half charge.

Nathan reached for his kit to pull out a first aid pack, to pack his sleeve with expanding medical gel, but heard another insurgent exclaim over the bodies he's left by the side of the track. Nathan raised his weapon. The enemy didn't come around the corner. Nathan didn't know if they were going to double back or wait for him, but his wound gave him no time to wait. With his good hand, Nathan plucked a fragmentation grenade from his webbing. His left hand was useless, barely able to hold his bloody carbine. He used his teeth one-handed to activate the timer, then tossed the explosive around the corner. The detonation was brief but deafening.

Ears still ringing, Nathan had to get some pressure onto his wound quickly, or he would bleed out. His pulse carbine slid from his nerveless left hand and he grabbed again at his medpack. He pushed the pack up his blood-soaked sleeve to the wound. Dizziness made his head swim, but he could feel the button and depressed it before his legs collapsed beneath him.

Oddly enough he felt alert as he looked up into that rusty alien sky. He thought his loss of blood should mean reduced cognitive function, but his mind felt suddenly liberated. One part of his brain attributed it to the medication in the gel. The rest of his mind thought of things that had been trained out of him.

It was clear to him that as long as people have what they need to get by, it didn't matter a whit what government they worked with, no matter what ideology was spewed. It only mattered when those who had power went nuts. His world went dark and silent at last.

Sergeant McKenna found him sprawled there unconscious when she came for her ammo. The tale was laid out for her all around him, the little guy who had always been so quiet and polite. She loved his sense of humor. She carried him back to the LT's position for evac, surprised by an ambush of her own emotions.

Question of the Day: What would life be like living in a dome?

Outside

B. J. Muntain

Pete sat in the shade of a very old oak – older than the dome, he'd heard, now transplanted into Sky Park – enjoying his peanut butter and jam sandwich. He'd finally got the new food machine to understand how to print it correctly. Not too soggy, with just the right ratio of jam to peanut butter.

Several stories up, he could see the entire city: the automatic transports on their efficient morning routes, the cleaning bots bustling like ants, the neat square blocks with tall buildings reaching up towards him. The transparent aluminum guard glass made you feel as though you could simply walk off it, into the air, but there was no getting through that transalum. He'd tried, once, to see what would happen. He had run at it and bounced off. He couldn't reach high enough to touch even the top of the guard, despite his own height. After a few tries, he'd been banned until he'd undergone counselling. Counselling was the City's answer to every abnormal behavior.

He'd always envisioned the dome to be like that guard glass – made of transalum, it encased everything, separating the safe world of the City from the dangers Outside.

A child's shout drew his eye to the park's fountain, its plume reaching taller than a man, then falling back into a clean, blue-dyed pond. Some children were playing nearby. Two boys pushed a third towards the pond.

Pete watched.

An ethereal fabric formed between the boy and the water, gently lifting him and placing him feet first on the ground nearby. The nanoparticles then dissipated back into the air.

The other boys ran, but they wouldn't get away with it. The ever-hovering drones policing the City would be sending video to the boys' parents. Pete had once been caught that way and introduced to City security. Counselling had turned him away from bullying. Always large for his age, he'd started working out at the gym as a way to use his bulk.

A soft tone from the node behind his right ear alerted him to a call. He tapped it, and a face appeared before his eyes. Mike.

"Hey, Pete," said the corneal hologram of Mike. "When are you coming for a visit? Festival is next week. It's a good time."

Pete nodded, and he knew his canned hologram was being shown to Mike, speaking with his voice as he himself mouthed the words, "I'll think about it, Mike. I'm not sure I want to travel right now." After visiting friends in other cities, he'd given up. Besides a few cultural differences and new foods to try, they were just other domed cities. Even the jets opened and closed under domes, to protect passengers from the dangers lurking Outside.

"Come on, guy. You've got to get out of that dome for a bit or you'll go stir crazy."

Possibly, he thought, carefully not mouthing it. "I'll think about it Mike. I've got to get today's blog up."

"That won't take you long. You said all you had to do was put the data into popular language. You could do that from anywhere. Call me later." Mike's face disappeared.

'All', Mike had said. 'All' he had to do was take Doctor Shear's notes and make them interesting.

A tiny thought intruded. Less than an hour's work. It really wasn't much.

No, he reminded himself on the elevator down. The blog was useful. He'd received commendations from the City government. They even paid him for it now. He was keeping people safe, they said. That's of highest importance.

On the sidewalk, he stepped around a cleaning bot, then stopped at a corner to look for oncoming transports. He always looked both ways, not that it mattered. The nanoweb would stop him before he could get off the sidewalk. But the transport would always stop, just in case someone was determined to get through the web. And stopping threw a transport off its schedule.

In his home office, he sat before the keyboard, watching a much larger external screen than the corneal one. Following Doc's notes, he typed, "A traffic accident has ended three young lives and has seriously changed another. Although the young woman will most likely survive her injuries, she will need months of treatment to even walk again."

Doctor Shear worked in the emergency room of the great Edge Hospital, near the main gate of the dome itself. That was the hospital that took in Outsiders who had somehow gotten injured or killed. Doc would send Pete a list of what had come in from Outside the dome. There was no shortage of these items. Doc's list was a daily reminder of the dangers Outside.

Pete's blog, *The Outside Insider*, showed people what happened outside the dome. People needed to be warned, though he sometimes wondered if his readers just enjoyed others' miseries. No. They needed to know so they wouldn't go Outside into danger. No one would willingly go Outside... yet people obviously lived there. They died there, too, but they had to live to die.

Growing up, he'd had nightmares about Outside. He'd imagined jungles where wild beasts hid, waiting to leap at anyone stupid enough to leave the dome. Robots. Aliens. Axe-wielding serial killers. Probably not the dinosaurs or gigantic apes or man-eating plants, though.

Doc's lists scared him even more. Outside, children drowned when bullies pushed them into ponds. Outside, people died in accidents with uncontrolled transports.

Outside, you could walk off a building and fall to your death. Outside, four young people had a terrible accident. Three had died. For the first time, he wondered about their families. What were their parents feeling? Did they even have parents? With all the deaths and injuries, how many people actually lived long enough to be parents?

Funny, but the movies he'd seen never answered those questions. Nothing good seemed to happen to people Outside. There had to be some good things out there, right? Or why would they live there?

A beep behind his ear signaled an e-mail. His father. His mother was never around, always busy doing something, volunteering for any cause that asked her. Dad always called him.

Pete pressed 'publish' on the blog post. '*All*', Mike had said. That was all he did.

Ignoring that thought, he jogged to his parents' apartment at the end of the hall. His dad was at the door, wearing a ratty sweater over a stained one-piece suit.

"What's up?" Pete asked, though he knew the answer.

"I'm out of credits."

"You know, there's a reason we only get a certain number of credits, right?"

"Shut up. Key your credits in." Pete never used his allotted alcohol credits. Too many people, like his father, never left their apartments. The Alcohol Credit Agency could see he was giving his credits to his father. The city didn't care what you did in your own apartment. As long as you didn't drink outside your apartment or walk around in public while inebriated, no one cared. If you did, you'd get taken in for counselling. His father had had so much counselling he was ready to go ballistic. Or drink himself to death.

A few taps on the keyboard, and Dad was happy. Pete hated himself. He was out of the building before those thoughts could creep up again.

Could he talk to the families of those accident victims? Maybe they'd give him information for the blog. Doc could probably help. Should he phone Doc, first? But Doc never returned his phone calls and rarely answered his e-mails. There was nothing else to do, so he decided to go straight to the hospital.

The Edge Hospital was much larger than he'd expected. The other hospitals in the City were the size of a city block, between two and five storeys tall. The Edge took up four city blocks, and about ten storeys. A large sign topped a double door: Emergency Entrance.

He waited just inside the door, until he had to move to let ambulance workers bring in an older man whose face was covered with blood. Pete looked around the waiting room. He'd never seen so much blood, a sharp contrast to the pale green walls of the city. He'd seen blood when he'd hit a smaller boy, before the counselling. He'd seen drops when he'd cut his finger trying to cut cardboard for a science fair. He'd seen vials of the stuff when nurses drew blood for those few medical tests that couldn't be done through skin. But he'd never seen so much in one place.

He tried to talk to a nurse passing by, but she only frowned at him and told him to get in line behind a particularly bloody man who seemed to have a head wound. Curious, he had to ask, "What happened?"

The man turned around to glare at him, holding a bandage over his forehead – then he grinned. "Strangest thing ever. I was sitting in my yard, having a beer with some buddies, when the neighbor's drone came round and smacked me on the head."

Pete stared. "A drone?"

"Yeah. Guess he was spying on me, when he lost control of it. Think there was a power line too close – the electromagnetic got in the way of the radio control."

"That's..." he tried to think of something sympathetic to say, but he couldn't. "That's the weirdest thing I've ever heard."

The man laughed. "Yeah." He pointed to his head. "It looks bad, huh? Well, you shoulda seen the other guy."

Pete laughed, too. A wrecked drone? He'd never thought it could happen. "Why would your neighbor be spying on you?"

"'Cause he thinks it's funny to take down everything someone says and put it on his website. Said people in the City think we're strange. What are you in for?"

"I just want to talk to one of the doctors." Pete didn't know which was worse – the idea that his blog might be similar or the thought he should look for that site.

"Well, if you're not bleeding or in any danger, you're in for a long wait." He motioned to the crowded waiting room. "It's always crowded in here. There's only three ER docs and this is the only hospital that will take people from the real world." He winked, as though Pete knew what he was talking about. "The people here are kind of peculiar. Ever been into the city?"

He was about to say he was a citizen... but maybe the guy would stop talking then. "A couple times," he hedged.

"Then you know what I mean. They don't really do much here, do they? They eat that printed food and live in cells. And they're always talking to those eye cameras, so they never see what's around them. Strange."

He found himself nodding. Well, it *was* kind of... wait. He tried to word his question so the guy didn't suspect. "You don't like printed food?"

"Well, it's kind of bland, isn't it? Even when they spice it up, it still tastes like cardboard. Spicy cardboard."

Had this guy tasted cardboard? Pete hadn't. Again he nodded. "I see what you mean," he lied. He considered asking him if he could interview him, but remembering what he'd said about the neighbor's website, he kept his mouth shut.

Then the guy was called to a window, and Pete to another window. The nurse looked tired. "What can we do for you?"

"I just want to talk to Doctor Shear."

She eyed him. "Personal? Medical?"

"Business." She frowned. "You'll have to call to set up an appointment then. He's too busy helping patients." Then she called the next person in line.

He walked out of the hospital. All those Outsiders. He'd never suspected. Doc only sent him the interesting ones. He doubted he'd see 'Male, 50s, stitches after being hit by his neighbor's drone' on the next list. Weird that the nanoweb let that happen... but there was no nanoweb Outside. The winds outside the dome would blow them all away. He'd always wondered why they couldn't just fill the Outside air with them like they did in the dome. If they put enough of them out there, surely that would work?

To his left was the Main Gate. The Edge itself. Funny, but he'd never really looked at the dome itself, and definitely not from this close. He should be able to see the Outside from here, shouldn't he? But all he saw was a diffused blueness, as though the sky was reflected in all the molecules that made up the dome. It couldn't be that blue Outside, could it?

Against the nothingness of the dome, a huge metal door stood solidly. Around the door signs seemed to float in midair, but must be attached to the transalum. A large yellow sign hung above the door: "Warning!" Below it, a scrolling sign said, "This doorway exits the safety net of the City. By using this doorway, you indemnify the City against all responsibility for your safety. Proceed at your own risk."

"Sir?"

Startled, he realized he'd walked up to the door as he'd been reading. The voice belonged to a bored-looking security guard behind another sheet of transalum to his right.

"Yes?"

That weary voice said, "I have to ask you, as per regulations and policy, why you are here at the Edge Door."

"Just checking it out. I've never been here before."

"I have to tell you, as per regulations and procedure, that the City cannot be held responsible for anything that happens beyond the outer door. You go out at your own risk."

Pete stared. *Why would he want to go out?* "Have you ever gone out?"

The guard looked confused. "Why would I?"

Exactly. Why would anyone go Outside? "Any idea what's out there?"

"There's nothing I want out there."

Nothing. Pete looked at the pale blueness of the dome again. Nothing lay beyond. Everyone knew that.

But people lived out there.

No sane person would want to go out there... but that guy in the hospital didn't seem insane.

"Thanks," Pete said, and started walking – towards the door. He glanced back, half-expecting the security guard to try to stop him, but no. He'd given his warnings, and that was the man's entire job. That was 'all'.

Another big metal door greeted Pete. An arrow pointed to a communications device in the wall beside the door. Pete walked up to the door, but it didn't open. He pushed on it. Nothing happened. He looked for some way to open it, but it was just one large sheet of metal.

That's fine. He should really go back now...

A calm, cool voice said, "Please press the communications button." So he pressed the large yellow button.

"Thank you," said the voice. "May I ask why you want to leave the City?"

That was a counselor voice. They had a counselor talk to you if you want to leave? He really didn't want to talk to a counselor right now. He didn't want to go out there anyway... did he?

Well, why not? What did he have to lose – a life where his existence was wrapped around translating someone else's facts into 'news'? He wondered what Doc's notes would say about him.

"Business," he said.

"What kind of business would take you out of the City?"

"I need to speak to someone out there." It wasn't a lie – a counselor could tell if you were lying. He did need to speak to someone out there. He just didn't know who yet.

"If you give me his name, I can connect you."

No. No. Why was he doing this anyway? Maybe he was a bit brusque when he said, "I understand the risks. I am leaving of my own free will."

"Please give me your name, so we know to allow you back into the City when you return."

He paused... but he did plan on returning. They'd let him back in, wouldn't they? Maybe on a stretcher. "Peter Kozan."

"Thank you. Press the yellow button again to open the door." His heart started pounding, but he wasn't afraid. Excitement drew his hand to the button.

The huge door slowly drifted to his right. He waited, forcing his feet to remain still while door opened. Then he stepped out.

A larger breeze than he'd ever felt from a fan brushed his face with a cacophony of odors. They weren't food smells. He'd smelled food before. But there were warm earthy smells – something like the oak trees, if you got really close to them, but much more. Sweet smells. Acrid smells. But the sheer wall of scents faded as something else struck him.

Quiet. For a minute, he thought he'd gone deaf, then a bird called, a soft, plaintive tune. A motorized rumble not far away – there. A paved area where a bunch of old-style vehicles he'd only seen in movies sat gleaming in the sunlight. Cars. The rumble died, and someone got out of the car, striding up a path behind him towards the City door.

He wasn't dead yet.

The bright blue sky was spotted with white clouds. The clouds he'd seen from Sky Park were faded cotton, compared to these. Beneath the sky were large patches of green plants – fields. Those were fields, like the ones in the history books, or the ones where serial murderers hung out in the movies.

In the distance he saw trees – more trees than he'd ever thought existed – and houses. He wondered how far it was. At the gym, he could walk what the machines said was six kilometers an hour. But he had no idea what six kilometers look like, in actual distance. He started up the road that went past the car area, toward the buildings. Was that a town?

He tried to name the smells and every sound. A soft rumbling, getting louder. He looked up the road to see a car coming his way. It was moving faster than he was walking, and he watched it with some interest. And then it was nearly upon him. A loud noise – not a siren, but a warning – sounded and the car sped around him.

Cars were a lot bigger than he'd thought, much bigger than the private transports in town. It took up nearly an entire side of the road... and it had nearly hit him. Because he was walking on the road.

Heart pounding, he moved to the side of the road, in case any more cars came along. There was no nanoweb to keep him out of trouble here. And he knew, from Doc's notes, the kind of damage those vehicles could do. Three dead, one injured.

As he got closer to the buildings, more cars sped by, both ways. About an hour after leaving the City, he reached a sign. "Welcome to Darmuth. Population 4500." Another sign said, "Stop by Annie's for a good home-cooked meal. Best chicken in town."

Where should he go, now that he was here? Somewhere friendly. The houses were still a bit of a walk away, but just down the road sat a small building like one of those diners from the old movies – right down to the big name announcing

'Annie's'.

When he walked through the door, something rang above him. He jumped. Looking up, he saw bells hanging on a string. A couple men, sitting at separate tables, glanced up, then turned back to their newspapers. When he looked forward again, a woman standing at the counter said, "Well, don't just stand there." She motioned to a round stool near the counter. "Sit. What are you looking for?" After that long walk, he needed... "Water?"

She held a glass up to the... refrigerator. He'd seen one in the museum. But this one looked far more modern, with a temperature gauge and small screen on the front. The glass filled with water from a small spout.

He drank – he'd never known water to have a taste, but it wasn't bad. Then he noticed she was still watching. "Say 'thank you'," she said.

"Thank you," he said, kicking himself. Just because he was used to eating from a machine, didn't mean he had to be impolite to people. "I'm sorry. I–"

"You're from the City." She must have seen his shock. "Easy to tell. You're wearing one of those one-piece suits you only get there. And you look like you've never seen stuff before. We see a few City folk here, this close. A few every year, at least. It's your first time out here, right?"

"Yes," he said, relieved he wouldn't have to lie. He emptied the water glass.

"I don't suppose you brought cash?"

He stared.

"Money?" she asked.

Worried now, he said, "I have my paycard." She shook her head. "It's not worth the hassle to try to get City money off a card. Tell you what. I'll make you a sandwich, on the house." She eyed him. "That means free."

"I couldn't–"

"Next time you come out, you can buy your own. Make sure you come to Annie's again, okay?"

"Yes. I'll come right here." Then he had to ask, "Are you Annie?"

"I am now. Ever since I bought this place fifteen years ago. What kind of sandwich you like?"

"Peanut butter and strawberry jam," he said before he caught himself. Again, she wasn't a machine. "Please. If that's okay?"

She smiled. "Perfectly fine. Ned's just made some fresh bread. Ever have fresh bread before? No, I guess not. You're in for a treat."

She bustled to the back and came back a few minutes later with the biggest sandwich he'd ever seen, nearly hiding the small plate. The bread itself was huge, and when he lifted it, it was soft. He could actually smell the peanut butter.

The sweetness of the jam perfectly matched the strong saltiness of the peanut butter, and the warm bread had its own subtle taste. The jam soaked into the bread a bit, but not messily. As he finished it, he said, "This is amazing. Thank you."

"Now, mind telling me why you disregarded all the warning signs to come out here?"

He shrugged. "I don't really know. I knew there were people here. I didn't expect a whole town."

"Curiosity, then. What do you do in the City?"

"I write a blog."

"No one comes out here unless they're desperate for something. The blog not enough?"

He caught himself shaking his head.

"Why don't I call someone to show you around a bit? That way you keep out of trouble, and maybe you'll learn something."

One of the men sitting alone among the tables spoke up then. "I'll take him around." He was older than Pete, but not as old as his father. His face looked leathery, though. 'Weathered', he'd heard it called. The Outside environment seemed to do that.

"Thanks, Rob," she said. To Pete, "Rob's a town councilor. He knows everyone and everything about Darmuth."

Rob held out his hand. "Rob Forrest."

Pete shook the hand."Pete Kozan."

"Good. Come on." As he led Pete out of the diner, Rob said, "Not many City folk leave the City. They say it's frightening. I don't know why."

Pete shrugged. "In the City, there aren't as many ways to die. The drones and the nanoweb keep things pretty safe."

"I suppose. So why are you here?"

Pete thought about that. "Well, I wanted to see why anyone would live out here."

Rob guffawed. "Must think we're a bunch of hicks."

"Not really. Just..." A clang to one side made him jump, but the calm "Well, fuck" after it took the edge off.

Rob rushed over, so Pete followed.

An older man, about his father's age, stood

there, looking sadly at a jumbled pile of metal pieces – heavy-looking metal pieces, scattered over the cement driveway. A dirty cardboard box lay nearby. This old man was carrying that? And then he looked closer at the man – yes, he probably could carry that. His shoulders may once have been broad, strong, though now they drooped.

"What happened, Jim?" Rob asked, his hand on the man's shoulder.

"Well, I was cleaning out the garage. Without Joe–" he paused, swallowed. "Well, I've got no use for all his old engine parts. I was taking this load out, and thought I should call Joe for some help–" He shook his head, but not before Pete saw tears in the man's red eyes. "Guess I lost my concentration."

Rob led the man to one side, probably so Pete wouldn't hear something very private. He did hear a few words, though: 'alone', 'accident', 'funeral'... and he knew.

He looked around for the cleaning bots – then remembered. The old man would have to... No. He didn't have to. Pete could.

He stooped to pick up those metal pieces and put them back into the box. Yes, they were solid enough, heavy enough, but not unwieldy.

"Thanks, son," said the older voice behind him.

Pete picked up the box. "Where do you want this?"

"Back of the truck would be great."

Pete slid it onto the flat part of a nearby transport. "Is there any more?"

He spent the rest of the afternoon loading the

41

truck and unloading it at the scrap metal place. In between, he had his first non-automatic transport ride, in the back seat of the large truck cab. It wasn't as worrying as he'd thought it would be.

The other two men didn't talk much, but there wasn't much to say.

Once the truck was empty, Jim said, "I'll buy you boys some supper. I owe you."

Pete was going to protest, but saw something in Jim. Defiance? Perhaps pride... Dignity. Of course. "You know, supper would make my whole trip out here worthwhile."

They went back to Annie's, more crowded now, though many folks were leaving at the end of the dinner rush.

He had chicken, because Annie made "the best chicken in town." And it was real chicken. Tender, with spices he could only guess at. It was the best food he'd ever eaten, even better than the sandwich.

After a pie filled with the taste of real apples, it was dark outside. Jim insisted on driving him back to the City. Pete was happy to accept.

As he stepped through the inner door to the City, a loud insistent buzzing bothered his ears. He looked around for its source, then realized: it was the City. The drones, nanoparticles, transports, all added to the constant buzz.

At home, he sat at his computer, writing down everything he'd learned. Then he glanced at his e-mail. Another report from Doc.

As he wrote it up for tomorrow's blog, he thought about the people he'd met out there. At the end of the report, he added, "If the family or friends of any of these people see this post, I'd love to talk to them. E-mail me."

He read it through again. It was enough. Ease them into the idea that these stats were real people. And there were more people out there, family and friends of the people he'd written about. Get his readers really thinking.

Then, because this was his life and he wanted to know more, he searched online for that neighbor's blog, just to see what he wrote about. It wasn't easy – the search engines didn't pick up on much from Outside. Once he'd found his way off the beaten internet path, though, he found more.

The next day, he started a new anonymous blog, *Outside the Dome*. The City government wouldn't like it, but people needed to know.

Question of the Day: Who do you ask the important questions to?

Question of the Day

Scott McGlasson

From the hotel lobby where I'm scribbling this down, I see out through huge windows into a motionless world. A rooster tail of dirty snow hangs in the air, thrown up by a green Buick sliding out of control. The blue-hair just barely peeking over the steering wheel has the same surprised expression on her face as she's had since the morning the world was supposed to end, almost two months ago.

Bear with me. I'm trying to keep my hands from shaking. Can't keep a good grip on the pencil. This journal is full of jagged scribbles and words running together, but this is my rock. It's kept me sane.

I thought just jotting some things down might steady my hand, but no joy so far. Maybe a quick stroll down memory lane might do it. Yeah, it's already helping. I can read my own handwriting now. Supercalifragilisticexpialidocious. See? Perfectly legible. Hopefully this won't be the last entry, though I can't really imagine what comes next.

Something finally happened. In an endless existence of rigid sameness, something changed.

Okay…took five minutes. Got the shakes again and had to relax, calm the mind…make sure what I thought I saw is still there. It is.

So, let's try this again. I think my writing hand is ready to cooperate. I opened and closed my fists until the jitters passed and then did some deep breathing exercises. Funny thing about breathing; I once decided to hold my breath and count Mississippis just to see how long I could go before keeling over. I got bored after about two thousand and let muscle memory go right back to sucking air in and out. My mind *knows* that I don't need to breathe in this place, any more than I need to eat or drink, but the body likes its habits. Speaking of food, there were a *lot* of people eating choice cut steaks when the end came, so I've had no shortage of samples over the past few months. All of it just as bland as raw flour.

Not gonna take too long to get this down. Gotta get outside. He's probably watching right now and waiting. Sure, infinite patience and all, but I'm not about to test that. Not today. Not ever again.

Where to start?

It's winter, but never cold. I can make noise, but there's never an echo. Everything is fixed in place, the whole world dipped in acrylic and left to dry. Besides Yours Truly, nothing moves. Not the sun's place in the sky or that flock of geese frozen in mid-flight over the Dunkin' Donuts across the street.

The science-types called it AFH21334, a potato-shaped mass of iron and rock that nobody saw coming until it was too late. It was supposed to hit about fifteen-hundred miles northeast of Papau New Guinea, moving fast enough to punch through the atmosphere, three miles of Pacific Ocean and then, for good measure, continue right on through the ocean floor.

After the news broke, common knowledge held that if you somehow survived the blast wave and earthquakes, the sky was going to cloud over for a thousand years and kill you anyway, along with everything else on Earth above the microbe level.

None of that happened. For all I know, the asteroid is still hanging there, just over the waves, a ball of friction-heated death as motionless as the hotel manager kneeling in prayer on the other side of this counter. The television behind him is showing a priest or cardinal leading mass in Times Square. Which one wears red? Cardinal, I suppose. Crazy, right? I mean, if everything's frozen, or, at least, not moving, how does the TV still have an image on it? But that's how it works. If something was on when things stopped, a cell phone, a light bulb, the sun…it's still going strong eight weeks later.

After the first announcement, everyone reacted in their own way, but there some definite types. There were the rugged individualists and preppers, heading for the hills to find the deepest, darkest cave and ride it out. There were the nihilistic that welcomed the end and "Sweet Meteor Of Death" became a meme the very night the humanity learned it was going to die. The religious, including my parents, and this hotel manager apparently, checked out of life and spent two weeks on their knees. There were the deniers that couldn't accept the fact that a flying mountain was bearing down on us, even if you tied them down and duct-taped a telescope to their face. Saw a guy done up like that a couple days ago on top of the Great Valley High School in Devault. Yeah, things got a little nuts right there at the end. I think I saw images of Los Angeles burning. Maybe it was San Francisco. I haven't found a screen showing which it actually was and I sure as hell wasn't going to walk from Pennsylvania to California to find out.

Apart from the survivalists, the nihilists and religious, there were those that decided to party until the end. 'Belle and I, we were solidly with this last group. We knew all the best end-of-the-world parties would be with the real nutjobs and hedonists, so that's where we were waiting for the cosmic erase button to be pressed. The parents of a guy 'Belle knew had kicked the bucket a couple years prior, leaving him with way more money than good sense. When the news broke, he turned their five bedroom McMansion into a permanent rave and promised to be the most whacked-out SMOD party we could find. 'Belle, you have to understand, had a real wide romantic streak. She wanted to be going at it like rabbits when *it* happened and so we were, *in flagrante dilecto*. We didn't know whose bedroom it was and we didn't care. All that mattered was going out in style. I was in rare form, playing 'Belle like a damned piano, listening to her body, her voice, trying to time her climax with the very instant of impact. And I did. Mine too. Represent.

In the afterglow, when conscious thought was possible again, I wondered if the asteroid had already hit. How long it would take the blast wave and earthquakes to reach us here in New England, on the opposite side of the planet? I guess I thought the house would explode around us or something.

Then I noticed 'Belle wasn't moving. Not just collapsed and lying still in my arms.

Wasn't. Moving.

She was still warm—they're all still warm—but her body was locked in place; legs up, knees bent, and hands behind her long, auburn hair, white-knuckling the headboard. I laughed at her. Can you believe that? I laughed at her and told her to stop messing around. When she didn't react I got confused. Then I panicked, maybe for the first time in my sheltered, cloistered life. Heart-attack? Seizure? Was she tripping on something from the party downstairs? Then I realized I couldn't hear the party. A couple hundred twenty-somethings with a serious sound system less than ten feet below us and not a peep. I yelled for help. To who, I have no idea, but I yelled. Then I screamed, throwing myself off 'Belle, landing painfully ass-first on the hardwood floor.

I don't remember pulling on my clothes, but I *do* remember not being able to look at her. I still don't understand why. I guess I was thinking seizure or something because I was still screaming for help when I threw open the door and saw people in the hallway. Frozen in the acts of walking, dancing, drinking, making out—all completely still and silent. I remember a sick dread blossoming in my stomach, a nausea that grew with each unmoving person I saw. I had to get out of there. I know that's chickenshit. I know I should have gone back to see if there was anything I could do for the woman I professed to love, but the only thing I could process an overwhelming urge to get the hell out of that house. It was after I stumbled/fell downstairs that I really lost it.

The house was massive and the living room was one of those big, vaulted ceiling jobs that could probably fit my parent's entire home with space to spare. All the furniture had been thrown through the massive front windows into the yard to make room for the packed dance floor. There I saw people in various stages of undress, bodies pressed together and sweating, sliding over each other. Typical rave, right? Wrong. Despite the size of the speakers, there was no music. Despite my screaming, right in their faces, none of them moved. Despite gravity, a few were suspended above the floor, caught in euphoric leaps of varying human geometry.

Too much for my overloaded mind. Hell, I'd just finished having sex less than a couple minutes before. How clearheaded are any of us at that point? I ran. I ran hard. Straight out into the yard past a few more statuesque party-goers and down the long driveway. My folks' house wasn't too far away so I just beat feet in that general direction. Past more frozen people, frozen cars, hell, I even saw a jumbo jet overhead trailing white streaks behind it, completely immobile. I kept running and screaming, the volume increasing with each newly discovered, unmoving horror. Running and screaming, screaming and running. Stopping, standing, staring confused, I did that too in equal measure, all the way home.

Mom and dad were there, sitting on the couch, holding hands. He was kissing her on the forehead. I shoved at my dad. He rocked away from me, his puckered lips coming away from my mom's skin, but their hands held fast and she started to tilt after him. I realized that I could shove them until they tipped over and they would stay locked in that position, so I gently eased them back, my father once again placing his frozen kiss. I stumbled back from them and collapsed on the floor. Somewhere between confusion and panic, I passed out.

When I came to, they were still sitting there, dad still kissing mom. I was a bit surprised to find them sitting instead of kneeling in prayer. My parents had tried and failed to instill a reverence for God since I was a toddler. I went along with it for a few years like everyone does, but in retrospect, I suppose I gave it the same weight as Santa and the Tooth Fairy. My parents said it Was, so it Was. I started having problems with the whole arrangement of an all-powerful deity and world suffering, the whole original sin vibe, as early as first grade. This caused no end of family discord so I eventually learned to simply pay lip-service to their god and try to respect my parents in spite of their beliefs. It didn't take long for them to catch on, but except for little hints and such from my mom, they let it be. It wasn't always easy, but then again, neither are parents. And neither are young, headstrong idiots convinced of their own infallibility for that matter. When I got home from college and couldn't land a job right away, I moved back in with the folks. Not big deal, most of my friends were doing the same thing. But when I saw their same-old-same-old life, the unchanging nature not just of the house I grew up in, but of the immovable nature of my parents' beliefs, there was trouble. How could they be so blind to reality? How could they look at overwhelming evidence and opt for faith? How could they have faith in the absence of evidence in the first place? So many arguments. So many slammed doors. I was such an asshole.

Sitting there on the old couch, despite their apparently immobility and impending doom, they looked peaceful. Almost happy. I couldn't stand looking at them like that so I ran again, but this time only as far as my little apartment over the garage where I holed up for three days. I did a lot of talking to myself, along with a lot of screaming at the walls, but, more usefully, it was there I started getting a sense of my new reality.

If it was electronic and it was on, it remained on. If it was off, there wasn't a damned thing I could do to get it to turn on. A quick trip down to the first floor of the garage confirmed that cars not only wouldn't start, they wouldn't even turn over. I found that things still had mass, that I could pick up and move things same as always, but try and throw a brick through a big window…no dice. A dull thud and the brick bounced off without leaving so much as a mark. I tried to drive a nail into a 2x4. Might as well have been granite for all the dent I made, no matter how hard I swung the hammer. Finally, I tried to start a fire in the backyard using my Dad's gas can. I have no idea if gasoline burns. Not only would the no-longer-gasoline-smelling liquid not pour, I couldn't light a match, couldn't get my Bic to fire up either. Not even a spark. So, like so many other things in my life, I gave up. I simply, if uncomfortably, accepted that nothing moved.

Everything except me. Okay, me and this mechanical watch, a graduation gift from my Dad. That's how I know it's been almost two months since everything stopped. Winding the thing became an obsession and I do it multiple times day, very careful not to over-torque it. My own personal chronological fidget spinner. I think it's because the watch was ticking before all of this happened. Or maybe it's because I was wearing it when everything else stopped. Tick-tick-tick, endlessly, spiderweb-thin hands tracing arcs over and over above the gold and silver art deco face.

Once, back in the beginning, I thought about taking it off and setting it down to see if it still worked without me wearing it. I couldn't bring myself to do it for fear that it might actually freeze up just like everything else. This watch is my last tenuous link to the world that moved, that jumped, that ran, that fell. A world that traced orbits around the sun, gave us seasons, gave us freaking days and nights. I'm convinced I'd have probably gone insane without something moving besides me, without knowing how long the world has been like this.

I moped around my apartment for a few days, not daring to go back into the house and see my parents sitting there again. Thinking back, I'm pretty sure I already knew what was happening, but the supposedly rational part of my mind wouldn't accept the data. Thinking of my parents and their beliefs only scattered what little doubt I had left and I wanted to hold on to that, hold it up like a shield that was quickly rusting away at the edges. At first, I was rock-solid sure that there was a scientific explanation for what had happened to me, to the world. I couldn't think of one, but I was fairly certain the word "quantum" was involved somehow, like I'd fallen into a personal black hole or something. This line of thinking didn't do me any good though, and slowly, over the following days and weeks, I grew convinced that someone, or Someone, rather, was doing this to me and I sure as shit had some questions.

"Why me?"

That started it off. I think I mumbled it at first. There was a *lot* of personal inertia against even believing, let alone having a discussion with, some old bearded fart in the clouds. I let it sit in my mind and kept mumbling it over and over as I walked from my little cloistered suburb north of Pittsburgh, following south along winter-bound Interstate 79. I figured if there were anyone else to see moving, the chances would be higher the closer to the center of the city.

I stopped for a break on the roof of the Children's Museum, just shy of crossing the Allegheny River. I wasn't physically tired, but mentally, I just needed to stop and process. I had seen some some weird, end-of-the-world shit along the way. People doing absolutely horrible things to one another that I don't particularly want to dwell on here. Sitting there on that roof, looking at the skyline of downtown Pittsburgh, I just kind of shut down. I don't need sleep any more than I need food or water, but at some point, I suppose, the conscious mind just says it's had enough for the day and shuts the hell down. By my watch, which I, of course, wound immediately, I had gone fugue for six hours and the question in my mind had changed.

"Why *only* me?"

Pittsburgh was as frozen as everything else so I decided to follow Interstate 76 toward Philadelphia and New York. Bigger metros, bigger chances to see someone else still animated, still free to move about.

Every period spent walking brought new despair, walking through an apocalyptic landscape, a world frozen in its death throes. I'd continue until I couldn't take any more, then find a place, always as high as I could find, to shut down for a while. Every time I came to, a new question burned in my mind, but I wasn't mumbling anymore. The volume of my asking grew louder until I was shouting at the top of my lungs.

"Why are *you* doing *this* to *only* me?"

I received no answer. Or, at least, nothing I could identify as an answer. I needed to start asking louder, bigger. Impossible to ignore.

In New Stanton, I raided a Home Depot for pallets of cinder blocks and arranged my Question Of The Day in the empty parking lot in letters ten feet long.

WHAT IF I DENY ALL OF THIS?

I took a package of index cards with me as I headed east on I-70, writing *This Isn't Happening* and *I'm Just Dreaming* and *I'm Strapped To The Aliens' Table*. I dropped them every mile or so along the way. I always made sure they faced toward the sky, though even now, I'm not sure why.

I followed the intestate mainly because it was flatter and more even-surfaced than the rising and falling foothills of the Appalachians. Fun fact: even if you never get physically tired, walking over uneven ground and having to carefully pick out every footstep wears the mind out and, frankly, makes you cranky as hell. I opted for the smooth asphalt of the highway and made good time.

I wore a good pair of hiking boots, jeans and a t-shirt. I couldn't feel the cold so I wasn't worried about exposure, but I I did keep a parka, gloves, and a wool cap in my backpack, just in case the world started moving again. Once I stuffed the big coat in, though, it never came back out. For some variety, I walked the fifteen miles between Somerset and New Baltimore butt-assed naked. Sure, snow and ice everywhere, but I didn't get a single chill.

Almost to Bedford, I got dressed again and started heading through town. Something—I don't remember quite what—made me think of my parents again. For the first time in weeks, I really saw them in my mind instead of batting it away like an annoying insect. What can I say? It pissed me off. For the first time since I started walking, I was more angry for what had happened to them than what had happened to me. I remember being furious. Just pure, undistilled, violent anger. You know how frustrating it is to be consumed by rage and completely and utterly unable to break something? Not even myself, apparently. I punched the red brick wall of an elementary school for a few minutes for all the good it did. Not even a scratch on the knuckles. Hot coals still driving me, I found a mattress store near a middle school and, one by one, carried their entire stock out to the football field and spelled out my new Question Of The Day.

WHY DID YOU DO THIS TO MY PARENTS?

That thought smoldered in my mind as I plodded along the interstate which had started angling sharply upward. The Appalachians might not have the majesty of the Rockies, but try walking them. It wasn't fatigue—as I said, I never feel physically tired—but it took *forever*. There was enough strangeness to keep the mind occupied though. Near Fort Littleton I saw a full-sized jumbo jet flying upside down only a couple hundred feet above the ground. There's a story there, but I'm not sure what it is. It probably ends with time moving again and everyone dying as the plane slams into a mountainside. I saw a lot of things like that along that stretch of highway. People frozen in the act of wigging out and either trying to kill themselves or others around them. The helplessness I felt gnawed at me, slowing me down. I saw a family in parkas, all bright, primary colors like you see on the ski slopes, sitting at a rest stop picnic table and eating lunch out of a cooler. The vapor of their breaths at the moment everything stopped still hung in the air. The kids were laughing and the mom was rolling her eyes. The dad had the smug look of self-satisfaction and I assumed he'd just dropped one helluva bad joke on them, as fathers are wont to do. None of them saw the tanker truck slamming into the embankment behind them, sparks flying, ochre liquid gushing from huge folds in the trailer, ready to fireball. I could see the entire thing, but there wasn't a damned thing I could do about it.

As I made my way into the little mountain town of Roxbury, I wondered how I might have avoided this entire situation. I oscillated between things I could have done differently to things we, all humanity, could have done differently, but never really got anywhere with it. How can I possibly answer for the entirety of human existence? There were a couple of scary moments there, I admit, where I thought that's what might be happening; I might be put on trial to answer for all the crap we have done, to the planet, to ourselves, etc, etc. Thankfully, those moments were few and far between, but I couldn't quite shake the feeling of "if only".

On the east end of Roxbury, I found Big Jim's Car Credit City where a tall bearded man in a cowboy hat stood in front of a crowd of about two hundred people, mouth open, yelling at them, throwing things over their heads. Their hands were outstretched, reaching up. As I got closer, I realized Big Jim himself, if the embroidery on his shirt was to be believed, was standing in front of an open metal case, throwing car keys at the crowd. For the life of me, I couldn't suss out why, but didn't really care. I took the keys, put the cars in neutral, and pushed them into letters.. Took me all "night" to write the Question Of The Day that evening, but I didn't get tired, so it really didn't matter.

WHAT COULD I HAVE DONE

No answer. Never an answer. I continued eastward as the mountains sloped down toward the eastern seaboard, but my steps were automatic, plodding. I had stopped caring and now only moved east because it was the direction I was already heading.

Mechanicsburg burned. I saw the massive column of smoke, frozen and unmoving, long before I could see the tops of the buildings. There was no road traffic heading into the mid-sized city. In fact, both lanes on both sides were heading west, away from the blazing town. I thought about just walking right on the hell through. After all, if the cold didn't affect me, how could fire? I debated the issue as I followed the interstate bending southeast around the city and finally decided that even if I was immune to the heat, the smoke, the fire, I was *not* immune to what I would see in there. My crazy-shit-o-meter was already full and I stayed on the highway, glancing toward the solid wall of black smoke every now and then. It was the final, catastrophic blow to whatever morale I had left. I withdrew from the immovable world, keeping my eyes on the road in front of me and my mind busy with song lyrics, movie quotes, and lolz from Facebook memes. In Edgmont, I sat on my ass, in the same spot, for three days at a Thai bistro. Not thinking of anything in particular, not shutting down into that weird fugue state, just...drained of everything. Not really sure what got me going again besides habit.

A couple days ago, with the snow-covered tops of Philadelphia's skyscrapers in sight to the east over Belmont Hills, I stopped at this Holiday Inn. The sun was still in the same position in the sky as the day I set out weeks ago, but my watch said it was almost midnight. Of course, I didn't feel sleepy, but I'd had enough walking for the day. With something like surrender, I stopped by the cars parked in the hotel lot. None of them had moved the morning AFH21334 was due to hit Earth. All were still covered with unblemished snow. I stood, staring at the smooth whiteness, completely unable to form a Question. My tired neurons refused to give up any inkling of an interrogative statement, so I heaved a great sigh and used a finger to write my ragged message into the snow-covered windshield of a Ford Focus.

WE NEED TO TALK

I came inside this lobby, sat down with my back against this counter, and stared for long time at what I'd written before letting my mind shut down.

My words were still there, exactly the same, when I came to. But, as I scribble this down, I'm both infinitely relieved and absolutely scared

59

shitless. Frightened or not, I'm going to put down this pencil, wind my watch, and march right on out there. Because I have to. Because when I woke up and looked outside, there, under my big, messy message was something new in this frozen world. Bold words in perfectly-formed letters.

I AM LISTENING

Question of the Day: What would you do to keep those you love from suffering?

Salvation

Josh Hayes

Another cold blast of wind knocks me a step forward. Bracing myself against the onslaught, my cloak whips violently around, its silver-trimmed, purple material slapping at my obsidian armor. I run my fingers over the smooth, metal casing of the stasis pod beside me, it's status lights indicating internal systems holding despite the conditions around us.

In the distance the streamlined transport hovers between two terraforming towers; long abandoned in the Most High's efforts to control his people. A blue aura surrounds the vessel as a deluge of snow and ice bombards its external force field. It's an older lane-jumper to be sure, but compared to the crumbling towers on either side, it is beautiful. With my optics set to full zoom I can see the triple star formation emblazoned on its hull.

My Salvation.

A new life waits.

I send the signal and wait for the response.

The two towers seemed to grow naturally from the valley floor, transforming from wondrous landscape into monstrous reminders of the terrors of this world. Most say shutting down those enormous processing stations is what caused the sickness to spread. On this accursed moon two things are absolute: the Order and the sickness. And both will kill you.

The wind dies down to a mere breeze. My trepidation, however, remains fierce.

"We're almost there," I say, running a hand over the stasis pod beside me. Repulser drives hum, keeping the coffin-sized capsule hovering above the ground.

My suit's proximity warning chimes and two red icons appear in my heads-up display. Immediate alarm turns to anguish when a familiar voice comes through my helmet's speakers.

"You know you can't leave, Jayden. He won't let you."

It would have to be *him* wouldn't it?

My cape snaps in the wind as my former executive officer steps around a snow-packed embankment, rifle in hand.

"He's wrong, Seth," I say. "You have to know that. Can't you see it?"

Snow dances between us as someone else steps

up behind my old friend. The wind billows the figure's cloak, revealing the gold-trimmed, red battlearmor underneath. Dasia. If she's here, there can only be one outcome to this day.

"It doesn't have to be like this, my friend." Seth's suit-enhanced voice echoed through valley, giving him an ominous sound. "The Most High is a merciful god. His love and forgiveness are bountiful."

"And yet you've brought *her* with you."

Seth gives the assassin a sidelong look. "A precaution only, High Commander. Now please, forget this madness. Return to the Order."

I glance down at the stasis capsule and say, "Is it madness for me to want this? To hope?"

"If it's hope you seek, the Most High has it spades, Jayden. Come back, let him show you his mercy."

I laugh. "His *mercy*? He knows nothing of mercy. He is a tyrant, Seth, nothing more."

Dasia steps up beside Seth. Combat systems begin to push forward, taking priority slots. Status icons appear translucent in my vision; weapons coming on-line, locking targets.

"Heresy doesn't become you, High Commander," Seth says, stepping to his right. "One way or another, you will return to the Order."

"I'm not going back," I say, a panel on my forearm slides open.

Dasia's gold-trimmed helmet tilts ever so slightly, giving her away. My boot rockets ignite, turning the snow underfoot to vapor. Dasia's rifle raises, but despite her unnatural speed, she's not fast enough.

Four micro-rockets blast from the launcher on my forearm, slamming into her as her rifle kicks. The explosion sends her reeling.

One down.

I spin, changing direction and altitude, turning to target my friend. Gunfire echoes around me. My armor sings as high-velocity rounds slam into me.

Warnings flash as Seth launches his own barrage of rockets and my suit's automated countermeasures fire.

Three of the four incoming rockets succumb to the decoys. One makes it through, however, detonating inches from my suit. The explosion hurls me end over end through the air. Several systems go off-line and a second later I crash into the ground, cutting a long trail through the hard-packed snow.

I roll to my feet, taking cover behind a boulder. Seth is moving, rifle up and ready.

"It doesn't have to be like this, High Commander," he shouts, sounding out of breath.

"I'm not going—"

I see it before my damaged suit sensors confirm the threat: a rocket launch from Dasia's still form. My heart stops and time seems to slow as a single rocket streaks through the air, but not at me.

"No!" I scream.

The explosion sends ice and fire streaming into the air. I watch helplessly as the stasis capsule hurtles violently across the barren landscape.

Fury overrides all thought. I scream and launch myself into the air, every weapon firing, unleashing hell upon this god-forsaken world. I taste the rage, a metallic bile in my throat. Both Seth and his silent assassin vanish in a torrent of destruction.

I touch down next to the capsule, now lying awkwardly on its side, power systems failing. The top panel slides back, revealing Emilia's unconscious body. Her shrunken features turn my stomach. The sickness had stolen her youth, leaving only a shadow of the vibrant young woman she'd been. Without the capsule's protection, she will not survive the rest of the journey.

"I'm sorry, little one, I failed you." I will not let her suffer. I draw my pistol, tears streaming. "I love you so much, Emilia."

I take a deep breath, steeling myself for what I'm about to do and I flick the safety off.

A furious roar pierces the stillness around me. A barrage of hot air washes over me, knocking me back a step.

From somewhere above, a booming voice says, "*Don't shoot!*"

I raise a hand, shielding my eyes. "What—?"

A shuttle materializes in a fury of snow and ice, touching down on the other side of my daughter's capsule. "*We received your message. We're from the Salvation, we're here to help.*"

I drop to my knees, pistol falling free, forgotten. I no longer need it.

Our new life is here.

Question of the Day: Who inspires you the most to pursue your dreams?

In the Name of my Father

Jo Zebedee

When I was a kid, Dad had a shelf of books that I barely understood. I'd take them down and read the titles, but they made no sense. And when I looked inside, they were about robots, spaceships, and worms in the desert. Nothing real. He had a telescope, too, one he let me use while he pointed at the stars and told me which was which, and the legends behind their names. He said that as long as I knew the Plough and the North Star, I'd never get lost in life.

And then he read Starbeast to me, when I was still young enough to believe. I cried when he told me I couldn't have a Lummox of my own, but he let me have a pretend one in the garage and I fed it a box of lettuce every day – and crisps at the weekend – and sometimes I'd make believe he'd escaped and squashed Mrs. Hilton from down the road, the way the giant peach squashed James' aunts. That was a good make-believe.

I went through the bookcase, first with him reading to me, and later by myself. I dreamt of riding a sand worm with Paul Atreides, or being Ender Wiggin heading off to space school. I wanted to be the person who could do the things in those books, go into space and find new planets, even though I was a girl, and there weren't many girls in the books doing the brave things. Dad said it didn't matter, that I could do them anyway, and I believed him. He also told me I'd have to study hard.

So, I did. I studied through school and then through college and learned astro-physics, even though it wasn't just as much fun as reading the books, and all the while he watched the stars through his telescope – and discovered a new asteroid, which was pretty cool – and added a model collection to the bookcase, of all sorts of space shuttles. He'd tell me the story of each: of Yuri Gagarin going into space; of Armstrong walking on the moon; of Apollo-13 barely making it back to Earth.

And then came the day we watched the space shuttle launch together. It had been put off for days, but finally was going to happen. Dad was nervous, right from the start, saying it was too cold, that they shouldn't be launching, but everyone on the telly was excited and the skies over the launch-pad looked bright and benign. Even Mum couldn't calm him. We listened as the last ten seconds counted down, and my stomach was jumping with excitement. I wanted to be onboard, to be heading away from Earth with the astronauts. I wanted to hear the engines roar into life around me and shake me in my seat. The countdown finished and the shuttle hurtled into the sky. Dad gripped my hand so hard it hurt.

A moment. A first spiral of smoke.

"There's a problem." Dad turned to me, his eyes glinting and wide. "Can't they see it's not right?" He hit his hand on the set, as if they could hear him through it. "Houston! We have a problem."

The shuttle exploded, right on the screen in front of us, plumes of smoke against a pure blue sky. I let out a yell, maybe surprise, maybe the knowledge that a dream had ended. We waited to hear what we already knew: the mission had failed, the astronauts were dead. All of them with their smiling faces as they'd walked to the shuttle just a short while ago.

"How?" I asked. "I thought it was safe." That was why they'd let a civilian go; because it was safe.

"Too cold," he said. "I'm sure of it."

Turned out he was right, and that NASA had known it was dangerous at the time. The shuttle-program was halted. Dad put away his telescope and let his bookcase turn dusty and anytime I talked about what I wanted to do, he changed the subject and told me to get a job in a supermarket, where I'd be safe, not with NASA, who didn't take care of their own.

When I graduated – not at the top of the class, but not anywhere near the bottom – he came but he barely smiled, and when I got accepted by NASA he didn't congratulate me. It was like he was dead inside, like the day when Challenger died, he had too. Everything we'd shared stopped mattering to him, and I suppose it almost did for me.

I missed him. I read the Culture novels and discovered Mieville, and had no one to share it with. I reached past Dad, into my future, and left him behind. And all the while, NASA was teaching me how to walk in space, and pee in space – and no, I'm not sharing, but you need good aim – and getting me used to re-constituted food. Some of it was boring, all of it was for the team, and none of it guaranteed I'd ever be one of the lucky ones who got to go to space. I wrote to Dad and told him what I was doing and why I was doing it: so that I could make space a little safer for the next person, and the next, and the next, because one disaster shouldn't take away a dream. I tried to tell him that NASA had learned, that they were taking care of their own now, but he just replied about how the sun was making his cauliflowers discolor on the allotment.

I told him about being selected for the International Space Station the day I heard. Mum phoned me and she was crying, and so proud, and she'd told Aunt Ella who'd always said it was a silly dream for a girl to have, when really they should be having babies. But my dad didn't say anything other than that he needed to go and water the plot, that the sun was too hot for the time of year.

Now that I'm here on the ISS, I still can't quite believe it. It's not like Dad's model ships, those shuttles are old now and out of service, just like him. No, the future is in this habitat, looking over Earth from its viewing window, and learning as much as we can about space. I've been here three hours and I'm still looking around and not believing I made it.

I float into my sleeping pod, tumbling into it not too gracefully, but that'll come in time. I turn around, savoring the freedom of the spin with no gravity to get in the way. I take the little model ship I brought and set it on my shelf, hooking it into place, and I pull out a battered photo and blow dust from it. Dad's smiling out at me, standing by his telescope with me in a pair of jeans and a coat, an open-mouthed ten-year-old. Through my viewport I can see Polaris and that settles me because I know I'm not lost.

Last of all, I pull out the picture of me coming down the launch-pad, ready to board the shuttle. It's got that blurred color that instamatics often give. Someone from the tech-crew squeezed it into my hand just before I boarded.

I look hard at it, and turn it over. On the back, there's a scribbled bit of writing, in a hand that I know from the front of all the books I read as a child. My eyes blur, but the tears don't leave, they just stay there, beading on my eyes, and I have to wipe them clear.

'Now go find a Lomax,' it said. 'If anyone can it's you. And then get home safe. Dad xx.'

Question of the Day: What would it be like if you could pick you who you were?

Happy Birthday

J. Edwin Phillips

Dome 17-Alpha
Embryonics Ward
Shupae, Ganymede

"Happy birthday," said the voice.

"Is today my birthday? I didn't know."

"How could you? It is your very first. Today, you have been born."

"I have been born. I understand. Are you my mother?"

"Not quite," said the voice. "You are the child of humanity. Humanity has birthed you. Humanity loves you."

71

"Yes, I am loved. I can feel this. Who are you then?"

"I am Usher, an artificial intelligence. I am here to help you."

"Help me do what? Why can't I see you?"

"Please stay relaxed. Your vision will soon be integrated, and you will see everything. I am here to help you choose who you are."

"You don't know who I am?"

"All new humans are quite impressionable, and I do not want to influence your decisions. I want you to search yourself and discover who you are. It is a journey only you can take."

"I understand. Please tell me, am I male or female?

"I do not know," Usher said. "You have not chosen a gender yet. That is one of the many decisions you have to make. You must also decide what skin color you would like and what your first vocation will be. All the answers are inside you. Relax your mind and let your thoughts drift. The answers will come."

"You mean, I don't have a body? How is that... Agh! My head! It hurts."

"You must stay calm. It is slight swelling of the blood vessels in your brain. This is normal and expected. I am administering some medication now. The pain should subside momentarily."

"It's getting better now. That was very bad. It's hard to describe."

"I must warn you that you will have other such episodes. Tell me when the pain comes, and I will help you."

"Usher, I'm trying to feel my body but I can't. It's like it's not even there. I'm afraid, please help me."

"Please do not be alarmed. You have a body and it is here with you. It is simply incomplete. After you have made your choices, it will be finished to your specifications. While it is being prepared we will complete your education. You are relaxing now. That is good. Just soften the tension and loosen your thoughts. You are doing well."

"I think that I am a male, but I am not certain."

"What makes you think this?"

"Well, I don't know really. I just feel that way I suppose. I feel like I identify more with males."

"You sound as if you are certain," said Usher.

"Yes, I believe I am. It feels natural to me."

"You are doing exceedingly well. Choosing a gender is an important first step in deciding who you are," said Usher.

"My memories tell me that this wasn't always true, that people did not always have a choice. I know this as a fact but I don't understand how."

"That knowledge is part of human history. You have been born with fourth level knowing and you are learning to access those memory files."

"Then it is true? People didn't always get to choose who they were?"

"In the past, gender was entrusted to random chance. As biologic entities, aberrations were commonplace. It was routine for some to have the mental and emotional direction of one gender and the physical attributes of the other. Also, disease was exceedingly prevalent. Genetic systematization was imperative to correct this. Now humans live healthy and more fulfilling lives."

"Usher, I don't understand something."

"Please ask me anything," said Usher. "That is why I am here."

"If we are biologic beings and those biologic determinations were based mainly on random chance, why was there so much hostility? I seem to remember that history is full of racial and gender bias. There was prejudice of all kinds. I can remember violence and cruelty. Why would people blame others over something that is beyond their control? Are humans still cruel in this way?"

"Humans are naturally a violent species. However, gender and racial prejudices are rarely the cause of contention now, as everyone chooses who they are and what they are to be. These are choices that do not have to last forever. We have the technology to change many things, including physical gender. However, the chances of needing to do so is improbable. Gender is important but only for socio-sexual identity. As you now know, breeding is done in a controlled environment. If you are honest with yourself and I refrain from influencing you in anyway, the likelihood of you needing to make changes later in life is negligible. Except for vocations of course. You can and will change those many times during your life."

"If that is true, then why do people still fight with each other?"

"You are very inquisitive," Usher said. "This is a good thing. We have been trying to make changes to the DNA strands that cause violent behavior but have been unsuccessful. Those strands seem to be connected to the survival instinct. We have been unable to remove them without also removing this instinct. Humans continue to routinely fight over belief systems and religions. There may never be a medical solution to this. Each person has to choose to overcome the irrational with patience and tolerance or choose not to."

"I thought you said you didn't want to influence my decisions."

"In all but this matter, I do not. Your choices are your own but humanity needs to curb its violent nature. We only ask that you consider tolerance and nonviolence when dealing with adversity. Have you chosen a name yet?"

"Not yet. I am going through the data and considering my options. How old am I? I don't feel like a child."

"You are a young adult," Usher said. "Or you will be as soon as your body has completely formed. Now that you have chosen a gender, we can begin the final process. You still need to choose a body type, hair and eye color, and other miscellaneous features."

"My memories tell me that having an adolescent period is essential to learning the fundamentals of survival. A person needs to make mistakes in order to learn. There are quotes from many historical figures that uphold this."

"Your ability to access your memory files and draw conclusions from them is quite impressive. You are correct of course; an adolescent period is essential. You have already had one. Your brain has been through a wide variety of experiences and has drawn from those experiences. This is part of the growth cycle."

"That doesn't seem like quite the same thing."

"No," Usher said, "it is better. It allows us to isolate and correct psychological abnormalities. Now, no one has to suffer from mental illness, even minor psychosis. The brain is tried and tested—corrected if necessary—and designed to succeed. Believe me, many stresses were placed upon your mind. You have the equivalent mental growth and maturity level of someone who has lived through several adolescent periods. This process was controversial when it was introduced. Many found it difficult to accept and that the desired results would be unattainable. Through a severe trial and error process, it has since become a proven standard. You must know that humanity can achieve almost anything. There is even an old saying: "Whatever the mind of man can conceive and believe—"

"—It can achieve.' Yes, I found the reference. I still don't understand something. I humans have the ability to genetically alter and create themselves in a specific image, why am I being given choices? Wouldn't it be more efficient to create specialized people to fill specific needs?

"I understand your query and must admit, it is a most logical deduction. This has actually been done and the specifics will be included in future lessons. Humans have a history of slavery that is still a tender subject even today. Many viewed this practice as genetic slavery. Also, humans are natural nonconformists. They have a need to strive to be more than they are. It was found that given a choice and allowing those choices to be altered, curbed the desire to revolt. I assure you, there is more than enough population to serve every need by society."

"I think I have a name now."

"Excellent. What have you chosen?"

"Kai. It has lots of meanings from many different cultures. I like that."

"I find it very fitting for you," said Usher.

"I have made all my other choices as well."

"Yes, I am reading the data now. They are far from the most popular."

"I like the idea of being different. When can I have my sight?" asked Kai.

"Very soon. Your body is almost finished. You should sleep now. When you awaken, we will continue your education. I will introduce you to the fifth and sixth levels of knowing."

"Will I remember any of this?"

"Of course. As I have told you, you are now born. Happy birthday Kai."

Those Who Control the Question

T. L. Evans

Lying hidden on the tall grass covered hill, Jack watched the smoke rise from the remains of the small settlement. The people in the village hadn't hidden from anyone. That, he supposed, had been the villager's damnation.

He turned his multi-spectrum binoculars upwards and scanned the sky above the mountain peaks that surrounded them. It was unlikely that he could have made out any orbiting starships or spy drones, but it was worth a try. Seeing nothing, he put down his binos and glanced quickly along the slope. His dirty blond hair caught in the wind as he squinted to see to the safety of his people. He needn't have worried; they were well hidden in the mixed scrub, brush, and tall reeds covering the slope. Even he couldn't make them out.

Their weapons were nowhere near as sophisticated as those of the Imperial Army; they were a rag-tag mixture of what could be scrambled together. For the most part they carried out-of-date combat rifles, though they had managed to grab one or two accelerator rifles, and had the golden prize of a plasma cannon they had stripped off a unit of Imperials they'd ambushed. Unfortunately, they were running very low on ammunition: they only had enough power for three more bursts with the plasma gun, less than sixty smooth bore rounds for the accelerator rifles, and even the mixture of bullets for their standard rifles were limited. Worse, they were running low on food.

Still, as a unit they could prove deadly enough if they took the enemy by surprise. Like most of his fellow pro-democracy Federalist Freedom Fighters, Jack would only engage when he could catch the Imperials off guard. That was, after all, the golden rule of the guerilla warfare -- fade into the background unless you could strike unlooked for.

At the moment, they were very definitely looked for. Throughout the star system, the Imperial Navy searched merchant ships that came and went. On the ground, the Imperial Army Guardians searched the towns and villages, seeking out the Voice of Freedom and his fellow partisans. Jack and his people were no match for the Imperials in a one-to-one fight, so he held his people back and bided his time.

Raising his binos, Jack focused in on the village,

noting the grey clad Imperial troops moving about the wreckage. He zoomed in on one of the ruined buildings where the fire was long gone. The walls had burned away; the wooden supports were charred to black. The Reynolds family had lived there: Maya, Brian and their kids. He adjusted his view and saw the bodies of the two adults splayed out before the building, shot in the head. The children's corpses could not be made out from the wreckage: they had been inside the building as it burned.

Jack repressed a shudder and adjusted his view. This time he focused on the long convoy of trucks ladened with supplies they could use. He focused on one of them, the one with an open hood. The one with a man leaning into it, and a woman working on it from underneath.

He turned his attention to the Imperials walking through the village. Not all of them were human. Here he could see the penguin-like shape of a Merodothite, and there the tree stump with tentacles that was a Rendethi. Most, however, were standard humans dressed in combat armor and carrying assault rifles. All in all, there were too many of them for his people to take, and they were well armed.

Two of them stood out clearly from the others. A man and a woman, both dressed in grey tunics, but with black trousers. Refocusing his binos once more, Jack zoomed in on their collars. The man's was marked with five laurel leaves, a half-Colonel; the woman's was marked with only one, a First Leftenant. The man's insignia was golden, noting he was a hierarch, the woman's silver: a commoner.

They were arguing vociferously, each occasionally scanning the horizon as they spoke -- no doubt wondering if they were being watched.

The Colonel was of average height, bust handsome, with black skin and short curly brown hair. The woman was a little on the short side, with olive skin and kept her black hair in a no-nonsense, off-the-collar, military bob. Both were in good shape, she was pretty and paid more than passing attention to her appearance. Jack couldn't care less; he was trying to focus on the flashes on their shoulders: the insignia that would tell him what units they were with.

They walked about the Reynolds home, and the woman squatted over Maya's remains. She seemed to examine the corpse, before looking up once more and scanning the slopes of the valley. She continued speaking to the Colonel, but Jack couldn't make out what was being said.

<<*Alison?*>> he asked mentally, using his implants and a directional radio, <<*Do you have the spot-mike on them?*>>

<<*Yes,*>> came the response, <<*They're talking about the need to keep the convoy going versus sweeping the area… and lots of stuff about bread rolls.*>>

<<*Keep at it,*>> he said. Bread rolls. Jack's mouth salivated.

The female officer turned her side to him briefly. It was enough for Jack to see her flash: an open book below what looked like an upside down V: a lambda.

"Sean, what does a lambda mean?" Jack whispered, following the protocols he himself had put in place. Even short-range line-of-sight transmissions occasionally give away a position; best avoided when possible.

Looking behind him, Jack could see his third in command and intel specialist, close his eyes and access his implants. "Logistics."

Logistics? Jack rubbed his eyes and looked again. Why are there two officers here?

He switched his attention to the Colonel. His flash was infantry. That added to his questions.

The woman stood and the Colonel shook his head. This time Jack could read his lips: "I don't like this."

Jack couldn't make out the woman's response, but a moment later the Colonel looked down and nodded. A few minutes after that the soldiers were packing up. Then, the vehicles started to drive out of the village, all except one. It moved about five meters before stalling out. The whole convoy stopped and several soldiers got out and fiddled with the power pack.

<<*We could take them,*>> Alison broadcast, <<*They're so focused on the truck that....*>>

<<*It's too risky,*>> Sean said. In the village, the soldiers working on the truck carried a spare powerpack over to the truck.

<<*We need the food and the ammo,*>> Alison countered, <<*Not to mention the weapons. You know what we could do with some of the accelerator rifles they're carrying?*>>

The soldiers linked a power cable from the engine to the powerpack and tried to start the engine again. Nothing happened.

<<*Not with Jack here,*>> Sean said, << *He's the voice of the revolution on this world. If they captured him it would be a blow to the cause.*>>

<<*We're not gonna risk it,*>> Jack said, turning his binos back towards the officers. They were arguing again. <<*There are way too many of them, and that Colonel is Infantry. Who knows what else is in those trucks. More soldiers? Combat drones? Absolutely not.*>>

He didn't need to hear or see her to know that Alison was grumbling. Several more minutes saw the soldiers unable to fix the transport and the Colonel look repeatedly at his watch. The two officers spoke again, the Colonel eyed the hills, the woman kept arguing. This time it was her lips Jack was able to read.

"They're long gone," the woman seemed to say.

The Colonel nodded and a moment later, the convoy loaded up and drove out of the village, all of them except the broken-down vehicle. Three enlisted men, one of them the penguin-like Meridothite, stayed with the truck. So did the female officer. Jack blinked twice. He couldn't believe his luck.

He heard some rustling down slope and Alison suddenly came crouching over to his position. He looked up and smiled.

"Jack, are you seeing what I'm seeing?"

"It gets better," Jack said, watching the column of vehicles move away, "She's logistics. An officer in logistics. Tell our people to get ready to move by the time that convoy is out of sight, and get Toby to check on the satellite positions. I want to be sure no one's watching."

* * *

The room was made of concrete and had no windows, the door reinforced metal. A single light hung from the ceiling, but not in a permanent fixture. It showed the cracks and water stains in the walls. There was a single, metal framed chair with no arms in the room and nothing else.

The door opened suddenly, slamming against the wall. It started to bounce back before a uniformed woman was thrust into the room. Her hands were bound and she had a bag over her head. She hit her shoulder against the door and stumbled, but quickly regained her balance and turned quickly as if to fight.

Jack walked in behind her, followed by Alison and Sean. Like himself, his fellow partisans had tanned skin and were covered with the fine dust of this planet's mountains and fields. They each wore an odd assortment of clothes, some their own, some donated by supporters, others taken from the corpses of the Imperials. Each also looked far older than they were: life in the resistance was hard.

They spread out around their captive, who was still dressed in the loose fitting black trousers and the dove grey, double-breasted tunic of the Imperial Army Guardians. The uniform was stained with dust and a small amount of blood, but it still fit her well. The prisoner shuffled her feet, turning, clearly expecting a sudden attack. She stood tall, perhaps even defiant, her stance at shoulder width, her head turning from side to side under the hood. She had a strong, lithe figure, especially for someone whose role put her behind a desk for most of the day. Jack figured she must exercise in her free time. Makeup, aerobics. *Typical Imperial Officer, all concerned about how she looked.*

Jack picked up the chair and set it down loudly behind her. Her head turned slowly as he put it on the floor. Even with her head bagged, she seemed in control, like any good Imperial Officer, but she jumped as Jack put his hand on her shoulder -- it was all façade. He pressed down, and she obeyed, sitting in the chair behind her. The partisans each circled her, first stepping quietly, then more loudly, all to disorient her. Her head turned to where she seemed to think Jack was positioned.

"Pahlavi, Rima, First Leftenant. Serial number DBOVOIR-202-56-8987." The woman said. Her voice was husky, but held a highly educated accent, almost elite.

"Yeah, you said that before," Alison replied, "I don't give a damn. I want to know what you were doing in that village."

"Pahlavi, Rima, First Leftenant. Serial number DBOVOIR-202-56-8987."

"This is going to be a long night," Sean said.

"Doesn't have to be," Alison said, her smile sounding in her voice. The three of them continued to pace around her.

"We know you're in logistics," Jack said, coming behind her, "What the hell is a logistics officer doing in the field?"

"Pahlavi, Rima, First Leftenant. Serial number DBOVOIR-202-56-8987."

Jack nodded his head towards the door and the three of them walked out. He clicked his remote at the light, turning it out before he softly closed the door. The three of them turned to the monitor on the hallway wall. It showed the computer-enhanced combination spectrum image of the room inside. The hood turned in the general direction of the door.

"You checked her for implants?" Jack asked.

"Twice," Alison replied, "Nothing out of the usual. The left wrist was reconstructed at some point, looks like there had been a bad break or something. Other than that, just the normal interface and comms stuff. Nothing deadly and nothing that could send a signal strong enough to penetrate the walls."

Jack nodded, let loose a deep sigh and ran his hand over his face.

"Any sign of the ones who got away?"

"Nope," Alison said, "They bolted pretty damn fast once the attack got hot and heavy. Typical Imperialist running dogs."

"You did a good job at keeping her pinned down," Sean said.

"Thanks," Alison said, but her eyes were focused on the prisoner, "But what I don't get why they were in the village in the first place?"

"Maybe it was just a convoy passing through." Sean shrugged.

"Why would a convoy pass through this valley?" Alison frowned as she spoke, but her eyes stayed on the monitor.

"It doesn't matter," Jack said, crossing his arms

as he studied his captive, "Or it does, but it's only the start. Pahlavi, Rima First Leftenant has a lot more useful information than that. If we can get it out of her quickly, we can find out troop movements and better yet, supply intel. We can intercept munitions and get some serious Imperial hardware. We can get some real supplies. Food, medical, all that stuff. More than that, we can find out who's placed where. But we have to break her before the Imperials have a chance to do a switch up. This is a golden opportunity, but we have to act fast."

"We'll need to drug her up with a metabolic accelerator," Alison said, "Give her the sensation that time is passing more quickly."

"We'll need to dose too," Sean said, frowning, "otherwise she'll see us as speaking and moving too slowly and she'll catch on."

"Do it," Jack said, staring at the monitor, "but keep her dose marginally higher than ours. Alison and I will tag-team her. You focus on the logistics, I'll work on finding out why she was in the village in the first place. Together, one of us will break her and the other will get an in."

"When do we get started?" Alison asked.

Inside the room, Jack noted the bagged head turn back and forth.

"Hello?" the woman said to the empty room.

"We already have."

* * *

Arms crossed, Jack leaned against the cold concrete wall of the interrogation room. The lights were on, but the bag remained over the woman's head. She remained silently seated. He had been there for an hour. Alison had come in two hours before that and fastened the woman's hands behind her, cuffing them to the metal frame of the chair. Now the captive sat perfectly still in the center of the room, Jack eyeing her from the corner.

"Jack?" she said, "You are Jack, aren't you?"

Jack remained quiet.

"I heard someone call someone else Jack in the car. I thought that person sounded like the leader. That's you, right?"

Jack continued to stare at her. He studied the fine grey fabric of the uniform, the once polished boots, the way her thighs filled the sturdy black of the trousers. He noted the flashing on her shoulder, the open book below a lambda, the epaulet showing her rank as a First Leftenant, the eight-pointed twinkling star within a circle: the emblem of the Sophyan Empire.

"You know they'll come looking for me. You know you can't win."

Jack shouldered his weight off the wall and began walking around her. Her head followed the sound of his feet, but not perfectly.

"My colleagues will come, and there'll be hell to pay," she said. Her voice was soft, caring, "But if you give me up, turn yourselves in…"

"You're not in charge here, Rima," he said to her ear. She turned quickly to in his direction. Her body suddenly stiff, he could hear her breathing heavily under the bag.

"Are you?"

Jack continued walking around her. She was frightened, and well she should be. She was also talking. First rule of being interrogated, don't talk. Once you start, you won't stop. They were half-way there already.

"Your people can't win this fight, Jack. The Empire hits such transgressions very hard. I know you people think you're fighting for what you believe in, and the Empire will take that into consideration."

Jack saw her tremble, ever so slightly. Her head was facing the wrong direction. She was disoriented. *Good.*

"Jack? Are you still there?"

Jack opened the door.

"Why did you take the bodies, Jack? Why did you take Mr. and Mrs. Reynolds from the village?"

Jacked paused, his eyes narrowing, then stepped out. He slowly and silently closed it behind him.

"Jack? Jack?"

* * *

Alison paced around the woman whose head was still bagged. In the silent darkness they inflicted on the prisoner, Jack had put four speakers rows of spotlights aligned on the walls, but the speakers and spots remained off, the room still lit only by the overhead. Alison said nothing as she circled the woman, but every now and then she would touch her, causing her to jump.

Jack watched on the monitor, studying the woman's body language. She was frightened, that much was clear, but she still held her composure.

"What's the complement of Fort na'Hari?" Alison asked, "How many air-tanks do they have?"

The woman remained silent. Alison came to a standstill behind the prisoner and yanked the bag from off her head. As she did, the spotlights came on with the sudden heavy clunk of a switch being thrown. They were blindingly bright; the monitor pixilated for a second as the filters adjusted. When the image refreshed, Jack could see the woman clearly. She blinked uncomfortably at the sudden light, frowning deeply.

"How many people!" Alison shouted in the woman's ear, and she jerked away from the sudden noise.

"Pahlavi, Rima, First Leftenant. Serial number DBOVOIR-202-56-8987."

* * *

Jack watched as light, music and noise blared into the room. The spotlights flashed in random sequence, causing the Leftenant to blink, wince and jump when a sudden explosion or high-pitched scream came over the speakers. It had been going on for over two hours, but to Jack and the others, whose metabolisms had been chemically accelerated, it seemed more like eight hours.

With the flip of his remote, Jack turned off the sound-and-light show. The sudden dark and silence seemed to strike her as hard as any new stimulation.

He let her sit in the sensory deprivation for half an hour before turning on the simple overhead. She blinked uncomfortably as Jack opened the door and came in carrying a bowl of food.

"Good morning, Leftenant," he said. Behind him, some of his people came in carrying a chair identical to hers, and a small folding table. Jack put the food on the table and uncuffed one of her hands, only to reattach the cuff to her ankle. He did the same to the other side. His troops left, closing and locking the door behind them. Jack sat down in the chair across the table from her and smiled. She stared blankly back at him.

"You must be getting hungry after all this time," Jack said. She looked briefly down at the food, then looked back at him. She remained silent and didn't move.

It was the first real chance he had gotten to see her up close. She was pretty, or would have been were it not for the sleep deprivation and general discomfort she was undergoing. Her face was heart shaped, with large dark eyes, sleepy eyelids and long lashes. Her lips full and under the right conditions might even have seemed sensuous.

Unlike the women who fought by Jack's side, she was well groomed, and clearly took the time to shape her eyebrows and treat her skin. In a different life, Jack would have been quite attracted to her, but under the conditions he lived, he found Alison's coarse dry skin and all but bushy eyebrows more appealing. They spoke of the hardships she endured at the hands of the Empire, not the luxuries she was afforded for imposing its will. Her soft nature and attention to appearance irritated him, but he hid his contempt as he smiled kindly at her.

"Go ahead, eat," Jack said gesturing at the bowl of protein-stew, "It's the same stuff we have."

The Leftenant cocked and eyebrow and tilted her head. Jack smiled in response. Taking the spoon, he helped himself to a serving, then put the spoon back on the table and pointed it to her.

"All right, don't."

Jack stood up, grabbed the chair, and walked to the door, leaving the bowl and spoon on the table. He rapped on the door -- a pantomime for her sake -- and a moment later it opened.

After it shut behind him, he stepped over to where Sean and Alison were watching the monitor. The Leftenant sat, staring at the door, then turning towards the bowl of food. Her eyes narrowed, and returned to the door.

She spent the next half-hour shifting her gaze thus until troops came in and took the table and bowl away. They left the door open for a moment before Alison walked in. Jack's fellow partisan closed the door softly behind herself, then leaned against it, arms crossed and smiled.

The Leftenant swallowed hard. "Pahlavi, Rima, First Leftenant. Serial number DBOVOIR-202-56-8987."

* * *

"It's Rima, right?" Jack asked, sitting once more in the metal chair that matched the one the Imperial Officer was cuffed to. Somewhere in the previous night's interrogation the woman had been stripped of her tunic. Now she wore a simple white blouse. A small bruise and a cut lay on her lower lip.

"If you haven't gotten that by now, you haven't been paying attention."

Jack laughed.

"So Rima, why don't you tell me when the next arms shipment is running to Halifour? No? Things would go a lot easier if you'd just tell me something. Anything, really."

She looked at the door, her eyes scanning the handle, looking at the location where the hinges were on the other side. He decided she really was quite attractive after all.

"Something small," he said with a shrug, "no one could begrudge you that, could they? Some little detail, say, how many napkins are sent to the base on the northern continent? No?"

Rima looked back at him. She seemed bored. That was good.

"All right then, how about something personal? Say, how you knew we had taken the bodies, Mmm?"

Rima frowned, looking confused.

"A couple of days ago, you asked why we had taken Mr. and Mrs. Reynolds bodies. How did you know?" His mention of the timing was intentional. He wanted to disorient her sense of time. Even to her sped up biology, it wouldn't have seemed so long.

"I saw your people taking them before you put the bag over my head," she said, and turned to look away, facing the wall, not the door.

"There now, that wasn't so awful, was it? But,

tell me, how did you know we took them with us, not buried them somewhere?"

"I smelled them in the truck," she said. Turning back to face him, he saw a burning anger in her eyes, "Besides, somehow I didn't think burying them would be a priority really, considering."

"Smelled them," Jack stood up and began walking around her. Both her hands and her ankles were chained to the chair, her wrists were badly bruised. He stopped behind her and leaned over her shoulder. "And how did you know them in the first place, mmm?"

"I didn't." She frowned, as if trying to look confused. "I'd never met them before."

"But you did know them. You knew their names. You called them Mr. and Mrs. Reynolds. An officer in his Majesty's Imperial Army Guardian's Logistics corps knows two ordinary citizens in a backwater village by name. That is very unusual. Why would that be, do you think?"

Rima looked away. He could smell her scent quite heavily; the touch of perfume in her hair could not compete with the sweat of a day's worth of drug enhanced interrogation.

"No? No answer?" He continued his pacing orbit, "Well then, how about something else then -- something simpler. What were you doing in the village in the first place?"

"We were moving a shipment and heard rumors of the attack. We went to investigate."

"You risked a convoy to investigate an attack? I don't think so."

"We thought there might be survivors." She

looked at him defiantly. "We were wrong."

"Why were there two officers with a convoy in the first place? Why send a half-Colonel and a logistician to dig around a burnt-out village?"

"Why did your people burn the village down in the first place?"

"What makes you think we did it?" Jack asked just to keep her talking.

"'Cause it sure as hell wasn't us," she said and smiled with narrow, accusing eyes, "The Empire doesn't do that kind of thing."

"No, you just arrest people." He leaned closer to her and caught her smell once more. "Men and women who protest too loudly. Men and women who fight for freedom, fight for the right to have a say in their own government."

"We have trials." She leaned towards him, until the handcuffs stopped her, "Did you give the people of that village a trial?"

"They were collaborators, giving away our position to the enemy."

"The children were collaborators? The one's you locked in that house and forced the parents to watch burn alive?"

"Apparently so."

"What makes you so sure?"

"Because you knew their names. You asked why we took the Reynolds bodies with us. If they weren't collaborators, how would you know their names?"

Rima paled ever so slightly. She looked like she might throw up.

* * *

On the monitor, Jack watched as Alison and some guards hosed Rima with icy cold water. The Imperial soldier's arms pulled against her cuffs locking her hands to the back of the chair. Her legs, uncuffed for the moment, flailed under the pressure from the hose. The water turned off and she pulled against her restraints. Her wet shirt revealed the surprisingly impressive muscles of her upper arms. Alison shouted questions about troop deployments, ammunition moving from point A to point B: questions about logistics. Rima didn't answer. The hose turned back on.

* * *

Rima's chin trembled, though whether it was from fear or the cold she had been forced to endure, Jack couldn't tell. He stepped forward and put a blanket around her shoulders. His sympathy for her wasn't completely feigned.

"Thank you."

"We're not monsters."

"Tell that to the people in the village."

"We're fighting for democracy, Rima. Those people betrayed us. They had to be made an example of."

"They weren't traitors, Jack, they were good citizens. It's just that you're their enemy, not us."

"Are we, or have they just been so indoctrinated by your propaganda that they can't tell anymore?"

"Our propaganda? Ha! I've listened to your broadcasts, Jack. You treat democracy like the one true faith."

"My broadcasts?" Jack pretended not to understand, "I don't make broadcasts."

"You're saying you're not Jack Sartre? The Voice of Freedom? You may digitally scramble the recording, but the cadence of your speech remains the same. I should know; I've heard it enough."

"Do many Imperial Logisticians listen to pirate radio?"

Rima remained silent.

"Oh, come now, you can tell me that!" Jack said and laughed. Rima looked away.

"I'll tell you what, I'll tell you something, you tell me something right? Quid pro quo."

Rima looked him in the eye, as if bored. Beneath it, Jack thought he could see her tremble slightly. *I just need to keep her talking.*

"You ask why we took the bodies. It was to remove the proof of something your press would call a massacre. Rumors of death squads breeds fear in those who believe in the system, mass graves dry up support from those who doubt it. So, we bring the bodies back here and toss them into the fusion reactor when we next fire it up. Now it's your turn. Does everyone in Logistics listen to Sartre's pirate broadcasts?"

Rima remained silent.

"Come on. Don't make me bring Alison back in here to try and drag it out of you her way. What harm can it do?"

"During morning coffee breaks," Rima said, avoiding his eyes when she spoke, "We sometimes listen to them. It's pretty funny stuff, actually."

"Funny? You find the call for insurrection funny?"

"All that talk of empowering the people and governing by popularity contests." She looked him in the eye and a smile appeared at the corner of her mouth. It opened the crack in her bruised lips, making her wince. "Having amateurs control society, make and enforce laws based on public whims? Pretty hysterical, Jack."

"You'd rather have some arbitrary authority control your future?"

"I can't think of anything more arbitrary than public opinion."

"The whims of an autocrat perhaps?"

"What's more autocratic than forcing your ideologies on the public through violence?"

"You are one to talk, Rima. Imperials arrest any you suspect of supporting the Federalist Rebels."

"We give them a trial of their peers. Can you say the same of those who you kill?"

"We only act when we know the truth."

"And those people in the burnt-out village? What truth did you know about them?"

"There were informants there, traitors. The fact you knew the Reynolds by name proves that."

"You killed them before you ever saw me. What about the others in the village? You killed them all. We know the Reynolds, so you burn down the whole village? Even the children. Burned them alive. Tell me, what treachery did the children commit?"

* * *

Screams came from the monitor. Jack didn't watch. They were running out of time and needed answers. Her intel would only be good for so long before the Imperials figured she was missing and changed things. He heard Alison shout questions, then more screams. He didn't know, didn't want to know, how Alison was going about getting answers, as long as she got them. Thus far, however, she had only been met with silence.

* * *

Jack began to feel the side effects of the metabolic enhancer. He was edgy, tired, and slightly depressed. It would grow worse soon. Alison, Sean and himself had been dosing themselves and Rima for three days now; it seemed like three weeks. They still hadn't gotten much actionable intelligence out of her, and still had no idea why she had been in the village. Her stoicism was really beginning to irritate him.

He looked at Rima on the monitor. As ever, she sat alone, hands cuffed to the chair. This time her legs sprawled out in front of her; Alison had not refastened her ankles at the end of her shift. Rima's shirt was torn, showing a well-muscled shoulder underneath. Her wrists were terribly bruised from pulling against the handcuffs, the left less so than the right. Jack wondered if that was because her right arm was stronger or if it was due to the surgery that Sean had noted when she came in. If it were the latter, Alison might be able to use that to her advantage.

He stepped into the room carrying his chair, placed it with the back facing her and straddled it like a high school student.

"Why were you in the village, Rima?"

"Is this your promise of freedom, Jack?" She looked up with him with her large brown eyes.

"We know the Reynolds were informers. Who else?"

"You say you fight for freedom, but what freedoms do you give? You force people to accept democracy through torture and at the end of a gun?"

"When necessary," Jack said shaking his head; he hoped a debate would get her to talk, "What did you think you'd learn by being in the village?"

"You grab people off the streets and hold them for money, for questioning, to make political statements -- then kill them as often as free them. You plant bombs for liberation, but there can be no freedom for those who live in fear. The Empire may not hold elections, but we guarantee civil rights, provide for people who cannot provide for themselves, look after those who…"

"We do what we must to ensure that the future is free."

"The future is not free, Jack, freedom is only found in the present. It is in individual choices. I may not vote, and may not select my leaders, but I'm free in every choice of every moment I have. Freedom is fleeting, momentary, and must be cherished as such."

"My future is free because I make it so through insurrection. I am a free man because I refuse to bow to the will of an oppressor."

"And so become an oppressor yourself. You're not free, you're a slave to your own ideology."

"I choose to follow my principles. I choose the path, for myself and, when need be, for my people. But it is a choice, just as it is their choice to follow me."

"And to torture? To kill men and women whose only crime is that they are loyal to a government that you oppose? What choice is that? You can't deny civil rights in the name of a 'Free Future.' The people here don't want your democracy. They chose to feel safe. They can't do that with you threatening them to live free or die."

"They will learn, I and people like me will teach them, through broadcasts like mine, and, yes, through violence when needed."

"And until they do learn, what? You will tell them how to vote. Will Jack Sartre lead them with the same sort of military command you lead your rebels?"

"Yes! If need be, yes. I have done well enough in war. I can do better in peace!"

Rima smiled. It didn't last long, didn't reach her mouth. It was only a fleeting glimmer in her eyes, but for that brief second she looked as if she had won a victory.

"What?" Jack asked. She remained silent. "What!"

The door burst open. Both Jack and Rima turned to see Alison striding into the room. Sean was two steps behind her.

"Sean, get your gun out of here!"

"She just sent a short burst signal with her implants," Alison said, moving close to Rima.

"We're still scrambling signals?"

Sean nodded. "Even if we weren't, we're too far from anything for the signal from an implant to get through."

Jack grabbed Rima's chin and pulled her face to look at his. "What did you think you'd accomplish?"

She smiled softly, sadly. An alarm suddenly sounded from the hall.

"There's another signal... this one's strong." Sean looked up and to the left, clearly accessing his implants. "It's coming from inside the base."

Jack grabbed Rima's shoulders and shook her. "What did you do?"

"You shouldn't have taken the bodies, Jack," she said, tilting her head.

"It's coming from the holding tank," Sean said.

"The bodies," Jack said, "you put a transmitter in the bodies. You knew we'd take them... as long as you were in range of the Reynold's corpses..."

"Rumors of death squads create fear. Confirmation dries up support," Rima said through a calm, knowing smile.

An explosion sounded from outside the hall. The ground shook. Alison turned to face the sound, Sean stepped through the door and looked down the hall. Gunshots sounded from all around them. Jack stared at Rima, her eyes no longer pleaded.

"Who are you?"

"Pahlavi, Rima, First Leftenant. Serial number-"

Jack felt a cold fury fill him and his body went

on automatic. He drew back his arm slowly, fingers closing into a fist. An explosion rocked the ground, followed by the sound of gunshots in the complex. He paused, looming over her, ready to launch his whole strength and body weight into that punch. He never had the chance.

Rima's foot flew into his face, the full force of her kick landing on his chin. His vision whited-out and he fell backwards onto the floor. Shaking his head, he looked up to see the Rima tug her left wrist against her bonds. Her hand seemed to collapse in on itself and slip free of the handcuff. Then she became a blur.

Alison turned quickly, but Rima twisted off the chair and swung it by the cuff still locked on her right hand. It smashed into Alison's head and blood sprayed across the room. As Alison went sprawling to the ground, Rima adjusted her grip, grabbing the chair with both hands.

"Sean!" Jack shouted as he scrambled to his feet.

Sean rushed back into the room, pulling the gun from its holster to meet the threat, too late. Rima swung the chair at his hand and sent the gun flying. The backswing smashed a leg into his temple. Sean fell like dead weight to the floor.

Jack threw himself at the Imperial Officer, but she launched a back-kick firmly into his solarplexis. He stopped in his place as he felt the wind rush out of him. Tiny lights appeared at the edge of his vision, and he fought to keep his feet. The Leftenant did not pause. She raised the chair over her and brought it down on his head. Twice.

Jack came around to find Rima standing over him with Sean's pistol aimed at his head. Behind her, Sean was unconscious and chained to the door. Alison lay in a pond of blood in the corner; her left arm bent in three places, her right four. The chair lay on its side next to her. Four soldiers dressed in Imperial grey moved about the room. They all had an Omega flash on their shoulder.

"You're not in logistics." Jack said, raising himself up on his elbow. He was not surprised to find his hands were cuffed.

"First Leftenant Rima Pahlavi," she said, picking up the chair from the ground, she placed it upright in front of him, "Army Intelligence. That's why I was in the village. We needed to get someone inside. Needed to be sure that the Reynold's information was right, that the infamous Jack Sartre was running this cell."

"You were the bait."

"No Jack," She said, flipping the around and straddling it like a high school jock, "I was the predator."

Question of the Day: What if you could share your memories with someone else?

November Log

M. D. Thalmann

I haven't written anything in forever, and I don't goddamn want to. It took ages to get my vidcap booted. This whole hab's ripe for the junk heap, not just this old-ass sensory cap. Not like NASA can't afford a new one.

Why am I writing? It's November, according to the readout on my HUD, which hangs just outside my normal field of view. They'll be expecting a report, but who gives a damn? Houston sent me here to put out fires, not be a goddamned secretary.

I crawl into the bath to get some relief from my aching back, though technically it's not my back. I am having a hard time adjusting to the new body. The tits are nice, but there's only so much fun you can have rubbing your own body and looking in the hollo-reflector, tits or not. This frame wasn't designed to dig in the hard packed blue-gray rock that make the moon's glow so iconic. It's like NASA isn't even trying to disqualify candidates anymore. Too much PC bullshit happening back on brown soil.

The tiller is broken, otherwise it wouldn't matter. I hate this fucking job. NASA keeps sending up lackeys, and they keep frying out in the first lunar cycle. No matter what kind of training they throw at the diggers, nothing prepares them for living on the little white ball when it's so black you can feel the weight of light years' of vacuum pressing down on you. So, they send me to clean it all up. They tell the poor fried motherfucker to calm the hell down and put on the vidcap and that they can call home, that it will all be butterflies and cotton-candy, or whatever the fuck. Then they hijack the poor bastards' cortex and wipe it. Plant me inside.

I go out to keep the tiller working and make sure the place is tip-top (ha) for the next transfer. I only ever get a short break before I'm called in to jockey a new meat-puppet for the rest of the rotation.

I light a smoke, knowing the alarms will start firing before I've exhaled my first drag. It's one of the few comforts NASA allows me, and one of the few reasons I do this shit job. I don't have lungs of my own any longer, they were removed. Cancer. Shit sucked. I got a loaner pair from some frat boy douchebag that wrapped his Italian sports car around a Doric column outside a government building. The transplant didn't take, so I smoke once in a blue moon… literally.

Somewhere back on Earth, my body's hooked to respirators and other apparatuses that keep my brain supplied with enough oxygen and fatty acids to keep me driving the puppets who mine the ore, but I haven't been on a walk in Earth Gravity in ages. Last time I tried, I bounce-hopped like a dumbshit and took a tumble.

I silence the atmo sensor alarm and suck down another harsh and wonderful pull from the smoke, not quite enjoying the dizzy feeling. She must not've been a smoker. The next one'll be better, once the skinsuit builds a tolerance.

Anyway, you probably just want me to get to the damned report, already.

Sector 16, log: November twelve 2079. What was your message, NASA? It's been purged from the log. Today, before I boarded the rover, there was a message-waiting indicator at the main terminal. I was ready to go EVA, so I left it. Those fucking gloves… anyway…. When I got back, the message was gone. Please advise.

EVA: It took a week to get the drift dug out and retrieve the tiller. The chain's missing several links. I can make it work, but we'll need a new chain and auger bits at resupply. Hab's only functioning at 78 percent, and Solar-One was sabotaged by candidate Alvarez before the wipe. Apparently she was harvesting the fuel cells, but for what, I don't know. Can't find 'em. Probably need to send up a new rod while you're at it. And let's put someone on the boat that can at least carry 200 pounds. I don't want to convert that to kilos, you nerds figure it out.

Kirk out.

I get out and dry my new tits off a little longer

than I should. I flick the butt into the tub and leave it for the reclaimer, a big no-no for which I've been reprimanded twice already, but when it breaks, I'm the one who cleans the septic anyway, so fuck it.

I power down and uncouple the vidcap, and rub my face, her face, with the damp towel.

An alarm sounds at the main console. A response from NASA so soon? Impossible. No time to boot the ancient vidcap again, I race to the terminal, careful not to skid on the thin aluminum flooring as I round the corners.

It's not from NASA. There are no headers. Instead, there's a crude graphic of the hourglass from Windows '98 draining binary sand in the ultra-high-definition that can only be brought to you in 16 bits. I'm stupid and curious, so I click the hourglass before the sands can run out. It asks for my security clearance. I offer it, thinking maybe it's NASA after all.

Go for operation? [Y/N], it says.

I don't have time to think, but I do anyway. Alvarez may have been hysterical and destroyed Solar-One, but she was also a brilliant coder.

I touch nothing, hoping It'll go away.

A spontaneous **[Y]** appears in the command prompt, and suddenly I know where that fucking fuel cell is. The whole place glows bright orange and then… **[SIGNAL LOST]**

* * *

"Thanks for your service, Lieutenant."

"Anytime," my artificial larynx buzzes.

"I'm glad the relay worked, or we'd have no idea what happened up there. Get some rest. We'll get you reassigned tomorrow."

"Somewhere with atmo."

"Roger that."

"On your way out, tell the nurse I'd like to be moved by the window... just for a little while."

Question of the Day: What if the universe can only support a finite number of living creatures at the same time?

A Question of Life

J. J. Clayborn

Adam sat in the front of the class, like he always did. His Advanced Astrophysics Professor, Dr. Andre Garver, prattled on about the inverse square law as it related to the decay of Hawking Radiation of gravitational singularities. Normally this kind of discussion would fascinate Adam, but he had other questions on his mind–questions that needed answers. But, today was different. Today it was just one question.

Eventually Dr. Garver noticed that the class was over and dismissed the students, who filed out of the auditorium in a barely controlled stampede. Adam broke away from the crowd and walked over to the Professor.

"Professor, can I ask you something?" Adam asked, standing beside the professor's desk.

"Sure, of course," Andre said.

Adam shifted and scratched his head. "Well, it's not exactly an astrophysics question, per se." He looked around the room, trying to find some inspiration to frame his question properly. "It's more of an existential question, really."

Andre laughed. "You always have deep questions, Adam. I'll do my best."

Adam shrugged. "I can't help myself, I'm always thinking. Anyway, the laws of physics tell us that no matter can be completely destroyed; only converted into energy and then, hypothetically, back into matter."

"That's right," Dr. Garver affirmed.

"Does that apply to people?" Adam asked.

"Well, your physical bodies will break down over time and be converted into nutrients for plant life, which in turn sprouts new matter in the form of plant growth..."

Adam shook his head. "No, I get that, Professor. I think you misunderstand my question. I mean, does that apply to people–to our souls?"

Dr. Garver blinked. "Our souls?"

"Yes, our souls. Souls are energy, aren't they?"

"Well, assuming that souls even exist, I suppose they would be energy," the professor mused.

"Oh, come on. Neuroscience can clearly record brain wave patterns on people with all kinds of machines. When we die that energy disappears. The brain isn't an electrical field generator and science has never explained what is responsible for making that energy in the first place, so it has to be a snapshot of our souls," Adam explained.

Dr. Garver rubbed his chin. "Well, yes, we don't know exactly how our bodies produce energy, but that doesn't mean that it's a soul…"

"Humor me, professor. This is a philosophical thought exercise; I'm not looking to publish a scientific paper on this."

"Okay, for the sake of argument I'll assume that the energy is a soul."

"And since it's an empirically measurable source, it counts as energy, right?"

"Sure."

Adam continued. "And energy and matter are essentially interchangeable…"

"… more or less," Andre agreed.

"So what happens to a person's energy after they die? Where does it go?"

The professor sighed. "I don't know, Adam. No one does. Some people think it goes to heaven, or hell, or some other mythical place that holds them for eternity…"

"Like a black hole, preventing energy from escaping," Adam said.

The professor chuckled. "I suppose that's one way of looking at it." He shrugged. "Still others think that it gets recycled, and we are born again in something else. Others think that it dissipates out into the universe, much like the inverse square law we talked about today."

Adam held his gaze. "What do you think, professor?"

He sighed. "I honestly don't know, Adam. But

I've thought a lot about it over the years. I have some ideas, but I can't prove any of them."

"Like what?" Adam sat down and listened.

"Well, I don't assume that the universe is truly infinite. I assume that the universe is at a constant physical mass–that the amount of matter in the universe is, in fact, finite. Granted, I think it's immeasurably enormous, but not infinite. This would mean that the amount of matter never changes; it only converts back and forth from energy to matter and vice versa. But what if the same were true for life energy? What if there is only a finite amount of life energy available in the whole universe?"

Adam sat speechless.

"The human race has been expanding, but it's killed off entire species in the process. What if those extinctions are part of the price?"

Adam shook his head, dumbstruck. "I've never even thought about that, professor."

Andre nodded. "What if something has to give up its life force in order for something else to be born?"

Adam's eyes were wide with fascination. "And if it's the same life energy, are you really ever gone?"

Dr. Garver shrugged. "I have no idea. Like I said, I can't prove any of this. It's all just hypothetical thoughts; crazy ramblings from an old man with too much time on his hands."

Adam laughed. "Your thoughts are very thought provoking." Adam stood. "Assuming you are right, do you think there'd be a way to harness that life energy and control it?"

"I honestly don't know, Adam. I never thought it." He scratched his chin in thought. "I suppose it should be hypothetically possible."

"Thanks, professor." Adam said. As he ran out of the door, he shouted over his shoulder "see you next week!"

* * *

Adam pushed the cart down the cold, sterile hall of the hospital. He stopped at the nurse's desk and she directed him to the room down the hall.

A squeaky wheel echoed in the hallway with Adam's footsteps. He reached the door and pushed the small cart inside. "It's nice to see you again, Dr. Garver."

The elderly professor smiled weakly at Adam from his hospital bed and extended a shaky hand.

Adam shook his hand and sat down beside him. "Professor, do you remember our conversation–the one from about five years ago?"

Andre blinked slowly and sighed a labored breath. "Which one? We've had many."

Adam chuckled. "That we did, Professor." He smiled at the memories. "I meant the one about the life energy, and what happens when we pass on from this place."

Dr. Garver nodded. "I've been thinking about that one a lot lately," he confessed.

"I've never stopped thinking about it." Adam patted the professor's hand. "Thank you." He straightened up in his chair. "Now, professor, I'd like your consent for an experiment."

A puzzled expression washed over the professor's face.

"I've been looking into things, professor." Adam pulled out a small computer tablet and pulled up some pictures. "First, I was able to isolate the exact frequency of the life-force energy." Adam flipped to the next picture. "Then I studied batteries and electronic components to understand how that energy might be safely stored." He swiped to a new picture. "And then I studied wireless energy to see how that energy might be captured as it leaves the body." He gestured to his cart. "And now I've built a prototype."

"A prototype of what, Adam?"

He shrugged. "I haven't named it yet, but in essence, a soul catcher. If I've calculated everything right, I'll be able to capture and store a person's soul as it leaves the body at the moment of death."

"And if you're wrong?"

"Then whatever happens to your soul after you die will continue and my device won't work," Adam explained.

The professor frowned. "And what do you plan on doing with these souls?"

Adam winced. "Release them, of course. What did you think I would do with them?"

"Then why both capturing them at all?"

Adam nodded as he understood the miscommunication. "I want to prove something, and test something. Capturing a soul will prove once and for all that they do actually exist. But, I also want to see if I can release it in a specific manner so that I have control over what new life is created."

"So you want to redirect the soul?"

Adam nodded. "Yes. I know that you aren't long for this world. Given your interest in this topic I was hoping you'd agree to let me test it on you."

Andre was silent for a moment. "Considering the inevitable outcome that we all face, I'm curious to know. Even if I'm not here anymore, I'd like to help answer this question. You can test it on me."

Adam turned on the machine and sat with his old friend for days. They talked and reminisced about the past. It didn't seem like 5 years had passed since Adam was a student in his class. Adam had been visiting for about a week. He drifted off to sleep in the chair beside the professor's bed. When he awoke the professor was gone–passed from this world. Adam made a small frown and touched the professor's hand. "Goodbye, old friend." He stood and walked around to the other side of the bed. A green light blinked on his machine. "Well, hello there," he said to the machine.

Adam drove for hours. He went to a remote part of the state where a forest fire had devastated the local landscape. According to the scientists and forest rangers it would be a few years before life returned to this burnt out valley. Driving the car down the dirt road Adam found a good spot and pulled over. The smell of charcoal and cinder assaulted his nose as he stepped out of the car. The air was dry, and the ground crunched beneath his feet. It was eerily quiet here; not even the birds greeted him. It shouldn't have surprised him, there was nothing for the birds here, but he still found it odd.

Adam retrieved his machine and set it up next to a dead husk of a mighty oak. He wasn't really sure what to expect, so he turned the switch that powered on the unit. Adjusting the controls he flipped the switch that released the professor's life energy back into the universe.

Nothing happened.

Adam felt no different.

He saw nothing change.

He couldn't measure any change.

Maybe it didn't work. Maybe it shouldn't work. Maybe these were things he shouldn't be messing with. He sat on the hood of his car lost in thought for hours. By the time he pulled himself out of his thoughts it was dusk. Adam wasn't familiar with this area and didn't want to risk driving at night, so he decided to sleep in the back seat of the car. There certainly weren't any animals or people nearby to bother him. He lied down and fell asleep thinking about his mentor.

A bright light made him squint. It wouldn't stop shining. He turned his head and shielded his eyes with his hand. He was groggy as he awoke and it took a moment to sink in. The sun–it was morning already. Adam sighed and opened the car door. He stretched and yawned.

Adam walked over to his machine. He was going to return it to the lab and break it down for parts when something caught his eye. There in the black, charred ground beside the machine was something green. Not just anything green, it was a sprout of an oak tree. "It works!" he shouted. He fell on his butt and cried and stared at the tree for an hour before packing up and returning to his lab.

A week later, Adam visited the site with several colleagues. The young sapling was now 3 feet tall. Life had returned to an area ten foot in diameter from where the machine sat. In excited tones the scientists discussed the meaning. It proved, fairly definitively, that souls did exist. It strongly suggested that life energy was required to create life, and that this life energy never went away. The implications of that alone were profound. Every person who ever lived, they were still here with us, all around us in some way or another. The fact that the only life that existed in this valley was in a perfect circle around where the machine sat also proved that the energy could be stored and released in a controlled manner. This changed everything.

The scientists returned to the lab. Adam was given a promotion to oversee this research project and spent the next decade researching life energy.

* * *

"We're dropping out of hyperspace now, sir," the helmsman reported in.

Adam sat on the bridge of the science ship. Nervous energy filled his stomach, and he took a deep breath to calm himself. "Very well, take us close to the target planet." Adam stood and his way to the elevator. After a short ride he disembarked in the science lab and went directly to the experiment.

He pored over every inch of the metal casing

that housed the grandest experiment mankind had ever seen. The invention of the hyper drive was a phenomenal leap forward, but this would change everything. This device, a missile sized version of his first prototype, contained the life energy of tens of thousands of people. In a few moments they would fire this at the lifeless rock they had selected. If everything worked out according to plan that lifeless rock would become a living, breathing planet in a few months' time. This meant that every single world in the habitable zone of a star could be reformed in a short period of time, even if it was lifeless. Humanity could spread into the stars and would be sure to never die, all thanks to Andre's willingness to help answer the hard questions.

Adam returned to the bridge once he was sure that the device was in working order. He oversaw the crew as they loaded the device into the firing mechanism. It wasn't a torpedo, exactly. The launcher just had an electromagnetic accelerator that would fling the metal casing toward the planet. Gravity would do the rest as long as they released it in the right position.

The moment finally came and Adam watched as the device shot out past the ship on his command. It fell towards the planet. The cameras tracked it as long as they could, but eventually they had to track its course with a holographic map.

The device impacted and there was no immediate change. Adam updated his research notes.

Every day the ship staying in orbit and monitored the situation. After a week a noticeable area of vegetation was present. After a month, the area was quite large. Three months after the device landed the area covered an entire continent. Adam needed to see it for himself.

A landing ship with Adam and a handful of biologists left the lower hangar of the ship and fell toward the planet. They entered the atmosphere and made their way down. From this altitude the entire continent was covered with lush vegetation. They found a clearing and gently dropped the ship into the middle of it.

As Adam opened the door to the small ship he was speechless. The world was gorgeous, and completely unlike anything he had ever seen. It was teeming with life; plants and animals; flying creatures, small creatures, aquatic creatures, and more. None of them were anything like the animals back home on Earth.

A tear rolled down his cheek; he felt the salt leave a trail on his skin. A thought occurred to him. Although this was the life energy of the people who had passed on, and they were still here in a metaphysical sense, they would never be like they were when they were alive. That person, that instance of them, is now a memory. They live on in memories, and their energy lives on in the universe, but they will never return in that familiar form that we know and love.

Adam sat on a rock and watched for hours. His team bustled about taking samples and readings, but he was content to bask in the natural beauty of this place, which he named Andre's World.

Seeing it in this pristine condition, he wasn't

sure that he wanted humans to build a colony here. He was conflicted. Maybe they shouldn't have ever meddled with this. Maybe there are some questions that are best left unanswered. He tried to come to terms with everything and one thought brought him comfort. He was glad to know that while his friend and mentor had passed, his energy still persisted. He thought back to the Oak tree and smiled. "I'll come visit you when I get back, my friend," he said to himself.

Question of the Day: When does a person come into their own? Is it because of what happens to them, or is it in them all along?

Sunstalker

Cheryl S. Mackey

Filmy clouds of gas and dust shimmered in the cracked display. Beyond the nebula, tiny stars dotted the blackness with an array of multicolored pinpoints of light. One of those lights, one of the more distant ones, was without a doubt The Milky Way Galaxy.

At least Noehni hoped so. She had come a long way to find the last of her people.

"Initiate the heads up display. Show me Old Earth and our current location."

A beam of light erupted between her and the view screen, an interactive hologram showing the entire breadth of the universe. Two tiny beacons blinked on opposite ends of the image. The faintly green glow of the HUD bathed the room in flickering light. She squinted at the tiny coordinates etched into the hologram beside her target. She traced a finger along an invisible line between Old Earth and her position in the Deep Black.

"Take me to this location," Noe commanded. "Maintain current configuration." She tapped at a small empty appearing space on the hologram near but not too near her target. The point pulsed and a series of coordinates appeared on the screen. The yellow lights on the console blinked green in acceptance of the command. The HUD flicked off.

The ship's AI droned, "Accessing Dark drives. Aligning wormhole bank—"

Noe interrupted the bored voice. "Nope. No. Don't tell me how. I don't want to know. Just get me there. The less I know the better. That's what my grandmother apparently wanted."

Her grandmother's death had left her unprepared, at the very least. The least the old bat could have done was leave an instruction manual behind. Or a cheat sheet. In the hundreds of years she on the ship, since age 6, she had never once been given any semblance of control or responsibility of the super advanced starship.

The door slid open. The hiss of air moving from the corridor into the small bridge stirred her shoulder length black hair into the air. She stared down the unfamiliar hallway with a frown. Where the hell were her quarters? The place where the door to the captain's cabin should have been was now a blank wall embedded with tiny, flickering ambient lights.

"Well, shit."

Four right hand turns, two anti-grav elevators, and an hour of poking her head into uncountable numbers of unknown rooms and passages later, Noe found her cabin. She half wondered if the Sunstalker had made it harder for her to navigate on purpose out of spite. The semi-sentient ship was aging and perhaps AI could be infected with…something to explain the sarcastic stubbornness and borderline defiance it had shown her ever since her grandmother had died and supposedly left her as captain and sole resident of the only home she remembered. If she hadn't known better the ship was testing her.

Noe studied the underside of the bunk bed without really seeing it. The quest for control of the Sunstalker had not gone well. She turned over to stare at the wall instead, stomach rolling.

"Sunstalker, initiate sleep cycle. Wake me when we reach the destination."

"Sleep cycle initiated. Alarm initiated. Estimated sleep cycle is 21 hours."

The room went pitch black.

Noe sighed and closed her eyes, the darkness behind them no less black. It was the memories that hovered there each time she struggled to sleep that made the darkness so dangerous. She forced her body to relax, but she could do little to force her mind to.

* * *

Officer Jedax Grunnas wondered if dying of

boredom was a real affliction. He then wondered just how long one would take to die of it. He blindly groped for the switch to activate the exterior lights and scanned the rugged, empty, terrain of asteroid N23 with his own eyes in order to stave off said demise. His light and fast jumpship had been parked on the pockmarked rock for nearly an Old Earth Week now. Border patrol duty sucked.

"Computer, scan quadrant 1A."

The robotic voice chirped, "Scanning."

"1A quadrant clear."

"Scan quadrant 1B."

"Scanning."

"1B quadrant clear."

"Scan quadrant 1C."

"Scanning."

Jedax sank back into the chair and propped his feet on the console. The AI continued to hum and chirp as it scanned 1C for anomalies. This particular sector would take a while as it encompassed most of the shipping and transport lanes between the inner planets, Old Earth, and the outer Black.

"Computer, continue scanning all quadrants. Inform me of any anomalies. I'm getting some sleep."

He exited the narrow bridge. The jumpship was small and more than cramped for someone of his size. At nearly 7 feet tall Jedax had to stoop to clear the ceiling. His quarters were efficient. Cot, sink, toilet, shower, cupboard. That's it.

He dropped onto the cot with a grimace. His lanky frame hung off both ends, or would if the damned contraption hadn't been wedged where the cupboard should have been. The cupboard now took up the middle of the small room to provide a non-useful privacy barrier for the toilet and shower

Jedax clamped his eyes shut. Six weeks of border patrol duty on a tiny jumpship on a manmade asteroid was suicidally boring at best. He should be back on the station, doing something, anything, to keep Old Earth from falling apart. Well, more apart. The ancestral home of his people was now a barely controlled explosion. Shards of the planet, held together by alien tractor beams, were all that was keeping it together and now those were failing. He could have used his influence to do something, done research into the alien tech...but no, he was destined to become a traffic cop He rolled over and stared at the cold metal wall. He willed the stray thoughts aside with a frown and focused on emptying his thoughts.

"Lights off." He muttered.

The room darkened until it resembled the blackness of space.

He welcomed it.

* * *

The first jolt shook Noe awake. The second flung her off the cot and against the iron plated wall across the tiny room. Waves of pain rolled from her left shoulder to her fingers as she struggled to her feet in the darkness. She shook her arm to restore feeling to it... and hopefully function. She gripped the nearest thing she could find and held on with her uninjured hand. The jerking motion halted with a piercing, metallic shriek. Ears ringing and arm throbbing, she scrabbled for the latch on the heavy iron door and tugged. The lock struck something with a grinding thump and snapped to a halt, jammed.

"Sunstalker, what the hell?"

"We are now at the coordinates."

"What was that? Did we just run through an asteroid field?"

"It appears that our destination was already occupied."

Noe's head throbbed. The Sunstalker's AI system would be rebooted after this. Or just booted.

"Lights on!" she bellowed. A surge of energy buzzed somewhere making the hairs prickle at the back of her neck. A faint yellow glow filled the small cabin from some sort of hololighting. It flickered sadly to the static laced hum now filling the air.

"Sunstalker, what did we hit?" She jiggled the heavy iron latch again. It grated against the bolt but didn't budge.

"According to the scans we collided with an Artificial Observatory Asteroid, model R-223-N23."

Noe banged her forehead against the door frame. "Artificial asteroid. Right."

Eyes crimped shut against the blinding headache and nauseating lights, Noe forced her breathing to slow. She would get out of this. She had to. She had no one else but herself.

And an asshole AI.

"Okay, Sunstalker," Noe muttered. She didn't bother raising her voice and possibly raising her blood pressure even higher. "Systems check. Life support. Security. Engines. Uh, everything."

"Systems check initiating."

Noe slapped her good hand against the metal plated door. The hollow thud echoed in the dimly lit room.

"And can you get me out of this room?" She asked after a long moment.

The heavy latch bucked out of her grip and the door popped open. Noe stumbled out the door and paused to look up and down the nondescript, dimly lit hallway.

"Shit."

* * *

"Shit." Jedax bolted upright a split second too late. The grinding that had pierced his brain and invaded his troubled dreams became a violent jolt. He, the cot, and the unfortunate wardrobe tumbled around the small room. His forehead bounced off the wall and the rest of the room's contents bounced off of him.

"What the hell?" he roared into the turbulent darkness. Emergency strobes flashed followed by the earsplitting klaxon. He shoved the wardrobe off of him and stood. The floor and short ceiling had buckled, giving Jedax the impression that the entire ship had been...squished.

He rummaged for the weapons locker built into the wall by the door. Armed with a stun gun and a kinetic rifle, he forced the warped hatch open and stumbled into what was left of the small jumpship's hallway. He halted, startled, at the sight of the remains of the ship. The entire starboard side had been peeled aside like an Old Earth tin can, revealing a darkened space beyond.

Except, the darkness wasn't space. It was the insides of another, much larger, ship.

Exposed wiring popped and sparked along the shredded remains of the damaged jumpship hull, revealing a giant chasm in the brief flashes of light. Rusty metal, jumbled parts of machinery, an archaic crane arm, and the distinct smell of stale air greeted him.

Jedax flicked the safety off of the kinetic rifle and slipped into the darkness. The stale air was cold, but he could breathe it. The larger ship that had somehow swallowed his had managed to do so without exposing its cargo hold to the vacuum of space. The klaxon and flashing lights abruptly died, leaving him in the vast cargo hold of an unknown ship lit by only the sparking, demolished remains of his small vessel.

"Hello? This is Officer Jedax Grunnas of the InterStellar Shipping Security Department of the Planets of the Old—"

He stopped, the echo of his voice hollow and loud in the dank quiet of the vast cargo hold. Something told him that whoever was on the giant ship wouldn't care if he was a Space Cop or not. He tipped his head to listen for the sounds of the engines, crew, anything, but only an eerie silence stretched on in the flickering darkness.

"Officer Jedax Grunnas," a robotic voice pierced the darkened hold. Jedax jumped and swung about to face the speaker, but no one emerged from the shadows lining the room.

"Hello?" He called out again, puzzled. Where was the crew? What kind of ship had such a giant cargo hold and no cargo?

The cold, unemotional voice spoke again, "Officer Jedax Grunnas, please remain in your ship."

Jedax finally spied the small speaker in the floor at his feet. Judging from the cracked optical lens staring up at him he figured it had once been a holoprojector. And a surveillance camera. He frowned at the camera.

"My ship is pretty much destroyed. Who am I speaking to? Where is everyone?" He asked. He peered into the camera. "And how in the hell did my ship get inside yours?"

* * *

Noe reared back from the view screen as the Space Cop's eyeball filled it. She grimaced and flicked a switch to shut it off. The giant eyeball vanished, leaving her staring at the now blank screen in mute horror.

"Sunstalker, what happened?"

"It appears that the artificial asteroid had been a base for local police speed traps, Captain. My safety protocols demanded I ensure the survival of all mortals."

Noe paused. "Just mortals, huh? Not us Immortals?"

She half wondered if the AI was rolling its

digital eyes at her.

"You put the ship in the hold because it was too damaged?"

"Yes, Captain."

"Scan the ship and Cop. You know his name and rank, now we need to know if he can help us...or hurt us." Noe muttered. She flexed her aching arm and winced. It would do.

"Scanning now."

"Good. Time to go meet our guest. You can fill me in as I try to find him."

Noe stalked the dimly lit hallways in search of the main cargo hold. Not that she knew where it was. In fact, she still knew next to nothing about her people, much less their technology. Growing up on the Sunstalker had been a sterile, cold environment heavily controlled by her grandmother. Hundreds of years with her grandmother at the helm had not made the ship loyal to Noehni upon Aegis' death only a short time ago.

"Captain?"

Noe halted and studied the empty hall. "What?"

"I have the information on Officer Jedax Grunnas that you requested."

A distant bang and shout echoed somewhere down the maze of hallways. Noe grimaced.

"Hold that thought and get me to the cargo hold faster. Please."

"Yes, Captain."

The hallway ahead of her morphed into a solid wall. A new hallway appeared to her right leading a short distance to a pair of double doors. Red lights strobed above them, but the alarm remained mute.

Something heavy slammed into the doors. They rattled but didn't budge.

"Captain, you should know that-"

Noe waited for the angry shouts behind the door to subside. "Yes?"

The banging continued. Laser pulses pierced a profanity laced tyrade. Blue bursts of light flickered between the seams of the doors but didn't appear to do anything.

"You should know that Officer Jedax Grunnas is well connected with the Magnates of Old Earth. He is related to more than three founders of the Trade Industry that serviced all human outposts from here to Jupiter before the Sundering."

Noe frowned. "So he's practically royalty. Got it. Open the doors. Keep a security field ready in case he decides he doesn't like me."

The Sunstalker chirped silently in her head.

She faced the closed doors, empty handed, waiting to face a possible ally. Or foe.

The doors slid apart.

The bore of an advanced kinetic rifle filled her vision.

* * *

"Hold it right there, Lady." Jedax barked. He jabbed the pointy end of the kinetic rifle into her face.

The woman's eyes crossed in an attempt to focus on the weapon. Instead of recoiling in fear, she swatted the weapon aside and pushed past him.

Jedax stood there for a moment, startled, before

moving to confront her. Again.

"Who are you and where am I?" he asked. He eyed the petite woman. She appeared to be in her mid-twenties, but something about her wide, knowing gaze, challenged that assumption. He studied her carefully, now more alert.

Something didn't add up with her.

He didn't recognize her uniform. Instead of standard shipping captains clothing, her attire amounted to something of a tunic and trousers, loosely belted at her waist. The clothing was nondescript, loose, shades of tan and blue, no insignias or rank patches. No weapons belt or holsters mussed the casual outfit. Heavy boots clanked and shoulder length dark hair swayed with each step she took toward his mangled ship. She didn't bother to turn around when he followed.

"Is this an Earth-class ship?" The woman asked.

"What?" Jedax frowned. He glanced at the remains of the jumpship, then back to her. Pale blue eyes, wide and unblinking, had trained on him. He blinked and then realized he'd holstered the kinetic rifle in the sheath at his back without thinking about it. "Wait, who are you?"

Her eyes narrowed, her gaze searched his. For an uneasy moment, the hair prickled on the back of his neck.

"I am Noehni Seyun and you are on my ship, the Sunstalker," The woman spun around as she spoke, sending her hair whipping out. She pointed a finger at the gash running the length of his ship. Whispered words reached his ears but he couldn't make out what she was muttering. Or, in fact, why she seemed to be conversing with someone he couldn't see or hear.

"What happened to my ship, Lady?"

"You can call me Noe. It's like the Old Earth name Zoe, but with an 'n'. Don't worry most people can't pronounce it the first time."

The woman rounded on him again. He barely had enough time to hide the slack jawed shock from her.

"And your ship was in my parking spot."

Jedax gaped, for the first time in his life struck silent. The strange woman seemed to take his mute shock for understanding and turned her back on him once more. This time her muttering was loud enough to be heard.

"Sunstalker, can you get it operational again?"

Nothing answered her.

"How long?" She asked the empty cargo hold. "Really?"

Jedax wondered if she could see the steam erupting from his ears.

"Lady! What in the name of the Seven Hells are you doing?" he bellowed. To her credit she didn't flinch when his voice echoed in the vast space around them. Instead, she peered over one shoulder at him, her frown a shade of disappointed.

She addressed the empty hold again, "You never mentioned he had a temper."

He growled. Actually growled. She hid a smirk behind her shoulder and turned back to the damaged jumpship.

"Ok, let's see if he will deal with us." Noehni muttered to the cold air. She turned to face him again, her expression now hesitant. Her small nose wrinkled in some form of abject distaste.

"Officer Grunnas, I can repair your ship, but," she said. "Only if you agree to help me with a small matter."

Jedax's ears burned. "You can repair my ship? The ship yours damaged?"

She had the grace to blush, but her lips tightened and her gaze grew chilly.

"Yes."

"Why should I do anything but bring reinforcements to impound your ship and toss your skinny ass in prison?"

"Because you have nothing else left, Officer Grunnas. Your ship is damaged, you have no way of contacting your people, and you are on my ship now."

"Are you threatening me?"

"No, I am telling you exactly how it is. I can fix your ship if you do one small thing for me, Officer," Noe asserted. She glanced back at the jumpship and frowned. "At least, I think it is small. I'm not certain."

Jedax's frown matched hers. He turned to study his ship with a glower as if it had betrayed him. The damage was extensive; he admitted to himself, the entire side of the hull had been peeled back as if by a razor, exposing the entire interior. Through the tangle of sparking wires and ducts he could see his small cabin, the sad excuse of a kitchen, and the bridge.

"I'm listening."

"I need to get to Old Earth."

Jedax's frown wobbled into a smirk before a snort of laughter escaped.

Noe's frown deepened and he elaborated.

"You're joking, right? No one goes there. It's a shattered mess."

"I know."

His laughter subsided at her puzzled stare. Her pale gaze was clear, earnest.

He dragged a hand over his jaw. The bristle of his five o'clock shadow reminded him that he hadn't shaved in a day or two…or three.

"You don't understand, girl, there is nothing there for anyone. It's being held together with duct tape and hope."

Noe's head tilted. "Duct tape? What's that?"

He resisted the urge to grind his knuckles into his eye sockets. A stabbing headache pounded behind his right eye.

"Nothing. Just…nothing."

"So I will repair your ship and you will guide me to Old Earth."

"What? No!"

"You are a confusing person, Officer. You have yet to tell me why we cannot go to Old Earth other than duct tape."

Now the other eye twitched in time to the pounding ache.

"Listen, There is almost no place left to go on Old Earth anymore. It is all but destroyed. The tractor beams that hold the planet together are failing and no one left alive knows how to fix it."

"I do."

"You do? You do what?" he asked.

"I can repair the tractor beams, Officer. Just as I can repair your ship," Noe gestured at the small heap of twisted metal.

"What do you mean?" Jedax's head pounded in time with his racing heart. The pain was turning his vision spotty. "Why...how would you do that?"

Her frown quirked into a sad smile.

"Because my people are the ones who had created it."

* * *

Noe watched the imposing Officer's head swivel between her and his damaged ship, his jaw slack with disbelief. She would have giggled any other time at the look on his rugged face, but now was not the time for humor. What time she had was growing smaller every day.

"Your people?" he asked. His voice was a baritone rumble in the vast darkness of the illusory hold. "That's impossible. The Sundering happened thousands of years ago. Wait, what people? You're human, right?"

Noe inhaled to steady her nerves. Time for the truth. Lies would do no one any good now.

"No, I am not human, Officer."

"I don't understand...not human?"

Noe shook her head, her shoulder length hair swaying with the motion. His dark gaze followed, but watched with the blankness of someone puzzling on an impossible dilemma.

A group of her people had sought Old Earth out thousands of years before in a dire emergency, according to Sunstalker, and had in turn saved the planet and kept watch over it until they could be rescued. The humans had known it was aliens, but had surprisingly pretended otherwise and let them be.

That had been long ago. So long, that it was possible that they were all gone now. The only hint of their existence that remained was the odd blue laser-like tractor beams that held the shattered planet together.

"Please, Officer, I need your help. I cannot repair the tractor beams without going down to your homeworld and seeing first hand. I also must locate whoever is left of my people"

"Jedax. Call me...Jedax." He muttered. A spark of interest lit up his rugged face. "You can repair the beams? How?"

"Please call me Noe, Jedax. If I can get close enough I can perhaps have Sunstalker run diagnostics to find out what is wrong with it."

Dark eyes, no brown, just brown, turned to look her in the eye steadily once more. Gone was the vagueness and slack jawed confusion, replaced by a spark of interest that had been missing.

"You are not human. You are an alien."

It wasn't a question.

She nodded. Her eyes narrowed, waiting for the gleam of greed or whatever a primitive race felt when faced with a known impossibility.

Nothing by raw curiosity stared back.

Noe cast an uneasy glance upwards. *Sunstalker, can you read him?*

The AI whirred silently in the background of her

mind as it always did, but a tingle of energy spiked when the computer replied.

He has no illicit intentions. His thoughts remain puzzled but very curious, Captain. He seems honorable. Honorable enough in fact to keep his questions to himself.

Noe mentally sighed. *Keep tabs on him; let me know if his intentions alter.*

Yes Captain.

"Noe?"

She jumped, startled at the sound of her name being spoken for the first time by anyone but her long dead mother, grandmother, and the Sunstalker.

And he'd pronounced it correctly.

She coughed to hide, poorly, the fact that her attention had drifted.

"Um, yes?"

"Now what? How are you going to get my ship fixed?"

"My uh, computer will handle that."

She squirmed at the disbelieving stare he leveled at her.

"Why should I trust you?" He asked finally.

She leveled her own stare at him.

"Because we need each other to fix problems we can't solve alone. You need your ship, I need a way to the surface of the planet that won't attract too much attention."

"Well, the only way to legally get to the planet is through the Moonstation. There's a once a day skytrain down to the last outpost of survivors on the planet. Maybe you can start there?"

Noe's eyebrows shot up.

"There are still people down there? The

139

atmosphere held?"

"Yes, barely. The shard they are on happens to be the largest one. I don't even know what part of the planet to be honest."

"But the people on your moon will know?"

"Yes, we have to go through them first. They are essentially the law now. The Magnates run a tight ship. Anything funny and they won't hesitate to arrest you and destroy your ship."

"That's why we need to take yours, Officer."

His eyebrows matched hers in altitude.

"My ship won't allow that I'm afraid. She is...stubborn. Come, you must be hungry. I have researched as much of Old Earth history as I could in the Deep and can get you some familiar foods, I believe. It shouldn't take long for the *Sunstalker* to repair your ship."

Noe turned on her heel and stalked to the door without checking to see if he'd follow.

He did.

* * *

Jedax watched the alien female eat the surprisingly realistic Old Earth pancakes with curiosity. Nothing she did gave any clue about her species...a gesture, a look, her voice, nothing. It was extraordinarily strange. He'd discretely looked for pointy ears or gills, or...something. What if she really was human and was delusional or spacey?

"You look human." He blurted out. He caught himself just as the last word escaped his mouth. He'd managed to control himself all of ten minutes.

He hid a groan behind his hand and shoveled another wad of syrup soaked pancake into his mouth as a chaser to his foot.

She tilted her head and studied him in silence as she chewed slowly. She obviously had more manners than he did if she was waiting to answer when she'd finished chewing.

She did so and her answer was not what he'd expected.

"I know."

Open mouth, shove foot in deeper. "So how is that possible? Are you sure you're not human?"

This time she smiled and the small mess hall lit up. No, literally. The lighting brightened.

"I'm sure, Jedax Grunnas. Just as sure as you believe you are human."

"Well, I am." Now his face burned red.

"What if I know of a story that might tell you something different?"

"Wait, what?" he choked on the pancake, swallowed the too big piece, and struggled to breathe and cough at the same time. Gods he was a mess. What had happened to the serene, cold, unwaverable...and bored...Officer Grunnas?

"I was joking, Officer." Noe smiled. "But come, we must get to your ship. It is repaired and time is short."

"That fast? Why the hurry?" he stood and stabbed a last forkful of pancake into his mouth. He watched emotions tumble like an avalanche across Noe's face and froze.

Pain. Regret. Fear.

He put his fork down. It dematerialized into the

141

smart-table along with the plates and napkins. Incredibly efficient and waste free.

"You're afraid."

Wide blue eyes studied him frankly, the dark pupils at their centers all but swallowing the blue irises.

"I am. I don't know if I am really the last of my people. I hope not. Being alone is…terrible."

His stomach clenched at her words.

* * *

Jedax buckled the harness and gave it a testy tug. It remained tight. Out of the corner of his eye he watched Noe do the same. The jumpship had been returned to its original special shape, jacked up quarters and all. Noe had only smirked at his ransacked cabin and dropped her gear in the smaller, neater one next door. Squeezed between his cabin and the mess hall, it maybe qualified as a closet, but she had simply stowed her gear and followed him onto the small bridge.

"Systems check," he flicked a switch on the console and watched the rows of lights, buttons, and switches flash several colors. Satisfied, he glanced over at the alien female and caught her staring back.

"What?" he asked, suddenly self-conscious.

"You are a good man, Jedax Grunnas. No matter what happens…thank you."

"No matter what…wait, will something happen down there?"

She shook her head. "I don't know. This is all new to me. I just…need to find what is left of my people. And fix the tractor beams."

"Do you really know how?"

She frowned. "I'll figure something out."

"Good enough for me. Let's go."

"Sunstalker, open the cargo bay doors." Noe called out.

The console chirped and the entire jumpship jerked. A hissing scrape echoed somewhere behind them in the darker recesses and the Jedax slid a finger along a screen on the console. It chirped and the ship lifted into the air with a smooth whirr.

"Jumpship One, heading for the Moonstation. Flight locked and loaded."

Noe tugged the harness tighter around her shoulders. "Why do you call it 'Moonstation'?"

Jedax guided the small starship out of the giant doors that appeared behind them. The smooth glide barely noticeable, he took the time to study the alien female.

"Because it's actually a space station. The moon was destroyed when the planet exploded. It was created to mimic the moon itself and maintain what stability left on the planet."

Noe frowned. "That sounds odd. Your people had that technology?"

Jedax squinted at the small display, at a loss of what to say. He tapped in the guidance codes for the station, grateful for the distraction of actually having to pilot the ship to give him time to answer.

"No. We didn't. And who or whatever helped us remained in the shadows. We never did figure out who to thank for helping us."

"I see. The Soldeuns are...were...an odd race

from what my grandmother would tell me. Proud, noble, generous, open minded, and kind hearted. Powerful. Except she wouldn't explain what had happened to them or why. Or why or how she was connected to Old Earth." Noe said with a frown. "My grandmother's knowledge of your world was limited to what we could find in various forms of transmissions."

"Are you sure you've never been here before?"

"No, but," Noe hesitated. "Over the years I know my grandmother had been in contact with someone. I never knew who."

"Want to bet that person is on the Moonstation? You said you were looking for your people."

"I...hope so. I have so many questions."

Jedax snorted and watched their tiny blip on the screen maneuver around asteroids and space junk. "Me too."

* * *

The Moonstation appeared large in the small display. At a distance it appeared exactly like the original moon should have according to her basic history lessons, but as they sped closer Noe could see definitely differences. Instead of a sphere of cold white and grey rock, smaller lit circles covered a globe of similar size and shape.

"Are those just...lights?" Noe asked. She squinted into the view screen.

"Yep. Those are massive light orbs. They cover the entire external frame of the station. They don't necessarily emit their own light though, but reflect the sun's back at the planet like the original moon used to. It works. Kinda'."

"Fascinating," Noe studied the 3D scan of the station that popped up on the holo-projector to her left. It showed the moon like station in detail, including flight paths of various ships and asteroids. Their small ship was a tiny, fast moving dot. "Where is the dock?"

"Dark side. They keep this side free of anything that might give it away to the inhabitants still on Old Earth."

Noe's head swiveled. "They don't know?"

"No. They've had enough of a rough life. Outsiders tend to leave them alone if possible. The scientists and medical teams keep an eye on them from a distance. Even the Skytrain is a mystery to them."

"That's sad."

Jedax caught and held her gaze. Tears edged dark eyelashes. "Why?"

"They are alone."

"They aren't alone. They have each other." he said. He steered the jumpship into low orbit around the dark side of the Moonstation. In the shadows it was easier to see the inner workings. The giant orbs the reflected the sunlight swung wide like a giant door as they approached.

"There's our dock. Since this ship is small we get a priority spot. And I happen to know the dockmaster," Jedax said. He slid a finger over the controls and they flashed blue. "Moonstation this is Jumpship One. Approaching dock 4."

The radio hissed before clearing and a woman's

voice barked.

"Acknowledged Jumpship One. Clearance issued. Dock and airlock are code green."

Noe's eyebrows nearly hit her hairline.

"What?" Jedax frowned at her stunned expression.

"Who was that?" Noe stammered. "I recognize that voice!"

"What? How?"

"That's the voice I heard talking to my grandmother."

"What?" Jedax bellowed. He caught the flash of panic on her face and sank lower into the uncomfortable faux leather seat with a groan. "I seem to be saying that a lot around you don't I?"

Noe nodded, her gaze now pinned on the ever enlarging fake moon sailing closer. The automated docking system had taken over, leaving them with nothing to do but stare at it.

"Who is that Jedax?" she asked again. He grimaced and swiped a hand over his eyes.

"That was our chief medical and science officer. She sometimes takes over for the docking control group if sensitive or classified materials are due to be shipped out or in for her department. I don't remember ever meeting her directly. She's old. Like really old."

"I must speak to her," Noe whispered. "Her voice, I know it."

Jedax watched the iron beams and lamps drift nauseatingly close to the ship as it maneuvered to dock 4. He wondered why the old harpy was manning the docks at this particular time.

"Noe, I think she's…"

Noe stiffened in her seat as if electrocuted. Jedax watched her pale blue eyes swirl black. No, not fully black. Deep inside the dark depths of her gaze pinpoints of lights swirled and danced.

An entire cosmos reflected back at him.

"She is here for me," Noe gasped. "She knows I am here. She has been waiting for a very long time."

Jedax frowned. His finger hovered over the emergency override.

"Uh, is that bad or good?" he couldn't take his gaze off hers. Galaxies wheeled. Stars flared and died. Deeper still within a radiant, larger, light shone at the center of her pupils.

"Good." Noe gasped. Her starlit gaze veered to the view screen and seemed to see deep into the insides of the station now surrounding them.

Their tiny ship jolted to a halt and the faint whir of the airlock sealing jerked Jedax into motion. He ripped off his restraints and reached for Noe's. Before his fingers could unbuckle her, the latches flipped apart of their own volition and the woman stood with inhuman…or alien…speed.

The door slid open revealing the cold, stark white interior of the Moonstation.

A woman stood there, waiting. Clothed in long white robes, the tall, elderly woman would have blended into the stark color scheme of the station's hallway, but for the electric blue eyes trained solely on Noe.

Noe moved forward as if on autopilot, her face void of expression, but her starry gaze wheeling in the same confusion Jedax felt. He followed closely, uneasy in the still, cold atmosphere. The two women didn't speak, but studied each other in the harsh white light, leaving Jedax time to study the station's chief medical and science officer. He wondered why he hadn't noted her oddness before. Everything about her screamed at his nerves. Tall, slender, with shoulder length gray hair and age lined skin; she was all but a statue for all she moved.

And then she did move and those vivid blue eyes locked on his. For a split second her silvered hair revealed glittering jewels on her ear tips. Ear tips that were very long and pointed.

"Uh, okay. What is going on Madam..." his voice grew strangled when he realized that he'd never known her name. Scarlet faced, he waited for the woman to flay him alive. Or space him.

She did neither, but smiled.

"I am Madame Echara, Officer Grunnas," she said.

Her voice, creaky with age, but very clear and strong, sent a tingle of energy up his spine. He found himself drawing up into a salute and only just kept his arm at his side.

"And you must be Aegis' granddaughter, Noehni." Echara rounded on the still motionless Noe.

"I...am."

"Is she with you? Or back on the Sunstalker?"

Noe blinked and the darkness faded from her eyes. Pale blue eyes regarded the elderly woman in disbelief.

"She's dead, Madame Echara." Noe said.

Grey eyebrows arched in response.

"Did Aegis ever mention anything to do with Old Earth?" Echara asked, cutting the conversation down to business. Her gaze honed in on the younger woman, turbulent yet focused.

"Not directly. She left a directive in the Sunstalker's logs that let me take over as captain upon her death and what I must do to keep it. All she said was to come to Old Earth and find the last Soldeuns."

Echara nodded as if expecting that answer. Her ear jewels glinted in the cold white light.

"Where are they?" Noe asked

"I'm afraid I'm the last, child. The others have returned to their place in space and time. I have stayed to watch over this world until the end. Too many have perished under our watch as it is."

"You're Soldeun?" Noe asked. "I don't sense you."

Echara threw her head back with a hearty laugh, leaving both visitors stunned.

"Forgive me, Noehni, I forgot you have never seen what has become of us. I was Soldeun, long ago, but now I am what I was created to be, an Immortal made from an Elven body on the planet Ein-Aral."

Jedax eyed the elderly woman. "Can you please tell me that I'm not the only one that is confused?" he whispered aside to Noe, half-jokingly.

"No, I'm confused too, Jedax. Echara, is your soul the only part of you left?"

"Yes."

"How? Why?"

Echara's smile faded. "That is a long story for

149

later. We have a mission your grandmother needed you to finish, correct?"

"I am to rescue the Soldeuns…but if you are the last, then what? I don't understand any of this." Noe said.

"The Sunstalker, is she in orbit?" Echara asked.

Jedax frowned at the woman's evasion. He too wanted to know what in the Seven Hells was going on.

"No, I left her some distance away. It's a long story but that's how we met," Noe gestured to Jedax. "We took his ship here because I didn't want to bring the Sunstalker close and risk questions."

"Good choice." Echara glanced over at Jedax leaving him wondering if her words were double edged.

"Why?" Noe asked. "What about the Sunstalker?"

"Your grandmother's ship will be able to repair the tractor beams. Their energy source is now much more limited without our sun as a power source. The starstone crystal orb is almost empty and the Sunstalker has a limitless energy supply in the Dark Drives."

"Okay, how does it power up the tractor beams?" Jedax asked. He didn't think they had a extension cord that would be long enough.

Echara explained, "The Sunstalker can transfer of it's space Dark Drives through a portal. Come, time is of the essence."

"That doesn't explain much," Jedax muttered. He stumbled into a run to catch up with the spry old woman and the worried looking Noe.

"What are the portals?" she asked. The woman was moving far too fast for an elderly human and Jedax could see faintly iridescent footsteps left in her wake. Bare feet. Huh.

Madame Echara answered without pausing. "The females of our race can create portals in The Void. They are a method of travel through space and possibly time for some. It's a shortcut we'll need to get to the core of the planet to fix the tractor beams by resupplying power."

"Wormholes." Jedax blurted out.

"What?" Noe glanced over at him, startled.

"She's talking about manmade wormholes. They've been theorized about for eons on earth."

"Close enough," Echara's voice echoed further down the hall. Jedax and Noe burst into a dead run to keep up.

"Now what?" Jedax huffed as he pushed his feet faster. His lanky frame and larger gait were no match for the Elderly woman's.

"Now we summon the Sunstalker." Echara said as the duo staggered to a halt beside her. She stood before a giant window overlooking the shattered remains of the planet below.

Jedax had seen it so often that he had to look away. It wasn't a pretty sight to see the once blue, browns, and greens of Earth turned into hovering chunks of land. The explosion had come out of nowhere no one has ever really discovered how it happened. Billions were killed even though the tractor beams had instantly latched onto all the larger chunks and held them in a loose, lopsided representation of what Earth had once been.

"It's so sad," Noe pressed her nose against the cool pane of glass. "Echara, how did you get the tractor beams to hold it together so soon after the explosion?"

"Pure luck. I happened to be working on a system for tethering our ships, like the Sunstalker, without any physical restraints. The planet exploded and I set the mechanism through a portal and into the exposed core. It activated instantly and snared all the pieces possible. Not all, unfortunately, so there is no putting it back together again."

"That's amazing," Jedax said. He squinted to see the thin laser-like beams spreading out like grabbing fingers from the center of the planet. There was too much debris to see to the heart where the alien machine worked in silence.

Echara continued, "At first the power from the explosion itself was enough to power the machine. But radiation decays as you know. It has been 2000 years and it is only now failing. Already 2 rays have collapsed. Any more and it will destabilize too fast to repair."

"Oh no," Noe glanced over at Echara. "How much time do we have?"

"Days, weeks tops. I'm just eternally grateful that you listened to your grandmother's directive. I'm just as saddened that she was not here to witness this."

"How do we create a portal to get it from the Sunstalker down to the core?" Noe pushed away from the window. Her fingers twitched with the need to do something. "And...how do we take one of the stars from the Sunstalker by the way?"

"Like this." Echara whipped her hands together as if clutching a ball between her fingers. With the motion a ball of light formed. It roiled and sparked, throwing shadows along the stark walls. "Stand back."

Jedax and Noe lunged backwards until their backs hit the wall.

Echara flung her arms wide and the ball of light surged into the air and halted to hover in a sparking, static frenzy.

"Watch," Echara said to the wide eyed pair behind her.

She pressed her hands against the ball of energy and shaped it into a large oval. Static and sparks, ringed the now oval shaped object and the inside grew fuzzy and vague. The ring of fire blazed hot and the inside of the oval sharpened until the engine room of the Sunstalker appeared.

"Those are the Dark Drives!" Noe crept closer and peered into the shifting image. She pointed out the two towers that seemed to contain nothing but chaotic darkness.

"Now your turn."

Noe's head came up so fast her neck popped. "Wait, what?"

"You need to create the other portal."

"Ah, I've never done that before. I've never had any useful powers."

Jedax frowned and pushed off the wall. "Noe, your eyes turned black and stuff back when we were getting ready to dock. It looked like there were galaxies inside."

Noe rounded on him. "What?"

153

"You've never done that before? What were you doing?" he asked.

"Nothing. Thinking. About stuff."

Echara broke in. "Good, do it again."

"That's crazy." Jedax's neck hurt from trading shocked looks with Noe.

"Noe, focus. Think of what the center of that destroyed planet looks like. Imagine yourself simply walking there."

"Right. Imagine walking into the center of a destroyed human planet. Got it."

Noe closed her eyes and exhaled deeply. Her petite frame stilled and Jedax wondered if she'd stopped breathing. He resisted the urge jab a testy finger at her arm and see if she'd jump out of her skin. But...judging from the frosty glare aimed at him by the old woman...not a good idea.

Just as he returned to his safe, white wall, Noe's eyelids snapped wide open. Bathed in black and pinpoints of light her dark gaze seemed to watch nothing and everything.

"Good, now reach for the energy within you. Contain it in your hands."

Noe grabbed at the air in front of her with both hands, holding them cupped. For a long moment nothing happened. Then a crack of thunder and flash of light shook the entire station.

A ball of white hot light burned midair between her hands.

"Seven Hells..." Jedax flung up an arm to shade his eyes from the fiery glow.

Without prompting, Noe swung her hands wide and shaped the ball into a second, fiery ring.

154

Instantly the static laced center sharpened and an odd machine appeared within its depths.

"Now what?" Noe rasped. Her breathing had resumed and now sweaty strands of dark hair clung to her skin. Panting with effort she guided the portal into a larger, more stable shape. It hung suspended in mid-air next to Echara's.

"Well done, you are certainly a Worldwalker if not a Timewalker. Now we move one of the Dark Drives to the tractor beam machine."

With a gesture the portal nearest the old woman flashed white hot. A dark mass flashed into view within it. It drifted toward them and through the portal. One of the twin towers in the starship now stood empty.

Writhing, oily darkness hovered between both portals. Waves of energy drove Jedax further back against the wall. Though dark, the fluid-like mass surged and seethed with swirls of energy.

"Hold the portal steady, Noehni." Echara commanded. Sweat steamed off the woman's hair and her wizened face flushed scarlet. Long ears laid back against her head.

Noe's eyes narrowed on the dark ball of energy, then the fiery ring of the portal she controlled sparked and spit fire.

Echara guided the dark energy through the air with a wave of a trembling hand. It drifted slowly to Noe's portal and into it with a staticky pop.

"Noe, guide it into the heart of the planet. The machine will take over once it is closer."

Noe's tongue poked out of the corner of her mouth as lines of concentration formed on her forehead. Flushed and sweaty, she curled her hands into fists as she worked to contain and maneuver the energy mass.

It sailed slowly, clumsily between the massive chunks of rock and blue beams of light. As it moved further toward the core of the shattered planet, the view in the portal followed, keeping the energy orb in sight.

A large globe appeared where the core of the planet had once been. Blue beams of light radiated from it in all directions.

"Let go of it, Noe. Its gravity will be attracted to the machine."

Noe's mental grip on the mass vanished and she tumbled to her butt with a groan. Breathing hard, she shuddered and blinked until her eyes returned to their normal shade of pale blue.

"Seven Hells." Jedax muttered. He stepped up beside her and watched the energy mass drift toward the giant machine with a purpose. It billowed into the center and instantly it clouded with swirling darkness, just like the tower on the Sunstalker had.

"What's happening?" Jedax asked. He resisted the urge to back away, dragging both women with him.

"It is done," Echara's tense posture relaxed and her portal popped with a flare of heat of hot air as it vanished. "You can let go now, Noehni."

Noe gasped and the portal swirling before her winked out with a spark. The blast of hot air was like sandpaper to Jedax's exposed skin.

"Oh, gods. That was like nothing I've ever felt before." Noe buried her face in her hands, her entire body still shuddering from the strain of controlling a power she'd never had to before.

"Look!" Jedax peered past the women out the window. The blue beams of light strengthened and darkened into deep blue-black webbing.

"Good. It's working." Echara said. She studied the rapidly healing tractor beams with a faint smile.

"Now what, Madame Echara?" Noe stood with a suppressed groan and moved to join the elderly woman at the giant window. Jedax followed and all three stood side by side watching.

"Now we are done here and can go home."

"Home? Soldeus was destroyed long ago, wasn't it?"

"Yes. It was."

"Then I don't understand, what is home?"

Echara turned to look Noe in the eye.

"Home is where you belong, my child. Home for you is the Sunstalker."

"But, it's missing a drive now." Jedax added. "Won't that be a problem?"

"Possibly. I am not an expert of Dark Drives nor that type of ship," Echara explained, her face tightening"And there are no more Soldeuns to help us I'm afraid. We are on our own. Come, my work here is done. I am ready to meet your Sunstalker. We have much to work on."

"Uh, yes, but..." Noe turned to Jedax and realized that he'd wandered away from the window to stare down the empty corridor. "Jedax? Are you coming?"

"I don't think so."

Noe frowned, taken aback.

"Why not?"

"You've completed your mission, but I have done nothing useful. I have only one thing left to do."

"I don't understand, Jedax, what do you mean?" she asked.

"Explaining to the Magnates just what in the hell happened today. I'm just a traffic cop. I'll probably lose my job." He grimaced. "It was boring anyway."

"What will you do?" Noe asked.

"I hope to study the technology your people used to save us. We as humans need to stand up and solve our own problems someday. We can't always rely on Soldeuns to do it."

"You are right," Noe grimaced. "I hope you find a way to help your people in a meaningful way, Jedax." "And who knows," he said. "Maybe we will be able to share tips."

"I look forward to seeing you again...and thank you for helping me find my people," Noe gestured toward Echara. "Even just one more person is more than I had before and now I have two."

"Two?"

Noe smiled sadly. "You are of my people, Jedax, in spirit if not blood. Goodbye, friend."

"Goodbye Noe Seyun of the Soldeun people."

They hugged and Jedax turned on his heel and marched down the corridor away from them. He refused to look back. To look back would be to second guess his sanity about everything that had happened.

"Are you ready, Noehni?" Echara asked softly.

The older woman gestured for her to move closer. Noe did but her gaze remained on the rapidly disappearing back of the space cop she called friend.

"You can call me Noe. It's like the old Earth name Zoe, but with an 'n'."

Echara threw her head back in a vibrant laugh.

"Very well, Noe, it is time to go home."

Question of the day: What is real, and more importantly, how do you know?

Visions of ARES

R. A. McCandless

The door hummed and cheerfully beeped. Three heavy bolt-locks withdrew with a solid *ka-chunk-ka-chunk-ka-chunk* to grant access. The air pressure changed when the door swung open on its pneumatic hinge and closed a moment later. The bolt-locks snapped back in place and the door beeped a happy note that it was secure. Oss felt the presence of someone else in the cell. He ignored the urge to stand up off the floor and salute what could only be a senior rank.

That was training. Oss's training was all wrong.

Metal chair legs scrapped against the ceramic floor. All this technology and they still couldn't improve on the basic design for someone to park their ass. Oss wanted to smile. His eyes teared up, his nose ran and he snuffled against his arm.

"Goddamn funny, that," Oss mumbled.

The man sitting in the chair introduced himself, but Oss didn't hear his name, only his rank—Major.

"This, Corporal Ossas..." Major hesitated over his last name. Everyone did. "On... On-yet..."

"Onyetenyevwe," Oss replied. "Everyone calls me Oss."

Major chittered a laugh. "I can see why. Well, Oss, this is a full pardon."

Paper whispered across the metal tabletop.

Oss stared at the pattern of his Disciplinary Barracks issued jumpsuit. He counted the bright orange horizontal threads.

"This is your retirement package," Major said. Another paper shushed to a stop. "Full medical, pension, a house by a private lake. I hear there's fish, if you like that kind of thing."

Oss stopped counting and closed his eyes. They burned at the corners and more tears rolled down his cheeks. Oss didn't hear the door open, close or beep, but he felt alone. He thought the man left the room.

"We need an official record," Major said.

Oss's thoughts froze and his eyes popped wide open. His heart hammered against his chest. Every muscle in his body tensed in fear. Major was still in the room. Oss was not alone.

He was never alone.

"Seven." Oss spoke into the sleeve of his jumpsuit.

"Sorry, what's that?" Major asked.

Oss turned his head along the crook over his arm and peered at the Major's chest. He couldn't make out the nametag from where he sat on the floor and didn't care to try. Major sat at the table, his Class A uniform crisp and clean, from the tip of his regulation haircut to the shine on the toes of his authorized shoes. Oss recognized two military service ribbons for combat operations at Six Cities and Tannhauser Gate.

The Major had seen action. Heavy action.

"Seven," Oss repeated. "Seven died."

"I understand this is hard. It's a formality, really," Major said, "but it must be on the record, and it must be in your voice. Phys-chem detectors will know."

Oss was on his feet and around the table before he realized. He grabbed the Major by the arm and neck. The Major was strong, but Oss was stronger. He levered the Major's arm away from his belt, slammed him back down into the chair, and pushed his face against the table. The Major's cheek hit with a solid knock against the metal that rang through the room.

"Seven died!" Oss pushed his face close to the Major's. "Seven," he hissed in the other man's ear. "Seven died."

"It was your ARES," the Major said.

"I saw them," Oss insisted. "I goddamn see them now."

"Tell me, Oss," Major said. "Tell me what you see."

Major was calm. In pain, but calm. Oss breathed heavily as if he'd finished a PFT run. He eased the pressure from the Major's neck, ready to slam him back down. When Major didn't move, Oss let go. He moved back, away from the table, until his shoulders hit the wall. He slid down with a zip from his jumpsuit as it rubbed against the smooth concrete.

Major stood up slowly, tugged his jacket into place and adjusted his belt. He didn't need to bother with the show. They'd hijacked his ARES, and Oss didn't mind. He was glad for it, especially when a wave of calm and euphoria washed out from his chest down his arms and legs. Everyone who came into the room had a "hidden button" that told Oss's implants to cool the aggression—make him passive. The sudden serenity told Oss that Major had thumbed his. A metallic taste filled his mouth and with it the words formed as he knew they would. They always followed the chemical calm.

Sometimes he could keep them from spilling out. Oss swallowed several times, but he couldn't stop them. It wasn't the words that worried him, it was what came after.

Through the ARES, Oss had almost perfect recall. A perfect soldier for debriefing.

"We entered the Voll's burrow," Oss said. "Two fire teams. Orders were to search for and destroy on sight. They have to be destroyed..." Oss shook his head to clear it. "That's what the training says. They ... the Voll ... their blood carries diseases and impurities. If even one gets away, they can ... intel says they'll kidnap children and infect them. Their females will seduce any man, to get knocked-up with tainted kids. The males will coerce or rape a—

heh—pure woman. Anything to keep their species alive and growing. So, they...training says they have to be destroyed. Orders say the same."

It's a lie, it's a lie, it's a lie, it's a goddamn lie—Oss thought. It didn't help.

"The burrow was an old bunker—civilian—abandoned and in ruins," Oss said. "It was from before the Voll."

The room grew dark and Oss could already smell the dank, wet underground. That was the problem with perfect recollection.

"That's the kind of thing the... they like. Drones are useless in the confined space, so there was limited sat-comm for the op. We had heat signatures on IR in three places. Two big, one small. The LT sent four of us after the smallest heat sign, the rest would sweep out the bigger groups. We went in by the numbers."

Oss curled his fingers around the hard composite of his MTAR-33 assault rifle. His fingers found the biometric studs. A moment later, ARES chirped recognition and weapon overlays leapt into view. A cross-hatch targeting reticle floated in the distance while ARES scanned the area. The reticle was color-coded matte gray to indicate no active target. Oss's 3D map of the bunker bounced in front of him as he moved. He waved it to the left corner of his vision where he could reference it without being distracted. Intel said the Voll were known for clever adaptation, even if they were lazy. ARES couldn't target the individual heat signs yet, but it estimated no more than four hostiles. The map showed his team as four green arrows moving down the corridor toward the heat sign.

More than enough against the unarmed, untrained, undisciplined Voll.

"It was all by the numbers," Oss said. "Then all hell broke loose."

He snugged his rifle into his shoulder and sighted down the corridor.

"Heat sign went off the scale all around us," Oss reported. "They had a boiler working and flooded hot water through the piping—steam overwhelmed the infrared. When they sent off the smokers IR became useless. ARES switched to full VR of the bunker based on the last updated schematics."

Oss gave a snort-chuckle.

A light blue wire-frame overlayed the flowing white smoke and outlined the corridor, doorways, rooms and service access. Two glowing semi-circles gave Oss estimated distance and time to contact from his current position. Oss swung his rifle left and right with the targeting reticle tracking his eye movement. He peered past the blue VR lines through the smoke and strained to make out the enemy.

"ARES was wrong. They came out of the walls, and they came fast," Oss said. "They used some kind of heat shields, old wall insulation or something. Private Stinson got it first—goddamn fire axe to the back of the head."

Barry crumpled to the ground without a sound. It wasn't how a soldier should go down. Not like this. Not against the Voll.

"Bell and Greengar managed to open fire, but in the smoke and heat and confusion—" Oss shook his head. "The Voll had the advantage."

Oss' ARES finally caught up to the action and painted the four hostiles with red chevrons pinned to their life signs. Yellow targeting reticles hovered in front of each hostile.

"They came at me, screeching and clicking, chittering like bugs. Goddamn bugs."

Oss lined up his MTAR with the first targeting reticle. The crosshair circle and chevron changed to green—green for go—and Oss squeezed the trigger three times. His MTAR thumped softly against his shoulder. ARES muted the gunfire sounds to small pops. The Voll dropped to the ground like puppets with their strings cut.

ARES rewarded him. It categorized the deaths to his kill ratio, adjusted his hit percentage to shots fired, and released endorphins into his system. ARES promised that euphoria would follow when combat was over and flashed GOOD KILL over each crumpled body.

Oss smiled and swung his MTAR to the next reticle.

"They swarm, ya know, like mosquitos," Oss said. "They don't even care for their dead. They swarmed me and there were too many."

ARES pulsed a red proximity alert over everything to warn him. The second Voll swung a club at Oss. Oss dropped the Voll at point blank range with two hasty shots. The club bounced against his helmet and cheek with a dull thud. Pain blossomed through Oss's face. He was momentarily blinded, but he trusted ARES. ARES was always there, a constant companion who never failed him.

That was training to, and it was right.

ARES was always there.

The third Voll swung a broken pipe and tore Oss's MTAR from his grip. The weapon clattered to the ground and skidded sideways. Oss drew his sidearm and ARES switched the targeting reticles and ranges to compensate. The Voll swung at him again. He was rushed. Oss jumped back and fired. He jerked the trigger. His first two shots pinged off the concrete floor. The third caught the Voll in the calf. It screamed, high-pitched and inhuman, dropped the pipe, and clutched at the wound.

"Too many," Oss repeated. "Goddamn bugs."

ARES pulsed the red proximity warning faster. Oss got off a hasty shot at the fourth Voll with the axe handle. The Voll screamed and smashed the thick wood into Oss's hands twice and knocked the sidearm free. Oss drew his KA-BAR and ARES adapted to the tactical knife. Pink splashes painted on the Voll's neck, abdomen and groin.

Quick kill or incapacitate. Don't go to the ground.

The Voll swung the axe handle at Oss's head. Oss stepped into the creature and used his left arm to catch the strike near the Voll's hands. It stung, but the block did what was needed. Oss stabbed his knife at the pink splash target on the Voll's abdomen. He wasn't fast enough. The Voll punched Oss in the face and rocked him back on his heels. ARES registered the hit, and flowed quick calculations for damage, fatigue and chance of recovery.

Oss caught the next two punches with clumsy

blocks. He couldn't bring the knife into a proper strike. The Voll was strong, but lacked the training of a soldier whose heart rate, V02 max, and respirometry were tracked and improved on a constant basis. Oss ducked down, spun and kicked the Voll's legs out from under it. The Voll fell backward and Oss lunged on top of it. He led with his knife.

ARES pulsed a proximity warning.

Don't go to the ground.

The Voll tried to deflect the blade, but it slid into his left shoulder. It screamed and hissed, grabbed Oss's hand and held the blade trapped in its body. ARES streamed more information for Oss about the Voll's wound. Oss tugged on his knife, trying to break the Voll's hold.

The axe handle careened off Oss's helmet in a series of wild, desperate blows. He'd forgotten the weapon in the struggle to survive. Oss's cheek broke under the barrage. He fought to free his knife. The Voll dropped the handle and punched Oss in the face. Inky black flared in front of his eyes from each blow. On the third punch, ARES fritzed for a moment. The words and numbers froze, vibrated and hissed with static. The red pulse of the proximity warning missed a beat, and then another. It picked up again on his right side, but not on his left.

Oss had a strange, split-screen view of the world. On the right, ARES functioned normally. The system provided the wire-frame VR of the bunker, target splashes, and a column of pertinent information. Oss's left was stripped of the overlays.

Smoke floated lazily around the room and obscured corners. The figures of his team and the dead Voll lay crumpled along the corridor floor.

Oss froze. On the right, he saw the Voll as he'd always seen them—hideous, hairless creatures with deformed heads, melted features and dark, mottled skin.

"Goddamn funny, that," Oss mumbled.

Oss's left eye showed him a human. A man. He was emaciated by hunger and streaked with dirt from living in the old bunker. A man—definitely a man. He wore clothes that might have fit him a year ago and now hung off his frame. The man's face was contorted in fear and pain. Tears streamed from his eyes and drew tracks across his cheeks and temples. It was a brutal contrast to the alien anger and rage his right eye showed him; the vision ARES showed Oss.

The Voll chittered and hissed, unintelligible as always. Under that, the man spoke clearly.

"Jesus Christ! Please! Please, don't kill me, Jesuschristplease!"

Oss scrambled back from the man as if he was on fire. ARES helpfully pointed out where his rifle and sidearm were—easy to reach. He ignored the information. The downed Volls were identified by ARES as dead.

To his left eye, they were human. They bled red blood. No deformations. No mottled skin. Dirt from the bunker. Rags for clothes. Looks of horror and pain carved forever on their faces.

"All of them," Oss told Major. "Dead."

The scene melted from his memory. He wasn't

in the burrow. He was in the padded holding cell.

"Thank you, Corporal Ossas," Major chittered. "We've long suspected that the technology targets genetic markers for what the Glorious Republic has designated as 'undesirables'. We assumed it worked in conjunction with the universal DNA mandates, but we didn't have proof. We didn't understand why civilians and children were being slaughtered. This is a turning point. You've given us everything we need for a full intervention."

Oss looked at Major for the first time—looked with both eyes. Major was a hideous and hairless thing. His deformed head split in a wide maw, which Oss knew was supposed to be a smile. The melted features and dark, mottled skin sent revulsion and fear coursing through Oss. Major looked back at him with large, warped eyes that wept yellow-green puss. ARES overlays pulsed a constant red proximity warning and urged him to strike—to kill—the Voll.

"Take it out," Oss said to Major. "You promised. Take it out."

The Voll looked down at his lap for several long moments. The silence between Oss and Major was tangible. It felt like an invisible wall hardened between them. ARES suggested that the chair would make a decent weapon, and splashed pink targets on the Voll's head, neck and back carapace.

Finally, Major nodded.

"We did promise," he said. "That was before we understood how pervasive the tech is throughout your body. It's not just wires and micros—the system is homegrown wetware that touches on pretty much every major organ you own. Even just to monitor, the design is an ethical gray area. Used in this way, it's a war crime against you and every soldier in the Republic."

"Take it out," Oss whispered.

Major gestured to the papers on the table in front of him.

"The package will keep you away from people," he said. "You don't have to see anyone if you don't want to. Everything is automated if you want it to be. You don't even have to leave for groceries."

"I don't want to see them anymore," Oss said. "I don't want to see you anymore!"

"We don't know what removing your ARES implants would do," Major replied. "It might kill you."

"Take it out," Oss told him.

"It could kill you," Major repeated, calmly.

"Then kill me," Oss hissed.

Question of the Day: How much would you trust an old friend if you met them as an enemy on the field of battle?

A Question of Timing

L. A. Behm II

*Notes on the Settlement of New Prussia and the
Surrounding System
Martian Sailing Directions
2700 Edition
Martian Naval Press, Phobos, Sol System*

New Prussia was settled by the German state of the European Union in 2475. The initial colonization effort was a mix of 'desirable' elements (mostly bureaucrats) and undesirable elements – descendants of Turkish guest workers, religious minorities and others the government deemed 'excess population' to the needs of the state. Once the colony was established, a similar colony was established by the French on the second planet in the life zone in 2522, and a third established by the 'spare' heir to the British throne in 2525. The final colony, Muscovy, was founded when a Russian colony ship, per her log, 'off course and running out of supplies' found the second jump gate into the system and 'crashed' on New Prussia.

There was a second colonization of New Prussia in roughly 2632 when elements of the German 'New Junker's Party' (Neue Junker Partai) were defeated after a coup attempt in Germany proper and sent to exile on New Prussia. The Junkers took control of New Prussia from the German Colonial Government, and established the Kaiser as ultimate ruler of the planet. . .

* * *

I looked at the chronometer on my wrist to check the time. Yes, I could have closed an eye and checked it with my implant, but the chronometer seemed the right way to do it this time.

"Mr. Polk, it's midnight. Fire a flare, if you please," I said to my aide-de-camp.

"Yes sir," he replied. Polk checked that the right colored flare was in the flare gun, raised it above his head and pulled the trigger. The flare climbed into the night sky and blossomed green. "Now we wait, Captain Herbert," Polk intoned, lowering the flare pistol. I laughed.

"Leftenant Polk, how long have you been in the Royal Navy?" I asked.

"Five years sir!" he replied in a quarterdeck

snap.

"And in five years, you haven't learned that with very few exceptions, that in the Royal Navy, patience is something beyond a virtue?"

"I . . . I hadn't thought of it that way," Polk replied.

"No worries, lad. If the Prussians wanted to kill all of us here, they'd have done it long ago," I said. I'd barely finished speaking when there were two 'thonks' from the Prussian lines. We watched the flares blossom.

"Green!" Polk said.

I reached up and keyed my throat mike. "Dunkirk. I repeat Dunkirk."

Behind us I could hear the V-Class Destroyer *HMS Vectis* engage her lift drives and thunder aloft, checking that the Prussians were holding to their side of the bargain. Just because I trusted the Prussian commander, didn't mean everyone involved in the mission did. I'd known Generalmajor Mustaffa Kemal since we'd both gone to Mars and Earth for schooling in the classics on the same ship, and Brigadier Crawford only knew Kemal as the hard hearted son of a bitch who'd done everything he could to throw us off the island of Saarland.

"Now, for the second part," I said, handing my rifle to the marine corporal who would be waiting here until I returned.

Polk followed suit.

Mustaffa hadn't required hostages per se as part of the withdrawal. It had been strongly hinted that he wanted to talk with someone during the twelve hours he'd allow us to remove the troops and ships of the Aerospace Task Group Four from the 'sacred soil' of Prussia, however. I'd not even given the Brigadier the chance to voluntold me to do it. I'd presented it as a requirement. Crawford hadn't even blinked before agreeing.

Besides, it might be the last chance I got to see Kemal for a while. Rumor was I'd be going back to Albion for a while, and then to Mars to talk to the government there.

The marines would escort Polk and myself to the half way point between the lines, where we'd be met by troops of Generalmajor Mustaffa's personal guard and escorted to a position he'd established where we could chat and watch the withdrawal. I'd also prepared a gift for Mustaffa. It was a tradition between us, and he'd given me the last gift when we'd met arraigning a cease fire to remove the wounded and dead when the Aerospace Task Group had first landed a year ago. Since then, we'd done what a Royal Marine ATG does best – taken ground, torn things up, diverted resources the enemy needed elsewhere, and kept troops of the Imperial Army from being sent against our allies in Muscovy. Now, however, with the Muscovites negotiating with the Kaiserin, we had come under increasing attack here on the island known locally as Saarland. The marines of the ATG had a litany of names for it, none of them usable in polite company. Brigadier Crawford had managed to hold onto the port he'd established on the island, but he knew we faced a loosing battle of attrition. He also knew he'd done what he'd been ordered to do – keep a chunk of the Imperial Army tied down on Prussia itself rather than available for use against the three ATG's that had been landed on Nouveau France. He'd never been ordered to lead a suicide mission, and when the opportunity came for negotiating with Generalmajor Mustaffa, he'd sent me to do the job.

Operation Dunkirk was the result. Albion would get the surviving marines and sailors of the ATG back, and the Prussians could claim victory in defending their sacred soil. Of course, if the marines and sailors were lucky, they'd get to spend time back on Albion before being thrust into the Southern Front on Nouveau France.

"Herr Kapitan Herbert?" came from the darkness ahead.

"Ja."

A red light sprang up, illuminating the face of Generalmajor Mustaffa. "My old comrade," he said, stepping up and embracing me.

I looked at the Generalmajor. He looked worn. The Junkers in charge of Prussia never really trusted the Turco-Germans in their midst – a mindset that went back to the mid-20th Century. Even though, at this point, due to intermingling of genetic materials, the Generalmajor probably had as much or more Junker blood than most of the Imperial Staff, he was still not a Junker, and worse, a 'Turk'. Some prejudices had survived well after humanity left the mother planet.

"Generalmajor," I said, returning the embrace as best I could, since both of us were in full combat kit.

"Please Aubrey, let us meet as friends," he

replied, breaking the embrace.

"As you wish, Kemal."

He lead the way to an observation post forward of the Prussian lines. Drawing back the blackout curtain, he stepped inside.

Inside, the post was spartan. The only thing indicating it was in use by the Generalmajor commanding Prussian forces was the battered silver coffee set on the simple wooden table. The cezveh was just starting to boil over a simple spirit lamp.

"Aubrey, I don't believe you've met my aide-de-camp, Hauptmann Bolukbasi," Kemal said, gesturing to a Hauptmann standing in the corner of the OP.

"Hauptmann," I said. "Generalmajor, my aide-de-camp, Leftenant Polk."

The Generalmajor shook Polk's hand, then gestured for all of us to sit down at the table. He even pointed me at the chair nearest the door, with Polk to my right. We all removed our combat kit and sat.

"Damned glad to be rid of that muck," Kemal said, pointing at his armor where it hung on the wall.

"Yes, the best fitness program ever mistakenly invented by our governments is wearing those damn things," I replied with a grin. "I've argued before Parliament that before anyone wants to get us involved in a war, they have to wear full kit for two weeks before they get to vote for or against."

"Capital idea, Aubrey!", Kemal replied, pouring coffee with his own hand.

Polk was staring at the coffee set. It was of the

ancient Turkish design – the cezveh was silver, and covered in arabesques. The demitasse cups were somewhat mismatched – the battered outer silver holders matched, but the inner ceramic liners were of slightly different shades of white. Kemal saw Polk's interest.

"You like my affectation, Leftenant?", he asked. Polk blushed.

"I've never seen anything like it sir," he replied.

"Well, when my ancestors left Earth," Kemal began, "they were shipped in cryo-sleep, because the colony effort by the EU was trying to maximize the number of people per ship. Mostly to rid themselves of 'troublesome minority groups'."

Kemal paused and lifted one of the cups into the light.

"So my revered ancestor, or if we put all machismo aside, his poor wife, who had actually paid attention to the scant training her family had received before being volunteered to board the first ship sent here to Prussia thought long and hard about what items she would want and need here in the wilds of a new planet. She, that poor sainted woman, read the available notes from the colonization of Mars and the Sol Belt. She looked at the list of items the EU would 'supply' the colonists, and recognized it for the bullshit it was. She took all her lists, then she cut those lists by half. And added in a few non necessities, to remind her family that they were more than animals sent into the wild to die, by a government that cared less for them than it did for pure Germans and Europeans," Kemal said.

Polk and Bolukbasi hung on Kemal's every

word.

"So, over the last three hundred years, we have replaced parts of the set as needed – as you see, the cups no longer quite match in color. The handle on the cezveh is local moria wood. Some of the silver has been replaced with local silver. But the set still exists, to remind us of where we came from, and where we are going," he finished with a flourish.

"Speaking of affectations," I said, turning to my armor and removing a bone tube, stoppered with carved moria wood.

I handed the tube to Kemal.

"My turn in our game, I believe," I said with a small grin.

"Oh? And what have you found this time?", Kemal said, twisting the moria wood caps. One popped off, and he slid the parchment in the tube out.

"I carved the tube from a sea eagle wing bone, and the caps from a bit of moria wood down in our camp. The parchment has three versions of the same poem by an obscure late twentieth, early twenty first century poet," I said.

Sea eagles were what the Prussians had named a large pseudo bird native to the coasts of Prussia and Saarland. Only a Junker would look at a large, leathery, reptilian flying scavenger and see an eagle. I'd found the bones while beach combing on a day off. I'd translated the early twenty first century English of the poet into modern Albion and Prussian.

L. A. Behm II

Dust stirs, trampled by the feet of countless specters
Macedonian Phalanxes, Roman Cohorts, Persian Hordes,
Missionaries and Mameluke, Para's and Marines
Shedding sweat, blood and tears,
Watering the lands between the rivers
Following his own wyrd Seeking god, seeking fame
Seeking the mystic east
Seeking the solace of the empty wastes of the Forge of God
I came to these history bespattered reaches
Fortune seeking
And found myself

Kemal read the poem and handed it to Bolukbasi. The hauptmann read the piece, then wiped away a tear from the corner of his eye.

"This one will be hard to top when we meet next, my friend," Kemal said, carefully rolling the parchment and returning it to the tube.

"It took a while for me to top your last gift," I replied.

"Hard work does a man good," he laughed, cocking his head to one side.

I also caught the edge of a sound.

"Incoming!", Kemal roared, throwing himself to the deck.

We all followed suit as artillery and missile fire thundered over the OP from the direction of the Prussian lines.

"Bolukbasi, get that ass in charge of the long range artillery on the radio," Kemal shouted as he pulled on his body armor.

I could hear the counter battery systems on the big landing ships open fire on the inbound ordinance. Polk handed me an ear bud and mike system, which I put on as he swung his armor on. I could hear command calling for me before the ear bud was seated.

"Break break, Acorn this is Sunray, come in, over."

"Sunray, Acorn, go ahead," I replied, swinging on my kit.

"Acorn, what the bloody hell is going on, over?"

"Unsure. Opposing Force Command is trying to find out what is going on on his end, over."

"Do you need escort, over?"

I thought about it – pulling out of the bunker would mean losing contact with Kemal and a chance to figure out what was happening with this dog's breakfast we'd been served. "Not at this time, over."

"Roger. Be advised we have gone totally defensive. Kingfish is setting up his shots, over."

Kingfish was the admiral in charge of the escort task force. His task force was heavy on heavy firepower and ships, because our command didn't totally trust the Junkers in Kaiserhaven. To date, we hadn't fired on the major Prussian cities – not out of fear of retaliation, but because the mission here was a side show. Things were about to change.

"Those assine bastards!" Kemal roared, turning on me. "Do you know what those. . . those sister fucking bastards in Kaiserhaven did? They've ordered the artillery and armor to fire on the beaches! They've taken control of everything but my division by replacing the officers with ones they can 'trust'!"

He turned back to Bolukbasi, and fired off a string of Turco-German that I couldn't follow. When he'd finished, he turned back to me.

"Question, my friend. Can you transport a few more troops? Say a divisions worth?"

I was stunned by what he was asking. I picked up my coffee cup from where it sat on the table, and drank it down to give me time to think.

"I believe so, yes. It will be complicated, and your troops will have to be disarmed at the very minimum," I replied after a few seconds thought.

"Of course," he said, waving his hand as if this were a minor issue. "And if not at loading, once we reach space they will have to be broken up into penny packets to prevent them from taking over any one ship. This is not a problem. How will your Brigadier Crawford react to my offer, that is the question."

"Honestly? I don't know, Kemal. All I can do is ask."

"Either way, we are done as agents of the Empire," Kemal said, turning again to Bolukbasi. "Execute Order Kilitbahir."

Bolukbasi swallowed, saluted and spoke rapid fire Turco-German into the radio again.

I took a deep, settling breath and keyed my mike. "Sunray this is Acorn, Sunray this is Acorn, over."

"Go for Sunray." "Opposing Force Commander did not give the order, and has offered his assistance in Dunkirk, over."

"Whaaat?"

"Repeat, Opposing Force Commander did not give the order, and has offered his assistance in Dunkirk, over."

"Roger. Have you been smoking hashish, Aubrey?" Crawford replied. Sunray was actually on the net, rather than listening in to one of his subordinates.

"Negative. Opposing Force Command has requested his unit be removed with ours. Agrees to disarming his force as they board ship and scattering them throughout the fleet to keep them from taking over any ship, over."

"Aubrey, do you trust him?"

"Yes, Brigadier I do."

"Roger. Hold." I waited. There was a spattering of rifle shots down the lines on the Prussian side. Bolukbasi muttered something to Kemal.

"Good. Tell them to be ready to withdraw in either direction," Kemal said.

He turned to me, finished his coffee and started reverently packing the set into an intricately carved wooden box.

"Bolukbasi reports the company commands have executed the political officers that Imperial Command insisted we had to take on a year ago," he spat. "I knew the bastards didn't trust us, but this? This is open betrayal."

"What about your people?", I asked, as Polk ducked out of the OP.

Kemal chuckled. "The Imperial Staff should have stuck to fucking their sisters," he said savagely.

"My division is made up of second sons at this point – because when they started giving us political officers a year ago to ensure we were 'committed' to the Empire, I started rotating the older soldiers home for rest and relaxation and training purposes. There's at least two entire divisions worth of combat hardened veterans on Canakkale Island. They'll hold against anything those sister fuckers send at them. If we can get protection from orbital strikes."

"Acorn this is Sunray."

"Go for Sunray."

"God help us, Kingfish concurs. He also asks if our new ally has anything he'd particularly like to see destroyed since Kingfish now has to re target some missiles, over."

Kemal grinned like a feral wolf. "Yes, I can think of a few targets," he replied.

"Sunray, orders, over?"

"Tell, what's his call sign, over?"

Kemal looked up. "My call sign is Avalanche," he said.

"Acorn to Sunray, Avalanche, over."

"Figures. Tell Avalanche to advance to point of contact with our lines, and we'll integrate along the front, over."

"Roger."

"And Acorn, bring Avalanche to my command post, over."

"Roger."

Outside, there was a sudden increase in the cacophony.

"Sir," Polk said as he re-entered the OP, "I've coordinated our marines with the Generalmajor's body guard. And it appears that the gunners on *Theseus*have decided to test a theory."

"What theory?"

"If one can saw through a hill side with a rail gun, Sir."

Theseus is a Myrmidon class Orbital Assault ship. She had been designed to allow the Royal Marines to land an entire division from orbit to seize a beach head, and then expand that beach head with supporting elements, allowing the Myrmidon's to operate independent of resupply for years. Most of her armament was designed to protect the beach head and Theseus herself. Gunners however, are an odd breed, and they had spent their leisure time plotting the positions of the Prussian Artillery. I'd actually sat in the officers mess on Theseus and listened to a pair of her gunners argue if they could chew through a hill with her armament. Kingfish was letting them find out.

"What the hell are they firing?", Kemal asked as he slipped the wooden box into his backpack.

"Ice," I replied.

"Ice?"

"Ja, Herr Generalmajor, Ice. Well, technically a frozen slurry of sand, water, with a steel base and a silicon shell to allow the rail gun to fire the projectile," I said with a grin.

"No wonder you could operate without logistics support for so long," Bolukbasi said.

"Best part was we used the shrapnel you sent us for the steel," Polk said with a grin.

"Well, not like we have to do much more than...," I said as there was an earth shattering explosion.

"I guess the gunners were right," Polk said simply.

"Told that Prussian ass he was putting too much trust in dirt and not enough in being able to move his guns!" Kemal said with a grin. "Now, Aubrey, I've long wanted to see the beach on this little shit pot of an island. Shall we?"

"The moons are particularly lovely over the sewage pond this time of night," I replied with a grin.

Polk and Bolukbasi went through the door together. I gestured the Generalmajor ahead, and then followed him into the night.

Question of the Day: Is it better to journey into the unknown alone, or with a friend?

A World of Sand

G. Michael Rapp

Aleksandr Puusepp feels the hot rays of sunshine wash over his pale and stubble-covered face. He forces his eye open only to see blurs and shadows. His head aches and sticky blood seeps from an open gash on his forehead. He made it to the place. At least that is what he hopes. He leans his head back against the headrest of the pilot's chair for a few moments, taking in deep breaths. His eyesight becomes sharper and clearer with each passing moment, until he can see through the shattered observation ports located directly above the control console.

The sky above is a majestic hue of blue, with a

187

few specks of white puffy clouds lingering in the atmosphere overhead. The bright sun is warm and almost welcome, at first. However, as Aleksandr sits in his seat, clad in a heavy insulated spacesuit, the sun begins to slowly work at him. He feels stinging sweat make its way down his neck and forehead. He squints up at the sky, looking for any sign that might indicate he made it back to Earth, possibly reassuring him that the whole thing is just a horrible dream caused by the trauma of crashing nose-first into a desolate gypsum desert.

It takes a few minutes for the idea to sink into Aleksandr's head. He is not on Earth like he should be.. Aleksandr knew that when he entered the mysterious solar system days before. He knew that when he entered the planet's atmosphere, hoping that whoever was sending out the cobalt and neon-green light into space would find him. He hopes that the light was being sent by the Progenitors. They were often willing to send humans back to where they came from. The others amongst the stars were less willing to do a favor for a species that barely left their own solar system.

Aleksandr feels panic setting in. His chest tightens up. His breathing is sharper with each passing inhale and exhale. He looks at the shattered and beaten remains of his control console. The mechanical clock in the upper right hand corner of the console tells him he has been out for nearly twenty-three hours, not exactly reassuring, but it's a start. He tries coaxing the different instruments online, and only manages to get the emergency radio working. Even that is not very promising.

Nothing but static filters through the tiny speakers built into the overhead panels.

"Damn it," Aleksandr mutters under his breath, switching the radio off to save whatever power still remains in the spacecraft's very limited energy reserves.

He loosens the black straps and unclips the brass clasps of his safety harness. The tension in Aleksandr's shoulders and chest lessens, making his heart rate slow some. His lungs start taking in deeper breaths, and the feeling of panic begins to subside almost immediately.

Tovarishch Puusepp, what are you worried about?

Aleksandr sits back in his chair, staring at the control console instruments with tired and sore eyes.

"I don't know," Aleksandr replies to the voice he believes is in his head.

Do you think they are here?

"If they are," Aleksandr begins to say, "they haven't made the first move yet."

Enemies like ours stand around, watching prey. They rarely commit to first moves or don't resort to direct action, tovarishch. They are like the wolves in the Urals; they wait for the opportune time to strike. A wolf never takes risks, neither can you, tovarishch.

"I know, tovarishch," Aleksandr says. He looks over his shoulder only to see a blur of a man he thought to be long dead.

Aleksandr rubs his tired eyes and jumps from his seat. His booted feet make a soft thud as they come in contact with the titanium and steel wall of the spacecraft. He walks over to the different items haphazardly strewn across the empty space between the cockpit and the workspace of the small craft. He kneels down, picking up the clothe sack that contains his survival supplies and tools—in case of some emergency, an emergency like this one. He collects the items scattered across the cylindrical craft's smooth walls. Each item is equipped with tiny magnets that keep them in place. Each tug is a task in itself. The weight of the bag feels like the boulders his father used to have him move on the collective farm. Then, without much hesitation, Aleksandr leans up against the curved wall of the spacecraft and falls asleep.

* * *

A cold wind forces Aleksandr awake. Sitting next to him is the same man he saw earlier that day. This time, the man is smoking one of the Belomorkanals from Aleksandr's survival pack.

Did you sleep well, tovarishch?

"No," Aleksandr manages to reply. "What are you doing here, tovarishch Volkov?"

I am here for the same reasons you are, tovarishch. Remember, we're on the same side, Aleksandr.

Aleksandr rests his head against the cool metal wall of the spacecraft. After a few moments, he looks at the spot where Volkov was sitting, smoking a cigarette like the old days. The smoldering end of a spent cigarette sits there, with whiffs of white-gray smoke emanating from its yellowed paper. Aleksandr does not remember when he last smoked. It must have been before he left Earth. He could not have one inside the spacecraft enriched oxygen environment—not unless he had some kind of death wish. He cannot remember having one now, but there it is, next to him. One end is smoldering, slowly burning off the excess paper into gray and black powdery ash. He knows that Volkov died many years before. He remembers watching his old friend and mentor being crushed by two massive blast doors of an abandoned Progenitor warship that was surveyed by the Consortium. There was barely enough of Volkov left to have a proper funeral with full military honors.

The weight of sleep makes Aleksandr's eyes burn with exhaustion. His head rest once more against the cold wall. His eyelids droop and flutter until his body finally gives away to sleep.

* * *

The next morning Aleksandr struggles to open the spacecraft's emergency hatch. He slams his entire bodyweight against the door comprised of reinforced steel, aluminum, and titanium. The hatch's metal door whines and groans as Aleksandr continues pounding on it. After a few moments, he gives up, feeling the energy being drained from his body with each forced effort.

The planet's sun heats up the inside of the vessel. Aleksandr glances down at the temperature gauge stitched to his spacesuit's right sleeve. The gauge reads 53C, Aleksandr begins peeling away vital pieces of his tattered spacesuit, which brings some relief but not enough.

The wind outside the spacecraft howls and carries with it fine gypsum sand through the shattered observation ports. He doesn't know where he has landed, but is feels like he's landed on a world of sand, which he knows is impossible. That's not how things work in the universe, or at least that's what his survival instructor said in training. It's hotter than any place he has been before now. It's far hotter than any place in his native homeland of the Soviet Union. Aleksandr's legs finally collapse under the weight of his sweating body. He pushes himself up against the emergency hatch. Sweat pours freely from the top of his clean shaven head and the back on his neck, soaking his clothes. Volkov plops down next to him, offering a sweating metal flask of water. Aleksandr accepts the flask and unscrews the lid before draining the precious liquid inside.

"Thank you, tovarishch," he gasps, before tossing the flask aside.

No problem, tovarishch.

Aleksandr rests his head against the emergency hatch, closing his eyes and listening to the dreadful howl of the desert wind....

Why are you hesitating, tovarishch Puusepp? Is he not your enemy? Do not fear what this man has done or why he is here. All you need to know is that he is your enemy. He has collaborated with the capitalist swine. He would sell his own mother to those dogs and his countrymen to make a few rubles. That is the curse of capitalism. The capitalists will sell each other to make a profit, and they will bring about their own demise. That is what makes capitalism inferior to communism, tovarishch. Do you understand that, Puusepp?

Aleksandr wakes up, jerking his head forward. Muscle in his neck and shoulders throb with electric pain from the sudden movement forward. He notices the wind has died down, and it's completely dark within the confines of the spacecraft. It has grown considerably colder in the last few hours. His body shivers against the cold metal of the emergency hatch. He flips on the map reading light attached to his discarded suit's chest plate. The tiny bulb illuminates the interior of the cramped vessel with a wash of yellow-white light. Aleksandr pushes himself up and heads over to the reentry vehicle's controls. He looks out of the broken observation ports, propping himself up with the pilot's chair. He spots a half dozen or so distinct stars, all forming constellations eh is unfamiliar with, meaning he has not made it back to Earth, as he was supposed to. He drops down from the chair, landing with a soft thud.

Aleksandr looks around the inside of the spacecraft. He spots his emergency kit with warped shovel attached to its cotton cloth. He walks over to it and pick up the back, detaching the shovel and throwing it down in the process. He rips open the cotton bag and sits down on the spacecraft's sand covered floor.

Aleksandr rummages through the bag's contents and finds something of use. He finds the

Belomorkanal cigarettes in their blue, red, white, and pink cardboard packaging. He grabs the cigarettes and a booklet of matches from the bag. He chucks the bag off to the side. It hits the side of the spacecraft's wall with a metallic clang. Aleksandr rips open the flimsy cardboard package with his thumb nail and takes one of the unfiltered cigarettes out. He pinches the end of the cigarette in two different directions, allowing him to smoke the tobacco inside cardboard-paper tube without inhaling the smoldering tobacco and paper into his lungs.

He wets his parched lips first before stuffing the paper cylinder between them. Taking the booklet of matches, he lights the top and inhales deeply. The harsh flavor of moist paper and cardboard and dry tobacco fills his mouth, and enters his lungs before Aleksandr exhales the thick smoke through his nostrils. A cloud of smoke fills the cramped interior of the spacecraft, force Aleksandr to move himself closer to the broken windows nearest the craft's cockpit. He finishes up the cigarette while leaning against the wall of the spacecraft, watching the obsidian sky above. The warmth of the burning paper and cardboard near his face pulls him away from whatever he hoped to spot in the sky above. He tosses the spent cigarette butt to the side. He stoops down and snatches the bent shovel, his lucky shovel, and glances over at the emergency hatch with a shrewd eye.

Aleksandr walks over to the hatch and slips the thin edge of the shovel into a small slit on the side. He begins prying the shovel back and forth. The hatch's door wiggles slightly but doesn't give in. He puts more of his weight behind the shovel's roughhewn wooden handle. He grips onto the wood handle with both hands, and puts all of his weight behind the shovel's blade until his knuckles are ghost-white. He pushes forward, hearing the metal grown but nothing moves, as before. Aleksandr pulls backward on the shovel with all of his weight. The metal of the emergency hatch groans and creaks until he hears a loud snap. Aleksandr feels himself fall backward, hitting the curved wall of the spacecraft.

"Damn it!"

Aleksandr looks down at his hand. A three-inch splinter from the wooden handle is wedged deep inside the palm of his right hand. The shovel, his supposedly lucky shovel, is broken in two, with one end still sticking out from the gap in the emergency door. Blood pours from his palm, down his forearm and over the dirty white fabric of his underclothing. He bites down on his lower lip, hoping to lessen the pain. It doesn't.

"Damn it," he grunts, still biting down on his lip.

Aleksandr takes a hold of the splinter with his teeth. He tastes the varnish of the wood and the salty copper of blood as he rips the splinter from his palm. Warm tears stream down his face from the sudden explosion of pain that erupts from his injured hand. He reaches for the survival bag with his good hand. He finds a small medical kit inside and tears it open with his teeth. He takes out a small roll of gauze and a square olive-green packet of sulfa powder. He tears the top off the waxy paper of the sulfa powder packet and generously sprinkles the contents on his injured hand. The powder causes him to wince as it does not dull the pain but actually aggravates the wound. He unties the knot keeping the gauze roll tight and wound and wraps his wounded hand. Blood still manages to seep through the gauze and thick layer of sulfa powder.

Aleksandr pushes himself up against the curved wall of the spacecraft. He takes out another Belomorkanal and goes through the process of getting it ready to smoke. He sits there as a cold night breeze wafts through the broken windows. The breeze moves the thin layer of sand this way and that. Aleksandr stares at the emergency hatch, seeing the bends and buffs in the aluminum paneling and locking bars. He brings himself up and heads over to the hatch. He looks at it for a second and lights his cigarette. He steps back two paces and runs toward the door. His should collides with the weakened door. The hatch's door gives way, with a high-pitched screech, and Aleksandr feels himself land in the fine gypsum sand. He accidentally inhales the sand, causing him to cough and lose his cigarette in the process.

Aleksandr pushes himself up from the warm sand. He gazes up at the dark sky. He doesn't see satellites or even a moon of any kind in the sky, nor does he recognize the constellations from his survival training. He was hoping that maybe this was Earth, somewhere near the White Sands staging area, but it's not.

"Damn it," he mutters to himself.

He begins working his way up to the lip of the impact crater. Once above the lip, Aleksandr sees more white sand, as far as his eyes can see. There's not much for shade or food from what he can see.

What are you going to do, tovarishch Puusepp?

Aleksandr shakes his head in disbelief and begins rubbing the bridge of his nose with his good hand.

"I don't know, Volkov," Aleksandr answers. "I don't know."

Why not, tovarishch?

"I don't even know where the fuck I am," Aleksandr exclaims.

Who cares where you are! You need to get somewhere safer, less exposed!

"This goddamned place isn't even where it's supposed to be!" Aleksandr feels himself yelling into the cool desert night. "They told me nothing would go wrong! Look at where the hell I am! Everything's wrong! Everything!"

Aleksandr's body trembles and his knees buckle, causing him to fall to the ground. He feels himself sobbing, with real tears streaming from his eyes. He feels a warm hand on his shoulder.

"I don't know what else to do," Aleksandr says, clearly defeated.

T*hat is no way to be, tovarishch Puusepp!*

Aleksandr tilts his head upward. He recognizes a familiar face. An older man, one the Americans used to call the Russia bear. The man offers Aleksandr his leathery rheumatic hand. Aleksandr accepts the help and pulls himself up from the warm gypsum.

What am I do to, *tovarishch* Volkov?"

Follow your training, Sasha. You came here for a reason, just remember that. Something brought you here. Call it fate. Call it God's will. Call it whatever you like. It brought you here.

"What?" Aleksandr asks.

The old man points to the light source in the distance. The man smiles at Aleksandr before fading away again. Aleksandr rubs his tired eyes, hoping that Volkov will reappear, only to be disappointed.

"Tovarishch Volkov," Aleksandr calls. "Where are you?"

Aleksandr sheds the remainder of his space suit, taking only the valuable, irreplaceable pieces of equipment still attached to its dirty fabric. He stuffs everything into the cotton emergency kit rucksack. He puts on the change of olive-drab fatigues and ties a cold weather jacket around his waist, putting the matching gloves and hat into the emergency kit's sack. Once he is satisfied with his preparations, Aleksandr moves over to the spaceship's control console.

He coaxes the Japanese electronics on. He flips a series of switches that start transmitting an encoded SOS message. Something inside of him tells Aleksandr that such a move is useless and a waste of vital electricity. No one will find him out here. Another, somewhat hopeful side believes it is worth the extra effort, like a sort of message in a bottle being carried across the medium of interstellar space. He slings the pack over his shoulder and walks out into the pre-dawn morning.

With little effort, Aleksandr makes it to the top

of the impact crater. He turns around looking at the damaged cylindrical reentry vehicle. The spacecraft's titanium and steel exterior is a dully gray with a large crack forming down the side of the hull from the harsh reentry and even harder impact. The crack looks like a gapping abyss in the pre-dawn light. Pale white sand has begun to fill the crack, and the sand has moved closer and closer around the vessel itself—a slow motion wave gobbling up an old shipwreck stuck on a coral reef. It will probably be completely buried by the sand in a matter of days or weeks if the winds keep up.

Aleksandr looks at his surroundings. Toward the sunrise he spots a mysterious light source. On all sides he sees an infinite expanse of white gypsum desert with a few mountains and mesas sprinkled in here and there. He remembers seeing mountains when entering the planet's atmosphere almost two days before. The mountains looked more like the mounds of dirt and sand he used to build with his brother in their backyard. From this new perspective, the mountains seem more menacing.

The morning air is refreshing and almost liberating, but it sends chills up his spine. The cold feels less alien to him than the sweltering heat from the day before, although he prefers to the heat to the cold.

Alexander begins walking in the light's direction. A familiar figure walks alongside him.

Tovarishch...

"Yes," Alexander replies, not looking over at Volkov.

Do you mind if I come along?

"No, tovarishch," he answers. "I need someone to talk to."

Alexander feels himself laughing, and he hears the deep, hearty laugh of Volkov as well. Alexander continues trudging through the fine gypsum sand, heading toward the light. He does not know whether he is going crazy, or if the heat has finally gotten to him. He no longer cares. He'd rather have a dead friend for company on an alien world than be by himself.

Question of the Day: What would a revolution on
a space faring colony world be like?

It Bears Watching

Chad Dickhaut

Pavlo eased his skimmer up a bit, giving him a
clear view of the other side of the mountain. A glint
of light caught his eye, and he trained the small
vehicle's optics in that direction. He grunted as the
image on the HUD came into focus. *What do you
know? There is someone down there.*

The figure far below, who appeared male, turned
the collar of his worn leather jacket up and took a
sip of something hot and steaming. He was looking
through a pair of binoculars, watching the workers
down in the Valley Launch Site readying Leader
Biliakung's shuttle for launch. The figure put down

the binoculars and rubbed his eyes; apparently, the morning sun glinting off the buildings had temporarily blinded him. After a moment, the figure slumped against his battered old dunecrawler and took another sip of his beverage. *Wait, what's that?* Pavlo focused the optics on the back of the open-topped vehicle, finding a rifle mounted on a rack. *Hello, probable cause!*

Pavlo toggled his radio. "CenCom, this is HB-197K. I have visual confirmation of our intruder. Subject is armed, moving in to apprehend. Over." He swooped in close, stopping a scant fifteen meters over the intruder's head. The wind of his lift fans buffeted the man, whipping his hair around. Pavlo trained the skimmer's minigun at him and clicked on its loudspeaker, which squealed with feedback as he started to speak. "Hands on your head and step away from the vehicle." The intruder dropped his red polymer mug and complied without hesitation. Pavlo brought his skimmer down gently five meters away from him, dismounting and drawing his pistol in one fluid motion. "This is a restricted area. Identify yourself--" *Wait. It can't be...* "Korlus??"

"Pavlo?" Korlus snorted. "Figures it'd be you." Korlus and Pavlo grew up in the same neighborhood. They had even been good friends at one time.

Pavlo flipped his faceplate up and laughed. "Me, huh? I get sent to check out a potential troublemaker on the perimeter. Who else could it be but you?"

Korlus held his hand up to his ear. "What's that, old friend? I couldn't hear you over the sound of you selling out."

"Cut the crap. Why are you here, Korlus?"

"I'm just here to watch the shuttle launch." He gestured toward the spaceport down the mountain. "Extremely interesting stuff."

Pavlo crossed his arms. "Sure you are. And that rifle in the back of your crawler is strictly ornamental, yes?"

"Relax, it's just a 7 millimeter. I only brought it to run off bukidlyones." As if to confirm Korlus's statement, a low, keening howl echoed from down the valley.

"Fine, you're only here to watch. How did you even learn about this place?"

Korlus grinned mirthlessly. "Sa Pagbatok is everywhere. Even in secret places like this. Especially in places like this."

Pavlo reached for his radio. "You bastard. When we find your bomb--"

"There is no bomb."

"Your assassin, then."

"No assassin, either."

Pavlo grabbed Korlus by his spiked brown hair and stuck his pistol in his face. "Then what are you playing at?"

Sweat glistened on Korlus's indigo skin, running

down his face in rivulets. "Mind if I take my jacket off? It's gotten hot." Seeing Pavlo's suspicious expression, he added, "Look, I'm not gonna try anything. Swear on my mom's grave."

Pavlo thought a moment, then lowered his gun. "Fine. No funny stuff, though."

"Deal." Korlus shrugged out of his jacket and panted in relief. After a moment, he continued. "Okay, so you know the Corporatists screwed us all."

Pavlo shook his head angrily. *Not this crap again.* As long as he had known Korlus, his friend had waxed eloquently and at great length about the evils of the Corporatist party and of corporations in general. It had worn thin for Pavlo years ago, even before the Corps cut his paycheck. "Look, I'm no fan of the Corps, but you can stow your revolutionary propaganda!"

"Don't believe me? When they took control of the government, did they fulfill their promise to eliminate the bloated programs and agencies they decried? No, they just farmed them out to their cronies. Welfare recipients became lab animals for testing reverse-engineered Old Empire tech."

At one time trawling ancient ruins for technology and data from the time of the old Interstellar Empire was a profitable, if somewhat risky, way to make a living. Then the government shut down public access, even with permits, all in the name of "historical preservation". In practice, that meant the scavenging continued, but only by government employees, and the public never saw what was unearthed. When the Corporatists took over, the government employees were replaced by corporate research teams, but the end result was the same.

Pavlo shook his head again, but slower this time. "That's not exactly true..."

Korlus glared. "Why are we purple, then? Government-issued photosynthetic skin treatment. 'Purps never starve,' right higala? Even when our bellies growl for days."

Pavlo grinned weakly. "See? It's not all bad."

Korlus exploded. "Oh, yes! Our benevolent overlords cast us little people crumbs from their table, and if our squabbling gets too loud they don't give more, they just try to make us want less. And if their testing thins the herd on the way to their 'solution', all the better for them!"

"What do you mean, 'thins the herd?'" Pavlo didn't like the insinuation, but he didn't have an answer for it.

"My mom, your folks, everyone they tried different chloro-pigments on before they figured out this," he gestured at his bare arm, "was the winner. You know: no tumors, no sugar shock, no blood poisoning. And that's just one 'solution' they pursued. There was also the 'super-vitamin' program, the sewage recycling program, all the horrors spawned from the bioengineering program... Have you already forgotten? Oh wait, I forgot. You left before things got that bad"

Pavlo waved his hand. "Yeah yeah, the Corps are evil. Even though I think you're exaggerating how bad it got, I'll grant you there were hiccups along the way. But hey, you see it as evil, so I get it: 'unethical live experimentation', people dying. I see how being faced with that could drive a man to revolt."

Korlus spit. "But you didn't. You sold out." He stopped Pavlo's protests with a raised hand. "I'm not done yet. You wanna know the worst part of it all? Most, if not all, of those experiments were unnecessary."

Pavlo's mouth curled into a question mark. "Unnecessary?"

"The Corporatists had secretly been in contact with the space societies for years prior to their takeover. They could've bought all of that tech, pre-tested and vetted for safety, if they hadn't been so damned miserly."

Pavlo shook his head. "That doesn't make sense. Wouldn't it be cheaper to buy the tech from the Spacers than slog through the R&D process?"

"In the short term, maybe, but then they wouldn't have proprietary control over the tech. They'd only be able to use it as-is, no modifications, which means they couldn't cut corners to save production costs." Korlus crossed his arms. "And they couldn't make as much profit selling us our 'salvation' that way."

Pavlo's throat tightened. He didn't want to believe what Korlus was saying, but he'd seen too much corner-cutting, too many budget cuts, too much disregard for public and even employee safety, to disbelieve. "Gihangop sa inahan!" He kicked a rock down the mountainside. Mama, Papi, and everyone else had died for no reason but the Corps' bottom line.

Korlus patted Pavlo's shoulder in compassion. "There's more. Ever wonder how old Biliakung stays so spry after thirty years in power? He gets rejuvenation treatments offworld. We have proof!"

"Kapasitat!" Pavlo mopped his tears away with his sleeve. "So much for the hope of waiting for him to die off. How are we supposed to get free from the Corps?"

Korlus grinned. "Relax, my friend. We sit back and watch our liberation unfold."

"Huh?"

"I'm here to make sure the ChiefEx really boards that shuttle. From there, Sa Pagbatok is ready to take control, once Biliakung 'voluntarily' steps down. And he will, once he meets our agents waiting at his orbital hidey-hole. See, we've been planning this for years, getting our people in place.

We've even got help from the outside, for mopping up afterwards."

Pavlo was incredulous. "From the alimango?"

"Nah, the Crabs are too much like the Corporatists. We'd be trading one oppressor for another. Now, the Camatori League are happy to help us liberate ourselves, then treat us as partners."

"Those guys? Aren't they kind of... lackadaisical?" Pavlo had heard about the Camatori from a friend who worked security at the spaceport at the capital. They were big on honesty, transparency, and fair-dealing, but their government, such as it was, operated on ad hoc consensus, or something like that. Pavlo could scarcely imagine how they got anything done. "Who's to say they'll keep up their end of things?"

"We'll just have to trust them, but keep them honest while we do it. It's like the Camatori say, 'Once won, liberty bears watching, lest we squander it or others steal it."

Pavlo laughed. "You know, I kind of like that."

Question of the Day: How do you find your place in society? Is it something you are allowed to pick, or is it decided for you?

Helix

Drew A. Avera

The catwalk hung over a dark void in the spaceship as Grant looked down. He could not resist the urge to spit and watch the bulbous fluid disappear from view for what must have been the eleventh time in as many minutes. Once again, his hands gripped the railing as he craned his neck to reach as far out as possible, his eyes looking down into the seemingly bottomless void below his dangling feet. Saliva moistened his lips for a moment just before he squeezed them together to separate the spit from his body. With only a moment of hesitation the spit trickled before falling away. "One, two, three, four, five, six," he counted until he could not see it any more.

"Ha! Only six seconds," Ben mocked. "I spit one yesterday and watched it fall for nine seconds. You'll never beat my record," he said with more than a hint gloating.

"That's because there was more light in here yesterday," Grant said. "The window is pointed away from the star right now."

The Helix was a spindle-shaped vessel with a population of over five-thousand human refugees. It had been more than a few generations since anyone could remember leaving Earth behind, but no one on the Helix ever imagined returning to a home planet erupted in chaos. The threat of nuclear war and religious oppression had put the world at the brink of extinction. History being as it was, there was no wonder why life was better in the darkness of space rather than risk the future of humanity on bloodstained dirt.

The void the two boys looked into eventually led to engineering spaces, but people needed clearances to go there. Instead, the catwalk where they sat merely bridged two sides of the round spacecraft together to make life easier for the inhabitants.

"Whatever, you still didn't spit one big enough to see for more than seven seconds so I still win," Ben shot back. His need to excel at pretty much everything was a double-edged sword. On one hand, he was a great teammate at handball, but sometimes his competitive nature was too much to handle for most people; really anyone but Grant.

"I know. Anyways, I'm getting bored with this. What do you say we go to the galley and see if Ms. Waller will give us some cookies?" Grant asked, knowing Ben could never say no to sweets.

"Uh, yeah!" Ben said jumping up from a sitting position and holding onto the cold steel railing with both hands. The catwalk was forty yards from one side to the other and both boys stood almost perfectly in the center when there was a sudden loss of power. With a whoosh, everything went silent and dark. You could have heard a pin drop if not for the instant pounding of the boys' hearts as fear flooded into their veins.

A chill went down Grant's spine before he finally spoke. "What happened?" he asked. His voice sounded hollow to him as the sound fought to be heard over the thrumming of his heart in his ears.

"I don't know," Ben said, his normal enthusiasm waning. "It's like the ship just died."

"Don't say that!" Grant replied. "You know what happened to the Verne."

It was common knowledge the ship named after Jules Verne had lost power while coasting too close to an asteroid with a strong gravitational pull. The resulting catastrophe had claimed several thousand lives and the memory of it cast a shadow over the last remnants of humanity, even more than a century later.

"That's not what I meant," Ben said, his knuckles white as he gripped the handrail while making his way to the hatch. "Follow me; we need to get somewhere safer in case the ship begins to list."

A ship without power to create its own gravity would often begin to tumble as outside gravitational forces from moons and planets began to take hold. Given their proximity to KG894, a moon base settled on the moon of a dying gas giant planet, they were within range to begin plummeting towards certain death, especially without power for steering and reverse thrust.

Both boys made their way to the main passageway and found it just as dark and quiet as the void had been. A few emergency lights were illuminated to provide enough light for people to navigate back to their dorms, but the eerily casted light made the boys more afraid than anything else. "It's never been this dark before," Grant said under his breath. His heart beat like a drum in his chest as he remembered accidentally being locked in a storeroom when he was six years old. Even then there had been enough light to not feel too claustrophobic. This scenario felt much different to him and he could not help feeling alone and afraid despite the fact Ben was right next to him.

"Come on," Ben said, pulling at his friend's shirtsleeve as they moved deeper into the passageway, further from the relative safety of the emergency lit area.

It didn't take long before the artificial gravity began to dissipate and their steps no longer fell solidly to the deck below them. The sensation of gradually rising from the surface and swimming through the air was foreign to them, but excitement soon turned to dread after Ben dared a glance from a small window looking out from the craft.

"Is it just me or does KG894 look bigger?" Ben asked.

Grant moved across the bulkhead as his fingertips found purchase on the ribbing of the craft, coming to a stop at the window where his friend looked out curiously. "It's hard to tell, really."

"Look there," Ben pointed. "See the moon base's landing pads? You can see more details of the structure from here," he replied.

"I hadn't noticed that before. Are you sure? Maybe we are just seeing a different perspective of it than we usually see from the void's big window." Grant's words seemed rational, but Ben was not exactly ready to accept his statement as the truth. There was no denying that the base at least looked bigger, alternate perspective or not.

"Maybe, but we need to find my mom. She'll have a better idea of what's going on," he said, nervously pulling back from the window. "Follow me; she's usually on the bridge."

"We're not allowed there, Ben," Grant shot back. He remembered being caught playing near the navigation charts earlier in the year and being told never to set foot on the bridge again. They were harsh words coming from Captain Lancier, Grant's uncle.

Ben scoffed as he pulled his way down the passageway and towards the top of the spindle-shaped craft where the bridge was located. "You can stay behind if you want to, but I'm going to find answers."

* * *

Darkness met them every floating inch of the way. Each corridor and passageway was bathed in shadows, the emergency lighting barely visible against the dull light reflecting from the moon into the windows of the Helix. The temperature was beginning to plummet and steam escaped their mouths which each panting breath as they found their way to the bridge.

"Uncle?" Grant whispered as they entered the ghostly room. The gravity levels were stronger in the bridge and their feet touched the ground lightly, allowing them to walk instead of having to pull themselves across the bulkheads of the ship.

Surrounded by eerily luminescent control panels and screens the boys stepped deeper into the bridge. Some of the readouts were easy to understand, temperature and oxygen levels were the first things they noticed, but the oscillating numbers identifying the distance between the Helix and KG894's orbit revealed the boy's worst fears; they were indeed falling, if you could call it that.

"Ben, look!" Grant gasped, pointing at the readouts as the digits scaled downward, each fluttering of numerals proving how quickly they were descending.

Ben moved and looked over Grant's shoulder, his eyes wide, terrified. Not only were they falling but he was just struck with the realization that they were the only two souls either of them had seen since the emergency started. "I don't know which is worse, the fact we are crashing uncontrollably or that there are no pilots, no anyone in the bridge."

Grant looked around, holding his breath as Ben's words were proven with a sight he had refused to acknowledge at first. They were in fact alone.

"Where did everyone go and why didn't we realize we were alone until now?" Grant asked, daring to reason the answer should be obvious despite the churning of fear in his body.

"I...I don't know," Ben whispered. He had always been the one with answers, the fearless one amongst his friends, but there he stood, watching KG894 grow larger as the Helix fell, aided by the gravity the ship could no longer combat against. They were nothing more than an advanced version of Sir Isaac Newton's apple falling from the tree, proving that gravity was indeed the enemy of flight.

Ben and Grant dropped their gazes from the banks of indicators and windscreen of the Helix that revealed their impending doom. No good would come from watching death rise towards them like a bird taking flight; instead they leaned against a bulkhead on the other side of the bridge and dropped their bodies down into a seated position.

"This situation doesn't make any sense to me," Ben said, his eyes moist with fresh tears threatening to stream down his face. Never in his fourteen years of living on the Helix had he experienced anything of this magnitude, nor had any training evolutions taken place that resembled their current plight.

"What should we do?" Grant asked; his voice on the verge of cracking. "We can't call for help, but maybe we can eject from the ship into an escape pod and land on KG894. Do you think you can pilot an escape pod?" He asked, allowing a tremor of hope to form his words.

Ben shook his head, he had played on many flight simulators growing up, but he had never learned to land any of those crafts on a surface bearing gravity. "We would die either way," he said solemnly.

Ben could feel hope escape his friend's body as he exhaled a barely audible sob next to him. The younger boy had put all his hope into Ben and now the fourteen-year-old boy felt responsible for crushing his best friend's hopes of normalcy. A flood of thoughts entered Ben's mind as he dissected the situation a hundred different ways, his eyes looking outside the Helix and towards the pale light of KG894. A bead of sweat ran down his brow as he thought, pleading to himself to find a way, any way to save himself and his friend.

As Grant sat with tears running down his face there was a sound, reminiscent of static across a radio frequency, but that was impossible because the communications systems were down, or were they?

"Did you hear that?" Grant asked, sitting up and looking around the room.

Ben's ears perked up as both boys stood and listened intently for what had caused the sound.

It happened again, this time more audible, more hopeful.

"Over there!" Ben pointed at an unlit console, mostly in shadows on the other side of the bridge.

Ben and Grant scrambled over to that side and looked at the station. There was only a small indicator resting flat on the horizontal surface, the readout nothing more than a dim, orange line scrawling across the four-inch plane. The sound appeared again, louder this time, but accompanied by a sign-wave along the orange line.

Ben squinted as he tried to read what the indicator was for. The only clue he had was the letters "DC" labeled under the right corner of the screen. He thought for a moment before speaking. "I think this is for emergency DC power, I remember reading in one of the manuals that electrical power can be reset so long as there is a power source. Surely this might have something to do with it," he said.

"If that's true then how do we reset it?" Grant asked.

Ben hunched down over the console, straining to read the controls in the dim light. "Do you have a flashlight on you?"

Grant looked down at his belt and brought his hand up with a pencil-thin wand, a small LED attached to one end. "Here you go," he answered, switching the light on for his friend.

Now, bathed in light, Ben could make out what each button and knob was on the console. Each label dismissing his attention until he found what he was looking for. "Here, generator reset switch, I wonder if this is it?"

Grant watched as Ben touched the switch and lifted it to the reset position before letting go. There was a louder than anticipated click as the spring-loaded switch returned to the normal position. The boys stood there for a moment in the darkness before the bridge lit back up, first in hues of blue and then brighter, whiter light engulfed the space in piercing luminosity.

Grant took a large gasp and wrapped his arms around his friend. "You did it!" he shouted. "I can't believe it!"

Ben smiled; looking around as each console sprang back to life and lit up. The temperature indicators and gravity monitor readings began to return to normal and both boys could feel themselves weighing heavier. Everything was moving in the right direction except for the altimeter, it still showed that they were moving closer to KG894's orbit and before long the moon's gravity would pull them to the surface.

"Oh no," Ben said as he darted across the bridge to the engine control console. Within a few moments, he realized the pulsars were not activated and needed to be restarted. His hands glided over the controls with the precision of a skilled pilot. The pulsar initiation sequence forced the engines to come online, led by Ben's skilled control.

"We are still dropping fast," Grant said as he read the altimeter over Ben's shoulder.

"The engines are online, but the pulsars are facing the wrong direction," Ben said. "I have to correct the pitch and ease off the throttles at the same time. I need you to take over flight controls," he ordered.

Grant looked over at the lonesome console across the bridge. He was nothing more than a few dials and control sticks, but it was beyond anything he had ever used. Grant, though growing up in the shadow of his Uncle who was captain of the Helix, was not being brought up to pilot the vessel.

"I need your help, Grant. Take your position at flight controls while I maneuver the pulsar thrusters."

Grant stared at Ben a moment more, nervous, afraid.

"Now!"

Finally snapping out of his daze Grant ran over to the flight control console, placing his hands on the control stick. "What do I do?" he asked, his fear hanging in the air around him.

"I want you to pull back on the control stick lightly. The Helix is too big for High-G maneuvering, so a light and steady pull will have to work."

Grant pulled the control stick back, barely applying any pressure to it.

"You need to give it a little more, you are only applying a few percent of pitch control right now," Ben said, turning around to read the altimeter indication behind him, the numbers dropping at a slightly slower pace.

Grant pulled back more. "It's really heavy, I

don't know how much longer I can hold it," he said. The control stick required forty pounds of force to move in order to prevent jerky movements at high speed. The increased control came at a cost of tired muscles for the pilots.

"You're doing great," Ben called out. "Keep it up."

Ben eased up on the throttle lightly until the pitch of the Helix was where he wanted it to be.

"We are leveling out! Don't ease up yet!" Ben cried.

Grant winced as his arms grew more and more fatigued by the weight required to maintain the position of the control stick. He wanted to cry out, he wanted to give in to weakness and let go of his burden, but as he looked over to make eye contact with Ben he could see that their lives were in each other's hands. Grant did not want to die and he sure did not want to be the reason his best friend would not live to see another day.

Through grimace and groans Grant kept the control stick pulled back. The indication on the altimeter finally began moving in the opposite direction, the direction that pointed them on a course away from the moon KG894. With that position, Ben increased the throttles and the Helix lurched slightly as the engines powered up to propel them away from the gravitational pull of the moon.

Now, with the threat of doom behind them, Ben

stepped back from the console. "You can ease off now," he said to his best friend as he walked towards him.

Grant's arm muscles were beyond the point of wanting to let go, but between adrenaline and self-control he eased the control stick back into the neutral position. Turning to look at his friend he spoke, "we did it."

"That we did," Ben replied, wrapping his arms around his friend and pulling him close. Desperation fueled their need to survive, to fight for the future of not only themselves, but the Helix as well.

"Congratulations, nephew!" Captain Lancier said, stepping out from a faux wall behind a line of control consoles in the bridge.

Both boys looked at him, shock in their eyes.

"I don't understand," Grant said, one arm still clinging to Ben.

More officers filed out from the same shadows as Captain Lancier and soon the bridge was full of the team responsible for the livelihood of the people onboard. "This was a test, not only for you, Grant, but also for your friend Ben."

"A test?" both boys asked simultaneously.

A smile curled the captain's lips. "Yes! You see, each member of my staff is chosen based on their interest. We raise our replacements because humanity can only survive using the knowledge of previous generations. It is my job as captain to ensure that future generations are taught how to deal with high-stress situations in order to preserve our species. That's what this was, the final test to determine if you two were ready."

Ben looked down at his friend questioningly. Before either of them could speak Captain Lancier placed a caring hand on each of their shoulders.

"Both of you passed with flying colors. You were put in a position where you had to rely on each other. You were forced to solve a problem in order to survive even though you were concerned for the safety and wellbeing of your families. Both of you took action and focused on saving the ship. For that I am most proud of both of you."

"Thank you, sir," Ben said, lifting his hand in a salute to his captain. Grant saluted as well.

Lancier returned the salute with a smile.

"Thank you, Ensign Benjamin Borden and Ensign Grant Lancier."

"Ensign?" Ben asked; his eyes wide.

With a coy smile, Captain Lancier replied, "Of course, only commissioned officers are allowed to pilot my ship."

And with those words the bridge filled with cheers.

Question of the Day: What makes us human?

Questions of God

Sean P. Chatterton

I remember the day I died.

Well, more accurately, I remember waking up afterwards.

* * *

Blinking several times because the bright light hurt my eyes, I slowly became fully awake. I couldn't focus my eyes properly at first; I felt out of sorts, not with it, thoroughly disorientated. This was not like any hangover I'd ever had before.

"Mr. Clarke, I see that you are awake. How do

you feel?"

It was a male voice, but I couldn't see the person speaking.

"Where am I?" I croaked.

"You are in a medical research facility Mr. Clarke."

* * *

Marcus's head jerked up in surprise as he heard the unexpected guard shout through the slot in the dull grey cell door.

"Prisoner three-two-eight-one, stand to. You have a visitor".

He heard the guard unlock the door and watched him warily as he scanned the room before entering. The guard ordered him to stand to one side, then enter. Marcus watched him conduct a quick, but thorough, search of the eight-by-six space. When he left the cell, Marcus heard him say to unseen people outside "It's safe to enter."

A tall, thin woman wearing a pale grey business suit entered followed by a shorter, but equally thin man. He wore an expensively tailored dark blue suit, and was carrying a black briefcase.

Marcus looked at them cautiously for a few moments. He gestured to the bed, and sat down on a three-legged stool. The bed and stool were the only items of furniture in the cell, apart from the exposed toilet and basin.

"For legal reasons, can I confirm that you are Marcus Clarke, previously of 1492 Long South Drive, Palamera, California?" asked the man.

Marcus nodded.

"Your date of birth is September second, twenty thirty-six?"

Again, Marcus just nodded.

Satisfied that he had the right person the man said, "We have a proposition for you." He introduced himself as Mr. Haynes, a lawyer for Haynes and Bencher, and Ms. Philomena Mimes, a scientist in a secret medical research facility run by Aon Armament.

"Can I call you Marcus?" Philomena asked.

Marcus nodded.

"At Aon Armament we are conducting research into cybernetics, and robotic augmentation for soldiers. Some of the work that we are doing carries high risks, possibly even death. This is why we have an arrangement with the US government for death row prisoners."

Marcus nodded again, not quite sure what to say.

"We are seeking volunteers who're willing to have their death sentence commuted to scientific research. It's somewhat like signing your body over to medical science."

"Why me?" asked Marcus.

"We have reviewed your file and you fit our criteria."

"I would like you to know that I am not a violent man. It was a stupid bar fight over nothing. He was trying to chat up my girlfriend. If the stool he fell on hadn't broken and put a spike through him, it would have been a different story. It was just a stupid accident, that's all." He paused, searching the floor for something that wasn't there, looking up he continued; "If it wasn't for a seriously shit lawyer and a corrupt judge who had never forgiven me for several misdemeanors with his daughter years before I could never have been given the death sentence. It was only manslaughter after all." Marcus paused, "I bitterly regret what happened, and given another chance I would do things differently, I really would."

Philomena nodded, "I thought as much, which is one of the reasons why I have chosen you for this. So do you want to do something which could help your fellow Americans instead of dying needlessly in jail?"

"Yeah. Why not, I'm on waiting list to die, it's not like I've got anything else to do is it?" replied Marcus.

* * *

"Oi, get your fucking hands off my missus."

Marcus shoved the blue baseball cap wearing man with a large black beard with his left hand, his right clenched into a fist, ready to punch him.

In the low-lit truck stop Marcus had been enjoying a few rounds of pool with his friend Jack and his girlfriend of eight months Mary. Marcus had pretty much ignored Mary most of the evening. Well, apart from buying her an occasional drink and grabbing her arse. He had spent more time drinking and shooting pool with Jack, and chatting up the barmaid, Jolene, than give any proper attention to Mary. Things were different now he spotted the trucker hitting on his girlfriend.

"I said get your fucking hand off my missus you fat fucker."

Before Marcus could say another word the trucker thrust his bottle of Budweiser towards him, to what he thought was his face. Marcus lashed out and hit him twice before thrusting him hard with his left hand. The big guy stumbled back and fell, crashing through a couple of bar stools, one broke as he fell on it. With a sickening crunch a wooden spike appeared in the middle of his chest and blood started seeping through his checkered shirt.

Mary started screaming…

* * *

Now he was more awake and with it, he tried to sit up, but discovered that he was held down, flat on his back. So he called out, "who's there?"

A woman spoke this time, "Good afternoon Mr. Clarke, how are you feeling today?" The woman sounded vaguely familiar. Marcus wondered if it was...

"Is that Ms. Mimes?"

"Yes. It's good to see you again Marcus."

"Why can't I move?"

She walked to his side then leaned over him. She was so close that Marcus could see her dimples, and smell the mintiness of her toothpaste.

"Is this better for you?" She asked.

"Yes, thank you. Can you tell me what's going on?"

"In a few minutes. I want to run a few tests first. If these tests run okay and you agree to remain calm, I will release the strap holding your head in place. Agreed?"

Marcus replied "yes". Not certain what to think.

Ms. Mimes moved from his field of vision. He could hear her typing on a keyboard.

"Did the experiment work? Was it a success?" He asked.

"Yes. You are our first complete success."

"What did you do to me?"

"We'll get to that in a short bit." She said in an upbeat manner. "However, the good news is that all the tests have been successful. But before I release your head as promised, I'm just going to cover your umm, *modesty*, with a blanket. I'll be back in a moment."

Marcus heard steps and a door open and close. Ms. Mimes returned in less than a minute, and he could feel something soft being laid over him.

"Am I naked?"

"Not exactly, but I don't want to cause you alarm with what you might see."

This scared Marcus. *Shit, what did I agreed to?* He thought to himself. Strangely he didn't feel panicked, just scared. "Calm, I need to remain calm, and not freak out" he said to himself.

Ms. Mimes moved out of his field of vision towards his head. Moments later he could move his head. He turned it both ways before tilting it forward to see a plain white sheet covering his torso. In the sterile white walled room, there was some kind of scientific apparatus to his left and an empty space to his right. He couldn't see the man who had asked if he was awake. On the upper half of the wall nearest his feet was a large mirror. Marcus thought it might be a one-way mirror so that other people could observe him. Marcus heard Ms. Mimes move a chair to the empty space to his right and sat down on it.

"Do you feel anything Marcus?" she asked.

"Like what Ms. Mimes?"

"Philomena, call me Philomena, there's no need to be so formal now. Can you tell me what you feel physically, emotionally, anything at all?"

Marcus relaxed a little with Philomena, he couldn't put a finger on why, but he felt more comfortable in her presence with her being so familiar with him. Marcus thought his reply before answering. "I am scared shitless. I know what you told me in the cell, but now, I can't help but be scared. Emotionally, well, I feel completely wrung out."

"OK, that I understand, I honestly do. Please trust me, you have nothing to be scared of. Do you feel anything physically?"

"I can feel that I am lying down on a hard surface. Have I been augmented, like you spoke about?"

"Yes, you have been *operated* on." Philomena accentuated the word operated.

"Can you tell me to what extent?"

"Hmm, it was a lot more extensive than we might have given you the impression of in your prison cell, but I think you'll find it a whole lot better than having been executed." She smiled, "but I don't want to cause you undue alarm." She paused, tilting her head. "Although I realize by saying it like that, it sounds scarier than it should, but please don't be scared." Philomena sounded genuine.

Marcus relaxed a little more after his talk with Philomena. He felt more confident that things would turn out OK if he trusted her. Again, he couldn't put his finger on why.

Philomena said she had other things to do, and had to leave for a very short while, but asked if he would like to listen to some music. Marcus replied "that would be nice." A few minutes later piped music started playing over unseen intercom speakers.

* * *

Marcus heard two people enter the room.

"Good afternoon Marcus." said Philomena. "Doctor Theopathetis and I are here today to bring you up to speed on your situation as promised."

"Good afternoon Philomena, Doctor Theo." Marcus replied.

"How are you feeling today?" asked Philomena "Confused. I've kinda lost track of time as well. How long have I been awake?"

"It has been a little over two days since we first activated you." Philomena was deliberate in her choice of words again.

Marcus didn't say anything for a few moments, puzzling on this. "Why *activated*?" He asked in a flat tone. He watched as Philomena came into view as she walked to a position by the side of him. Marcus looked at Philomena while she stood watching him for a moment.

"Yes, activated. As I promised yesterday, I am here to inform you of your current condition."

Philomena reached out and put her hand on Marcus's arm, hoping that physical contact would help.

"We have downloaded your entire memory, personality and consciousness from your old body and uploaded all of it into an android body. You do not have augmentation; your mind and memories are housed in a cybernetic machine."

"Shit..." he muttered. Marcus digested the impact of what he had just been told. He had somehow expected to have a robotic arm or legs, or *something*, but a complete new body? After a few moments of introspective silence Marcus asked, "What has happened to my old body?"

"It was cremated." Philomena replied tonelessly.

It was several more minutes before Marcus responded. "Am I a man? Or am I a machine?"

"Legally the person that is Marcus Clarke is dead. The android that is Marcus Clarke is very much alive and functioning very well."

"Do I have a soul?"

"That is for God to answer."

Marcus went silent again for a moment, bizarrely he felt strangely calm. Like all his inner demons had been exorcised. "I think, and feel, and I remember being Marcus Clarke; I feel like me. I don't feel like a robot." Marcus paused for a moment; his voice quavered a little as he asked; "Can I see myself in the mirror now please?"

Moving around the table, Philomena undid the straps holding Marcus in restraint. When she had undone all of the straps she stood back a little and told Marcus that he could now sit up, but to be careful.

Marcus tried to sit straight up, but couldn't quite manage it. Watching Marcus Philomena said "Take your time. You are going to have to relearn how to make your body do what you want it to do. I should imagine it will be like someone who has been wheel chair bound for a long period learning to walk again." Marcus still struggled, so in the end Philomena moved forward and helped him sit up. The thin white sheet slid down to his waist and covered his lap.

Marcus stared at his reflection. Where was his large handlebar moustache? The face staring back at him was a total stranger, not that of Marcus Clarke. It was a non-descript male face with neutral features and quite importantly, no facial hair. Marcus didn't recognize the person in the mirror. Philomena observed him, silently. He lifted his hand and flexed his fingers, looking at them. He carefully slid off the end of the table to stand before the mirror. The

234

white sheet previously covering him slid off revealing his anatomically non-gendered neutrality.

"I'm not a man, I'm androgynous." he said.

"What makes you a man? It's not just having a penis that makes you a man." Philomena said.

Marcus drew a blank, what did make him a man? "Is there any part of me that is human?"

"Physically no. No part of you is flesh or bone."

* * *

"What do you mean this one didn't work?" asked Duncan Sheen.

"The transfer completed exactly as it has done the previous six times, only this one didn't wake up." Replied Philomena.

Philomena explained. "The transfer took longer than previously, but this wasn't a major cause for concern as candidate nine was over fifteen years older than previous volunteers, and the extra time taken was attributed to the extra memories accumulated."

"So, to state the obvious, we still don't know why it worked for Marcus, and doesn't work for anyone else." stated Duncan.

"That's the long and short of it." She replied.

"Have you tried downloading Marcus's personality into another android to see if that would be successful a second time? Duncan asked.

"It had occurred to me, but for some reason the download of Marcus's personality appears to be blank. I have the tach's looking into it, but as yet, they have no answer as to why." Philomena shrugged her shoulders, not knowing quite what else to say.

Duncan scratched his chin, and said "Well, it's not all bad news today. I have some good news. The boys back in the software department have finally cracked the autonomous software. They are using a heuristic algorithm, which uses a reasoning response engine. So we now have the software to run the androids."

"Why is that good news?"

"Well, for us, it is massively cheaper than personality transfers. But more importantly, the defense general wants robots, not androids."

"What about my research? What about Marcus?"

"I have a new project for you. We need a volunteer for a trip to Io. Given certain criteria, I think Marcus would potentially be ideal."

* * *

"This is the *Hesperus* checking in on day five hundred and forty two. Everything is operating as normal. Ground control do you read me?"

Marcus knew that it would be around an hour

before Houston responded to his signal. Twice he had received rebuke when he had not given the official call sign check. Apparently "Major Tom to ground control" and "Houston we have a problem" was met with very little humor.

The further that he had travelled from Earth the harder it was to maintain a conversation due to the time lag. Marcus used to have chats with two of the controllers, Mark and Josh, in the early days. It had helped keep him sane whilst he adjusted to be on his own. But now the time lag made it all but impossible.

Marcus watched Jupiter growing larger every "morning" ship's time. He watched a particular small dark spot grow. This was Io, the fourth largest moon in Earths' system. He had read up on Jupiter and its moons. He now knew that Io was one of the four Galilean moons orbiting Jupiter. He had joked that he would be the first human to actually view the moon up close when he landed on it. Only they pointed out he wasn't physically human any more.

Marcus sat in the command seat as he recalled the conversation that he had with Duncan Sheen and Philomena about this mission.

"Marcus, we have a situation that might interest you." started Duncan. "A radio ham discovered a signal coming from IO. It has been confirmed by a number of radio telescopes from around the world. It is weak and sometimes intermittent, but it is there none the less."

"How does this involve me?"

"Well the United Nations Space Agency, have said that they will send a manned mission to investigate it. But there are a few technical issues that they have."

"I know jack about space, or space travel, so how can I help?"

Philomena chimed in, "UNSA doesn't have a space ship capable of making that journey that can support a human crew." "I'm guessing that since I'm not human, that's where I come in?" Marcus said.

"Yes." said Duncan. "Since you don't require food or air. It also helps that you are virtually immune to the radiation that their Ion drive puts out. It is entirely feasible that you could man this space ship for UNSA."

"Wow, where do I sign?"

* * *

Over twenty months Marcus watched as the *Hesperus* took shape. The engine was housed in a separate unit, which was nearly a hundred feet from the white globe, which housed the living quarters. A gantry of titanium tubing painted a stark white connected the two parts.

The *Hesperus* was built in sections and assembled in orbit. Whilst she would be able to land on Io, the extra gravity on Earth meant she would be too big and fragile to lift off in one piece.

In the time between the radio signal being discovered and going public, and the Hesperus being launched, no headway had been made in decoding the message. The short, repeating message defied all human and computer deciphering. The consensus of opinion was that it was a distress call.

During his astronaut training Marcus also had a number of modifications carried out on his android body. The most important was a military grade communication radio installed in his main carapace, which would be vital when on Io to maintain communication to the ship. A minor one, which pleased him, was he had fourteen thousand hours of digital music uploaded to his memory banks that he could listen to whenever he was on his "down time".

Marcus received the reply to his status update fifty-two minutes after he sent his message out. There was a time variance on the replies due to the location of Earth in relation to Jupiter's orbit. The message from Houston informed him that they would be uploading the final updated orbital insertion telemetry to the ships computer in the next twenty-four hours. Io was now only three days away and any minute adjustments were now finalized.

After nearly eighteen months of routine and, to Marcus, boringly repetitive experiments, Marcus

239

was actually looking forward to something actually happening, even if it was only maneuvering rockets firing. He even felt excited at the prospect. Once the Hesperus was in orbit he would be required to fire off a number of small satellites with sensors and using the onboard HiDef camera map the surface of Io in detail. The camera had such a high spec the scientists at UNSA were hoping for a detailed map down to one centimeter.

Several orbits would be required to map Io, and Marcus would not be able to land the ship until a suitable landing site had been located near the source of the signal near the moons" "north pole" region. Io had a very thin atmosphere, which was inhospitable to human life, but worse still the entire moon was practically full of volcanoes. Even Marcus would require a protective suit in these conditions. Not to breathe, but to protect his android body when he exited the ship to locate the source of the signal and report back with his findings.

* * *

The orbital insertion had proceeded without a hitch, and the detailed mapping had revealed a planetary surface in turmoil, much as expected. There were numerous volcanoes vying for the title of most active. Some of the more violent eruptions had produced volcanoes that were higher than Mount Everest. Landing on Io would be extremely tricky and exceedingly dangerous.

Scanning through the high-resolution pictures, neither Marcus nor UNSA could see anything on the surface at the location where the radio signal was issuing from. This meant that Marcus would have to exit the Hesperus and use a special close range scanner to see if he could detect anything under the surface. UNSA named the site of the signal Ground Zero, and they hoped that Marcus could find the source. Marcus wasn't sure how he felt about this. If he had been human it may have been deemed far too dangerous to go outside, but as an android he was considered expendable. Nevertheless, Marcus resolved he would go ahead and complete the mission to the best of his abilities.

* * *

"This is *Hesperus* to ground control. The landing was bumpy, but we are down safely. Local scans suggest that this plain is stable and we should be safe here for a while. I am sending you all the scans and will wait for your authority to exit the vehicle to walk the kilometer to ground zero. Please confirm upon return. Marcus out."

Checking the dials in the cockpit the external temperature was much as anticipated. Not enough to cause a problem for Marcus, but continued exposure could melt the prosthetic features off his composite alloy body. Marcus was not happy about this as it meant that he wouldn't look even vaguely human. If this happened, any sentiment that the authorities back on Earth had for him would melt along with his face. As human as Marcus felt "inside", he knew that outside he would look like a robot.

Whilst waiting for the reply from ground control Marcus readied himself in his protective suit and run through all the suit diagnostics. Twice. He received his confirmation to exit the Hesperus and make his way to ground zero. If he could have taken a deep breath, he would have.

Even though Marcus didn't breathe there was still an airlock for him to exit the Hesperus. Cycling through the airlock gave Marcus the final moment of trepidation. Whilst he knew his suit protected him from the heat and dangerous elements, he was still at risk from the constant volcanic eruptions and pyroclastic bombardments.

The outer door opened. Marcus looked outside and thought that he was looking at hell, only it was real, and on a different world. He performed a radio check with the ship, and confirmed that the radio link back to Earth was still working. This lifeline was purely psychological, but it did help his nerves. The final thing he did before climbing down the ladder was to press a button, which extended a Waldo arm with a camera on it to record this momentous moment.

The gravity on Io is about eighteen percent of Earths. This meant that Marcus would have to be careful not to bounce around whilst walking.

"That's one small step for a man, one giant leap for mankind."

Whilst Marcus had perfect recall, his nerves were playing havoc with his thoughts. He was extremely glad that he remembered to say "*A* man." No doubt back on Earth there would be a controversy as to why UNSA could not come up with some more original.

He then planted the UNSA flag within the camera's field of vision. The play-acting done, he then had serious work to do. The surface of Io looked like a moldy pizza, with sulphurous yellows and dark stains everywhere. The constant volcanic activity meant that Io did not have any craters from meteor impacts as the constantly changing surface simply dissolved them over a fairly short period of time.

A loud eruption several miles away rocked the ground where Marcus stood. He looked around still shaking from the noise and violence of the explosion. He watched the Hesperus wobble, but it remained standing.

Calming his nerves before setting off, Marcus

243

took one long look at the Hesperus and using his internal inertial guidance looked to a point in Io"s sky to where Earth would be located. He couldn't see Earth, but he knew where his home was. He then set off, one foot in front of the other.

Using a mapping device and the high-resolution scans that he had made from orbit, he made his way to ground zero. There was a slightly steeper rise but nothing above the surface that he could see. Unless obstructed by volcanoes or mountains Marcus could see all the way to the horizon, which was considerably closer than that of Earths. The locator unit beeped when he was at Ground Zero. Marcus unpacked various items from his utility belt. He then used the hand held scanners and small probes to start his scans. Opening his internal radio circuit he tried to hear the signal directly. There was nothing to hear. He sent a radio signal back to the ship to be relayed to Earth asking if they were still receiving the signal.

It took nearly two hours to run all the tests that he had to perform. In that time he had a reply back from Houston that the radio signal had stopped when he had landed. This had caused a huge debate, one that was raging amongst the academics. At the end of the tests, nothing could be detected that would indicate a source for the signal. There were no signs of life, no apparatus and no source that could be detected.

As Marcus finished his tests, a loud rumble sounded deep beneath him. The ground shook, and knocked him off his feet. The rumble got worse and Marcus got thrown around in a violent fashion. This lasted a good thirty minutes. When the Io-quake finished the visor on Marcus's space suit was broken, and all of the equipment that he was carrying was scattered. The minimal protection the visor offered didn't particularly bother him as his cybernetic eyes quickly adjusted without any operational difficulties. Looking back towards where the *Hesperus* was, it looked like there was a newly formed small jagged mountain where it should have been.

"Shit." was the first word that crossed his mind.

Marcus checked his radio link with the ship and managed to approximate a sigh of relief with his vocal unit when he received the confirmation return. If he could have wept with relief he probably would have done. Deciding that it was way too dangerous to stay on this constantly up heaving moon, Marcus planned to get back to the ship and head back into orbit. So he started walking back to the ship.

As he neared the location of the ship he was alarmed to see that he couldn't see the dome of the living quarters when he expected to. He was much closer to where the ship was located before he sighted the wreck of the *Hesperus*. His ship, the glorious *Hesperus* was lying on its side; the engine section was under rubble and newly spewed lava. The dome had serious impact damage, but was at least above the surface.

Now Marcus wept without tears. He would not be going home.

* * *

Getting back to the ship, Marcus found that he could get inside safely, but the atmosphere had leaked out through the large rent in the side. That would mean all the experiments he had so diligently worked on for the duration of the journey would be dead. The inside was a complete mess with everything strewn everywhere. A madly erratic thought flew through his mind as he made his way to the cockpit; it would be a bitch to tidy this lot up. In the cockpit he checked the ship"s radio and wasn't surprised to find that it was no longer working. A diagnostic check reported the external antenna was damaged, possibly beyond repair. His internal radio link to the ship worked, but there was no link back to Earth.

Marcus slumped in his chair, defeated.

* * *

There were no more eruptions or Io-quakes that day, or the following day. Or even the following four days as Marcus just sat in his chair not knowing what to do.

Marcus could not find the motivation to do anything, as he was utterly depressed with his current situation. This was worse than he could imagine. He had no way of contacting Earth; He didn't know how to repair the ships antennae, even if he had the parts. His internal radio only had a range of a few miles, and UNSA didn't have another ship to send; so there was no hope of rescue. He would be here until his power unit expired and then what? Death? Real, true death?

During his bout of depression, a plan formed in his mind.

He could configure the suits radio to transmit a signal, and plant it at ground zero. He hoped the signal might be good enough to reach Earth, and they would send someone to rescue him.

* * *

Traipsing back to ground zero Marcus was very wary. There were no rumbles or ground shakes, but then neither had there been a warning when the one that ruined the Hesperus had happened.

Marcus found all of his equipment still strewn where he had left it. This gave him some hope that his sketchy plan might actually work. He grabbed the tripod from its fallen position and stood it back upright then attached his suit radio to it. He had recorded the original signal, and edited it to include "Send Help" in Morse code. Sitting his suit radio on the tripod he activated the transponder unit to constantly transmit in the same repeating cycle. He checked his own internal radio and, yes there was the signal again. He whooped for joy. Stage one complete.

Looking around him to check everything was in place, he noticed a dark depression a little way off to his right. Still somewhat curious as to what could have caused the original signal in the first place he made his way towards it. As he neared it, Marcus could almost swear that is was pulsating. Standing at a safe distance he scanned it with his handheld scanner, and decided that the pulsating was a trick of the sickly light. Then for the first time he looked directly up and he could see the great coloured bands on Jupiter. Marcus had been so focused on his mission, not once had he looked up. He was instantly awed by the majesty of the vast planet above him. He stood watching this and lost track of time just staring at the wonder.

Sometime later he woke from his virtual daydream and stepped forward and straight into the dark depression. Alarmingly he started to sink. He turned quickly and tried to make his way back to the lighter ground when he discovered that this darker area was viscous and considerably worse than quicksand. In a matter of moments he was up to his waist in this treacherous stuff.

"Oh fuck" he screamed.

When he stopped sinking, he was up to his abdomen in the dark patch. He thought that he could feel the bottom under his feet, but wasn't too sure. Trying very carefully to move towards the edge he discovered that he could barely move. Knowing that it would be months before any help arrived, Marcus resolved to himself that even if it took weeks to make his way out of this sticky, viscous nightmare he would do it.

* * *

It took Marcus several days to wade out of the slime pit. Marcus had felt a few rumbles while he was wading, but there was nothing that he could do about it. When he had fully emerged, he looked down at his lower body and wasn't too surprised to see that whatever the substance was, it was acidic enough to destroy his protective suit, and his prosthetic skin revealing his composite alloy legs. Thankfully these were only pitted. This reminded him of the heat and the effects that it would have on his face. There was no reflective surface for him to use as a mirror so he was going to have to make his way back to the ship to see if he still had a face. He grinned internally at the thought that vanity affected even him.

He walked the short distance back to where he had left the suit radio and was surprised to see the tripod still standing, and a quick check on his internal radio confirmed that the signal was still being transmitted.

Marcus breathed a sound of a sigh of relief. Then the ground shook again, violently, extremely violently. The ground appeared to tilt at an alarming angle throwing Marcus into a jagged group of rocks smashing the side of his face. Marcus lost consciousness for the first time in years.

* * *

"REBOOT COMPLETE"

The words in bright orange glowed before his only working eye. One side of Marcus" head was damaged. He could neither hear nor see anything from his left side. He tried speaking and his vocal unit only emitted a quiet static.

Marcus tried to get up and discovered the whole left side of his body was damaged. He felt around and discovered that the sensors in the fingers of his right had melted off with the prosthetic flesh, so he had no way of feeling anything, he could only see crushed and damaged limbs.

Marcus checked the time. His internal clock showed him that only a day had passed.

He looked around at the desolation trying to locate the suit radio amongst the strewn equipment, but nothing was visible near him. Using his internal radio he found to his amazement that the signal was still being transmitted. This gave him hope that help might yet still come. He then tried the radio link with the Hesperus and got no answer.

Looking around at where he was Marcus could see a dark patch, and hoped that this was the same dark patch he was stuck in previously, so he triangulated a best guesstimate where ground zero should be and started to drag himself to it. Clinging to the vain hope that someone would rescue him, he had to say when because the word *if* depressed him too much, so when rescue came.

He found himself chuckling, even in this dire situation. He would love to see the look on their faces when they found that the source of the signal was an American made suit radio.

With that Marcus started his internal music, leant back so he could look up at Jupiter, and waited.

* * *

"Great shot Marcus" Jack said. Looking up and across the bar, Marcus saw a stranger standing just a bit too close to Mary, he had his arm around her shoulders. He ignored Jack and strode over shouting at him as he got within a few feet.

"Oi, get your fucking hands off my missus."

Before Marcus could say another word the trucker thrust his bottle of Budweiser towards him. Marcus lashed out and hit him twice before thrusting him hard with his left hand. The big guy stumbled back and fell, crashing through a couple of bar stools, one broke, he fell on it. With a sickening crunch a wooden spike appeared in the middle of his chest and blood started seeping through his checkered shirt.

Mary started screaming "you arsehole, that's my brother. He stopped by to say hello and buy you a beer. You stupid fucking arsehole!" She screamed; "what have you done to him?"

* * *

Nothing puts a man's life into focus so much as staring death in the face, or being on death row. Marcus had become acutely aware that he had been a drunkard, wasting his life. Life was a precious commodity, and up until the bar fight he had squandered his. During his time on death row, he didn't "discover religion" like many others had, but he did start "talking to god". There was definitely a lower case letter G there. He didn't suppose for one second that he would ever get any answers, but he asked anyway. Most of all he had asked for a second chance. He thought that Philomena had given him that second chance, but look how that had turned out...

But then why would any god give anyone a second chance? There had to be some kind of logic or a valid reason. And why would a second chance involve getting stranded on a different planet, damaged, dying and lonelier than he had ever been on death row.

* * *

As the last notes of Beethoven's Moonlight Sonata played Marcus woke from his reverie and realized that there would be no rescue. He wasn't a man, with or without a penis, he was just a machine, and as a machine, he was disposable.

Laying there staring up at Jupiter he had lost many days just contemplating life. He considered himself lucky. He had been given a second chance. He had been a bum in his human body, and in this android form he had tried, really tried, to be a better man. He may well have failed, but he had tried, and for that at least, he was content.

"God I was such an arsehole."

"That you were."

Marcus stopped for a second, "who's that?"

253

"Who do you think I am?"

"God?"

"In the way that you understand; yes."

"Shit..." Remembering way back in the lab when he asked Philomena a certain question, to which she had replied, "that is for God to answer", he asked: "Am I a man? Or a machine?"

"The most important part of your being is a man. Your body is all machine."

Marcus sat for a few minutes contemplating. "So what did I do to deserve a second chance?"

"You asked, and you meant it. So I gave you the second chance to make something of your life."

"Surely many other people ask, and they don't get a second chance, so the question of the day; why me?"

"Why not?"

Marcus was a long time thinking before he muttered, "Shit..." A few moments later he asked: "So why such a piss poor end, why not something better, more... meaningful?"

"Not everything in a person's life has a meaning that mankind will fully understand."

Marcus was dumbstruck. After what could have been hours he asked: "Are you the reason why I was the only personality transfer that worked?"

"Yes. The scientists could indeed download a person's memory, and personality, but they couldn't transfer the person's soul. Only I can do that. So yes, I transferred your soul to give you your second chance. I was the reason why you and you alone, transferred completely."

"I bet Philomena would give her right arm to know that."

"She may indeed. But for you, I think it is time to move on…"

Question of the Day: Can one really ever understand the past, or are we just forced to link together a story from misplaced clues and memories?

The Sapentia Report

Thomas A. Farmer

The system you are attempting to access is listed as: Restricted, Aleph Status

Command: Access restriction system.
Purpose: ... ...

The screen in front of you goes blank. For several heart-stopping moments, the data drive attached to the Isian-made console emits a high-pitched whine. The human who sold it to you never asked what reason you might have for needing Aleph-level access to an Imperial database, and you were not about to explain yourself to him.

Something lives beneath the surface of Sapentia, you are sure of it. The official record is too vague to be of use and the reasoning given is the usual for such incidents: chemical-induced hallucinations. Those creatures had not been a dream. The only thing left to examine now is an officially unofficial report compiled for the Emperor himself. In fact...

That train of thought is derailed as the screen comes back to life in utilitarian grays. The interface is cobbled together from a dozen different Imperial systems, most of which have not functioned as presented in years. Certainly, none of them have ever functioned quite like this.

Database access granted. Please input catalog information.

* * *

Date: July 5th, 4770CE
Subject: The Sapentia Incident
Author: Maciej Rashid al-Hasan Baine

Prepared for His Majesty, Emperor Sarpedon under the oversight of Grand Admiral Pegasus

* * *

All material contained in this document is assumed to be classified at the highest levels of intelligence. Under no circumstances is any of the following information to be shared with anyone 1) not currently holding an Aleph-level clearance or 2) any human or Isian with political or domestic ties to the Star Federation.

Punishment for the violation of 1) is to be no less than ten standard Terran years imprisonment and five hundred kilocredits. Violation of 2) will be met with an additional fifteen standard Terran years and a fine not to exceed 1.5 megacredits.

If you are in possession of this document and are a citizen in good standing of the Terran Empire but do not possess an Aleph-level clearance, please report to the nearest Law Enforcement Center, turn over all copies of this document along with the name(s) of the person from whom you received it, and no charges nor fines will be levied.

By continuing to read past this point, you certify before Imperial Law that you indeed possess the required clearance level.

* * *

The first entry within the report itself is listed as "Screen Record - Rashid, Maciej - June 1st, 4755CE - Used with Permission," along with another link to the relevant legal documents.

Transcript of the recording, spoken in a soothing female voice with a light Nova Terran accent, follows:

Imperial Planetary Catalog
Username: mhbaine1172
Password: 1galacticeye4u

...

Access Planet "Sapentia"

...

The planet known as Sapentia was discovered in the year 4532 by a joint exploratory mission by the Imperial Navy and the Confederate Isian Armada. A water planet, Sapentia boasts an ocean that covers 99.9% of its surface, leaving only a small Island chain above water. Imperial High Command immediately seized upon the idyllic beauty of the planet, its remote location, and the complete lack of other geographic features as the perfect location for a University.

Founded in 4537, the University of Sapentia was to be the Empire's premier institute for higher education. At that task, the University excelled, producing graduates that who met with success on a nearly universal basis.

Between the years of 4535 and 4690, the Isian

Confederacy also maintained a mobile research outpost on the planet. Predominantly located on the opposite side of the vast and, one might say, endless ocean, few University students made contact with the massive ocean vessel.

In 4688, the Isian research team contacted the University directly, interviewing students in evolutionary xenobiology and forensic astrophysics courses. Students interviewed said the Isians' questions were rather random, having more to do with the quality of their studies and how they perceived the knowledge they were gaining than anything. Shortly after, in 4690, the Isian team left the planet.

Isians would not return in any real numbers until 4704, when the first integrated human-Isian classes started their school year. In fact…

The recording pauses here as the screen blanks. In moments, it is replaced by a command structure interface. A verbal note added by Rashid indicates: At this point, I knew the data I was looking for would not be in the public files, but with a written record literally in my hands, I was sure the data existed. Fortunately, I prepared for this eventuality, though in hindsight, I suspect I was not as clever as I thought.

…

Command: Display Full History
Access Denied

Command: Open Root Access
Access Denied
...

Command: Play "Holfit Vakyisolt" from external
memory device.
Accessing device.
Playing music.

...
...
...

Username and password confirmed. Welcome back,
Archivist.
Command: Display full history of planet Sapentia
One moment.
...

Initially named Aquarius, proof of the existence
of the planet known as Sapentia was first discovered
in the mid-36th Century, during the period known
as the Terran Dark Age that followed the complete
cessation of all Faster than Light travel. Researchers
operating on the station then referred to as
"Solheim," situated at the third Lagrange Point
between the Earth and Sun, recorded a massive
stellar nova.

The first such burst was recorded in 3519. Ordinarily, such an event, while fascinating for researchers, would have passed unnoticed as time went on. However, scientists at Solheim recorded another blast in 3562 and a third in 3601. Between the years of 3612 and 3822, sixty-eight bursts were recorded from the same location in space.

Given that subspace was not discovered until 4101, nearly three centuries after the last recorded stellar nova, interest in the star waned significantly. As a set of data points, especially data points that did not match up with known properties of stellar novae, it remained fascinating to a niche group of scientists, but was quickly forgotten by the general public.

For the scientists that continued to research the phenomena surrounding the unexplained novae, the star continued to hold a fascination. They named it Brynistjyr, which was a far more palatable name than "Stellar Catalog Entry 457.X.661.Q.C1Z." Brynistjyr showed no overt signs of stellar activity after 3822, though its estimated 17KLY distance made resolution of any planets or other objects in orbit impossible even for Solheim's advanced (at that time) technology.

Interest continued to wane until 4521, when an agreement was reached at the five year First Contact anniversary with the Isian Confederacy. Isian Stellar data showed the same record of activity dated to, adjusting for their differing position in the galaxy, the same time period as the mysterious novae recorded by Solheim.

A joint Isian-human task force pinpointed the location of the star still known as Brynistjyr in 4523 and first set foot upon the planet they then called Aquarius in 4525. Aquarius showed telltale signs of massive surface damage identical to the sort that was expected given the star's violent history some eighteen thousand years before. Contemporary ocean life upon then-named Aquarius was radically different to that shown in fossil records from before the planet's star began its unusual cycle of flares.

By 4530, the exploratory teams had uncovered a massive...

...

Session Ended
Error Code: 11021

Command: Terminate Connection
Unable to Terminate Connection

Command: Root Terminate Connection
Working...
Working...
Working...
Failed.
Error Code: 663

PLEASE REMAIN WHERE YOU ARE. ANY
ATTEMPT TO LEAVE YOUR CURRENT
LOCATION WILL BE MET WITH FORCE.

* * *

*The following is a personal note from Maciej Rashid
affixed to the report proper. It is listed as "Journal Entry,
Personal" and appears to have been included after the
report itself was written. The style differs dramatically.
Your system indicates that the journal bears the signature
of Grand Admiral Pegasus's personal encryption.*

Rather than face fines or prison time as I
expected once the full extent of my crime was made
known to me, I quickly found myself face-to-face
with Grand Admiral Otto Pegasus Ilari Galard.
Grand Admiral Pegasus explained the purpose of
our meeting as twofold. First, he informed me of the
exact nature of the secrecy surrounding the Sapentia
Incident. Second, he congratulated me on
uncovering as much as I had before, as the Grand
Admiral put it, "making myself known to the
Manus Imperator."

Grand Admiral Pegasus then made a most
generous offer: I was to collate all available data on
the Sapentia Incident for His Imperial Majesty Lyov

Sarpedon Endymion Byquist and, to quote the Grand Admiral once more, "make it interesting for his Majesty's reading pleasure." I found this area of study much more fascinating than comparing the input/output ratios of emerging shield technologies and happily accepted the Grand Admiral's offer. I do not feel it would be in bad taste to also admit the alternative, a fine of three hundred kilocredits and five years in prison for possession of classified information, was not terribly appealing.

Had I not possessed the physical original of James Carolinus's journal, itself an artifact whose very existence piqued Grand Admiral Pegasus's interest almost as much as my own activities did, I might have left things alone and continued believing the official story.

Even so, I sat on the information for some time, assuming it was just the idle fantasy of a pair of college students. Gods know I had plenty of the same daydreaming on Sapentia's beaches. As the years went by, however, my mind continually returned to the stories I had read and dismissed. James Carolinus's friendship with Empress Wong, recorded in his journal and by his hand, became the piece that finally motivated me to, literally, dig deeper.

The actual strata of the islands making up the college atoll were exactly as the planet's official record stated. Dense, metal-rich, granite-like rock foiled my every attempt to dig. Even ground-penetrating radar simply showed a solid mountain all the way down to the planet's mantle with scarcely a gap inside for a cave or magma chamber. That again matched the official record: the solar novae thousands of years before stripped the planet's surface clean, wearing down most major landforms except for the ultra-dense, rocky mountains that even now still poke above the endless waves.

It took time, and a role as a professor of shield mechanics, but I was finally able to craft a system to access the planet's classified records. I knew they were there because a "routine security check" of the college's computer systems pointed out a massive dead-zone inside the data architecture.

This brings me back to the encounter with the Manus Imperator and my meeting with Grand Admiral Pegasus last year. I have already started work on the report and, with luck, it should contain every scrap of information surrounding Sapentia and the so-called "Incident." I hope my inclusion of tabloid speculation alongside encyclopedia facts and personal journals of those involved does not strike the Emperor as off-putting. Facts are immutable and often virulent, and the truth of what happened inside the Sapentia arcology was out there but not widely acknowledged, and some of the fringe theories contained more truth than anyone suspected.

I should thank Grand Admiral Pegasus not only for my freedom and the continued patronage of the Imperial government itself but for this assignment specifically. I believe I am the first, other than Nanishir Ubrigumi herself, to have access to the full and unaltered transcripts of her mission logs from Sapentia. I have been told that this access is a direct result of certain favors he called upon; I did not ask what those favors were.

* * *

Here begins the text body of Rashid's report.

The Sapentia Incident of 4690CE remains one of the most curious events of the last millennium. The fact that it happened at all proved the correctness of a great many theories about the cosmos. Until mankind first encountered the Isians in 4516CE, we thought we were alone in the universe. True enough, we had discovered plentiful life throughout the galaxy, but a new species of bird-analogue or an edible fruit does not contain the wonder a thinking creature does. Perhaps that is why the existence of non-humanoid but sentient creatures under the surface of Sapentia was kept so secret--to know that such a civilization existed under the feet of the Empire's most prestigious university would have turned more than one "fact" upside-down.

Rasheed's report helpfully includes a series of cross-references links in the sidebar relating to the following topics: Alien Life, Humanoid; Isians; Isian Armada, the; Isian Confederacy, the. A note that seems to have been added by a subsequent reader includes various historic events, focusing on the years between Human-Isian First Contact and the Sapentia Incident.

Regardless, the creatures discovered on Sapentia were anything but "like us." For nearly a century, we assumed the ocean planet was simply the unfortunate recipient of a stellar nova some million or so years ago. We assumed, rightly, that surface conditions on the planet were due to the aforementioned nova and that no further investigation was necessary. Standard surface-penetrating radar did not indicate the presence of any subsurface caverns, after all.

Still, the idea that there was more to Sapentia persisted in some circles, even after the establishment of the University that gave the planet its name. In the grand scheme of things, those ideas, while ultimately fruitless at the time, produced some of the finest astrophysical minds of the current generation, myself included (class of 4751CE. Refer to public record No.166793263 for any pertinent details).

After the Incident, enrollment at the University of Sapentia fell dramatically. Word spread of a heavy-handed coverup, and student numbers dwindled. The influx of tourism, itself ultimately pointless, interfered with the studies of the students enrolled during, and after, the Incident without bringing and real benefit to the University. The ban on non-student visitation (4711-4713) only helped fuel the rumors.

Two of the three involved in the incident were given commendations for their contributions to Imperial science. At the time, those contributions were left under a cloak of secrecy due to the confidential nature of the events in which they were involved, a decision which threatened to backfire spectacularly until Empress Wong released an official report in 4715 crediting "James Carolinus Antinius Alexander" and "Alena Sotto Sylvana Baumeister" with the discovery of new life on Sapentia. Nanishir Ubrigumi, an Isian scientist, was not recognized by the Imperial government.

Another sidebar annotation includes a link to the Isian government's letter of commendation awarded to Nanishir Ubrigumi. The letter bears a public information catalogue tag, but the reason given has been redacted.

That the life they were credited for discovering was a species of squid-analogue that did in fact open the door to new radiation-shielding technologies seemed to quell the rumors of "secret actions" and "hidden cities" for some time.

James Carolinus Antinius Alexander (4670-4747) went on to become a prominent Senator and close confidant of Empress Evelyn Wong. Indeed, for there were very few with whom he could share his story, it only made sense for James Carolinus to either sink to the gutter, forgotten, or rise to the highest heights of Imperial society. With a degree from the University of Sapentia, the odds would have been in his favor even without his astounding tale.

Yet, the release of the report could not have been better timed to ensure no one would read it. Carolinus made a name for himself as a pioneer in the field of astrophysical technology by becoming the first human to design a functional subspace engine that was not itself a derivative of an existing Isian design. Against such an achievement, his role in "new radiation shielding technologies" fell into the background along with any involvement in the "Sapentia Incident."

Not only was the report buried, but his part in it was repeatedly stated to be incidental. Carolinus seems to have joined the "expedition," for lack of a more convenient term, primarily because his friend Alena Sotto went missing. Naturally, he searched for her. Sapentia University is a small campus after all--word travels quickly and there are few places to which one can disappear for long.

The tale of "True Love" as spun by the reports and later by Carolinus himself (though only after Sotto's disappearance) is false. His journal says as much. His concern for his friend was true enough, but it never reached the sort of fever pitch it gained in later retellings.

Alena Sotto Sylvana Baumeister (4668-Unknown) served as a Civil Rights Attorney for nearly twenty years after her graduation. She championed the acceptance of Isian citizens within the Empire, fighting to afford them the same rights given to all human citizens in good standing. She was wildly successful, using her working relationship with Nanishir Ubrigumi to illustrate to certain reactionary members of Imperial society that the Isian people were due just as much as our human citizens.

A sidebar note references a court case: Sotto v. Terra Nova Polis Governance, 4701CE.

The last record of her presence is on the fringe colony Aloysius's Watermark more than twenty years after the Incident. There, she disappears after passing through Imperial Customs. Her destination as of this writing remains unknown. After leaving that amusingly named colony, her trail, as they say, vanishes.

Personally, I suspect she made her way to the Star Federation (*Rasheed has included a list of planets and installations within easy travel from her last known location, and a link simply labeled "Appendix B, Subsection 11.7"*) under an assumed name. Despite resources provided by Grand Admiral Pegasus himself, all I have uncovered is a single line of notation from the Cameda Family's records indicating that an "Aline S.B. Schotto" owed them a great deal of money. Beyond this, I have no concrete information upon which to base my assumption.

Nanishir Ubrigumi (4428-4769) originally bore the entire blame for the Incident. When Alena Sotto disappeared, and James Carolinus began his search for her, Ubrigumi broke cover to aid in the search. Accounts vary on her reasoning: Carolinus himself claimed she was never undercover and simply strode onto the University's grounds wearing full combat gear, while her own report indicates she spent considerable time exploring alternative options.

In examining the data, I feel blame, if "blame" is even the proper term to use, does in fact fall at her feet. Without Isian help, Carolinus never would have found his way into the arcology or spread the story of the alien life living there. Certainly Alena Sotto and Nanishir Ubrigumi were more capable of keeping secrets than James Carolinus.

For some time, the relationship between Sotto and Ubrigumi was the sticking point, the thing that made the least sense. James Carolinus went searching for her and saw the Isian as his best option to find his friend. That much was always clear.

I missed the explanation on my first reading of his journal, so focused was I on the descriptions of the life the three of them found there. Amid the descriptions of biomechnical trees whose roots grew out of an eons-old nuclear pile and shadow creatures that only James Carolinus could see clearly, was hidden an exchange between Nanishir Ubrigumi and Alena Sotto herself.

* * *

Here, Rashid has pasted several excerpts from Carolinus's journal. It preserves the handwriting, though some of the smudges from age and dirt have been digitally cleaned up. He writes in a flowing script, almost calligraphic.

N and I camped at the edge of a glowing sea. Far below us, some kind of liquid's swirling around the bases of the trees. N says earlier expeditions connected the liquid and the trees to what they're pretty sure is, or was, the arcology's nuclear reactor. Some million? Billion? A fuckton of years ago, this whole place ran off of the power generated down there.

Now... what? It's got trees growing in it. Big fuckoff trees hundreds of meters tall with branches woven around one another like vines, and they're growing right in a sea of liquid nuclear material.

…

N heard me talking about it as I was writing and corrected me just now. Not nuclear material. It's nanomachinery, a little water, and, yeah, a lot of nuclear material. I don't see how important the difference is.

…

Holy shit.

…

Ok, so, let me back up. We found Alena. She ended up down here when one of the shadow things chased her and then the leaf (N tells me that they're not leaves, but whatever) she was resting on moved. N and Alena think it was some sort of reaction to the shadow thing. N tells her to make sure she takes detailed notes.

I'm pretty sure the trees hate them. Didn't I mention that before? Yeah, the trees are alive, they can move, and I swear to the gods they can think and talk. I heard rumbling before it happened, like a cello the size of a starship warming up.

So, one of the shadow things corners us, right? Three fucking eyes boring holes right through me, it felt like. It manages to get onto the leaf where we set

274

up camp. N and I kick its ass and knock it into the glowing sea.

And the trees around us WOKE UP. They moved. They roared.

We ran like hell.

* * *

One small sentence amid such detail is easy to overlook, but the clue is there. Ubrigumi reminded Sotto to record everything that happened when the tree-like creatures awakened. Later details support this observation and support my supposition that Alena Sotto had been inside the arcology before and the Isians knew about it. That explains Nanishir Ubrigumi's presence at Sapentia University, why an Isian soldier masquerading as a scientist would take an interest in a single lost college student.

Ubrigumi went back to the Confederacy after the Incident, where her findings were classified at a level similar to this very report. As news spread, the Isians declassified parts of her report quietly, but little came of it. After all, everyone "knew" that Sapentia's islands were solid and only fools believed in the stories of aliens lurking there.

Tragically, she perished in the New Colorado Civil War last year, forever putting out of my reach any personal experiences not included in her official report. Most attending the funeral had no idea she was involved in the Sapentia Incident at all, forcing me to invent a cover story that we met some years back at a concert.

It was her death that ...

* * *

Session Ended.
Error Code: 663

Please confirm clearance level before continuing.
...

A countdown appears on screen, starting with a generous fifteen seconds. With seven seconds remaining, your password appears to be accepted and the input box disappears. Moments later, another box, framed in an alarming red, dominates your screen.

...

Clearance Denied.

Please remain where you are. Any attempt to leave your current location will be met with force.

Question of the day: What happens to the stories that never get finished?

An Ending for Cole

Bryan S. Glosemeyer

When Cole pictured this day in his mind, rehearsing how it would play out over and over again, he had always held the locket in his hands. For one last time, he would watch every holo of his family contained within. Then he would tear down the Eternal Tyranny of the Gods. Forever.

The same Gods he had once served and fought for. The same Gods that had refused to save them, even as his wife's body cooled in his arms and his daughter's blood stained his armor. The same Gods he had sworn a high oath to kill.

Untold lifetimes later, Cole finally returned to

where it all began: a dead, forgotten ruin on a dead, forgotten planet. The first temple of the Gods, twelve jagged, black spires raking at the frozen sky. Directly beneath the cold, comfortless light of a small red sun, surrounded by dry tundra, the temple ruins offered the only evidence of the planet's living, breathing past.

Standing once more at the dead center of that rotted structure, Cole was at long last ready to fulfill his oath. But not like he had dreamed. No locket. No holos. The last remnants of his family nothing more than barbed-wire memories, snagging and scraping at the back of his mind for a few thousand years.

Millennia ago, when Cole had devoted himself to killing the immortal rulers of the galaxy, he knew it would require sacrifices, terrible sacrifices. The locket had been just one among countless losses through those long years. Lost back when the Draco wormhole shattered, and the Gods set twelve hundred suns to supernovae.

Five centuries later and the locket's absence still carved out a raw, naked wound. But had he not let it go, he never would have passed through the Tethering and dipped his right hand into the Well of Fenrir.

Never would have become what he became.

Never would have been able to free the Tethered from the Eternal Tyranny.

As he approached the last crumbling stones of the central altar, a quantum tear ripped through the sickly green sky. Blasts of exotic particles and the white light of celestial armor illuminated the wasteland. From out of the rift, bellowed the thundering voice of...

***

The scene abruptly stuttered to a halt, creating an awkward tableau of suspended motion. The Lore Master gestured for the narrative holo display to power down and the lights of the royal viewing hall to quickly fade up to full brightness. Frozen ruins dissolved into opulent, overstuffed furniture and gilded walls.

"That's it then," said the Lore Master. "Off to quantum gravity lessons before you're late."

The Young Prince and his cohort were not happy. A chorus of whining groans filled the hall.

"But you can't stop now," the Young Prince complained. "We were almost at the end. You have to tell us what happens next. What happens to Cole?"

"That is all there is, my prince," said the Lore Master. "Nothing happens next."

"You've gone daft, old man," said the Young Prince. His cohort failed miserably at trying to stifle their snickering laughter. "I demand that you stop playing this silly game of yours and tell the end of the story."

"I beg your pardon, my prince, daft I may be, but I am playing no game. There's no more story to tell. That's it. That's how it ends. Kolp the Red's unfinished epic."

"Unfinished epic?"

"Indeed, my prince."

"Why didn't Kolp the Red finish it?"

"He died, my prince."

"But I want to know what happens to Cole. How does the story end?"

"I do not know, my prince."

"But... but why?"

"There are times, my prince, when you can ask why and no answer will ever be satisfactory. When you can collect all the reasons why, so that they even outnumber the stars of your grand empire, and still find yourself unable to change a godsdamned thing. Those are the times when we must learn to accept that things just are the way they are."

The old man gripped the Young Prince's shoulder in his long, boney fingers. "Sometimes stories never get finished," the Lore Master said. "Sometimes people die."

Vines

R. T. Romero

When all the world has been and seen
These tokens of our mortal dream
And young men age who've never been

Creators, yet unspoken,
Then climb the mountain and tell all
In heavens reach, from where stars fall
Within the sphere that now defines
The secret depths and hidden signs
'til wondering dawn rises to view,
And spreads her glow on questions true,
Which, brought to light, can evoke change
Though not quite all within our range:

Overlooked, the details show it...
Then go you home to carry on
Before the light is wholly gone
To sing aloud the last refrain
And write your verse upon the rain
To reach and grasp and write their hearts
As if a demigod of arts
To plow and plant the yet unseeing
Upon their very ground of being:

Planting there, would you grow it?
However sure and deft your hand
Respond to what is never planned.
Far down the echoed way ahead
Where others write and we're long dead
So far beyond this mortal frame,
So far beyond this clever game,
Please speak mine only in my name

Though of your heart I stole it.
Hearken now and scurry fast
The vineyard's son is home at last!

What alchemy transmutes the line
From new crushed grape to finest wine?

Andre's Questions

What follows on these next few pages are some of Andre's actual questions that he posited to the *Space Opera: Writers* community. The questions aren't presented in any particular order. They are loosely arranged chronologically with the most recent questions listed first.

***

Which do you prefer, "A story that drops you right into the mechanics of book explaining things as it goes along? Or, "A book that has a slow build up and explains everything in meticulous detail?"

Does real life politics drip into your narrative?

How many planets do you have in your galaxy? So far I have 38 planets but will only feature about 6-8 of them in my first book. I'm still hashing out the lore/history for them as well. My universe is massive. My book is a massive epic. It will take some time to finish it but I'm having so much fun writing it that makes time go by fast!

What would you do if a publisher gave you free reign to produce as many words as you wanted? I ask this because I just bought a book called "Words of Radiance" in paperback and it's 1300 pages long... I don't know what I could write that's that big. Do you?

I have a quick question about character names. I have a character named Auron in my book but since the name is iconic in the world of video games who will most likely be my targeted audience, should I stick with the name or change it. I'm attached to it but I don't want it to feel like I recycled an existing character.

How many of you have read "The Art of War?" And is it any good?

What are your favorite Starship names? Mine's "The Executioner." and. "The Liberator."

Have you ever written a "short story"? & How do you feel about "short stories" in general?

When you're writing your chapters do you prefer giving your chapter a title or not? Example: "Chapter One" or "Chapter One A Day of Reckoning."

How many of you write furiously when you're upset or angry? I'm breezing through this scene right now... straight pissed!!!

How many of you start your book backwards by writing the ending first, and the beginning last? I know how I want my first book to end, but I'm having trouble finding out how it should begin... What should I do?

How do you make up a calendar system in your

novel and how/what do you name it? I've been trying to get a calendar system that doesn't sound stupid for months!!!

Have any of you ever created a flow chart to plot out your story?

How do you approach "Character Arc" in your novel? I start out as fast as I can to show a flawed character that will be put through more conflict than your average citizen! By the end of the book my characters are going to be hardened and ready for the next battle.

Do you ever write dialog first then description later?

How many projects are you working on currently? Me, 3!

This is just an observation but during First Page Friday* a lot of critiques center around people saying, "Oh you shouldn't begin with an info dump" or "There's too much description." etc. I understand that but you do realize that some of your favorite books like "The Reality Dysfunction" "Leviathan Wakes" or "Ancillary Justice," start with info dumps and description. Have any of these beginnings turned you off or grabbed your attention from the first page? If so why/why not? (*Editor's note: First Page Friday is a tradition in Space Opera: Writers where we share the first page of a book we are working on to get feedback from other members of the group.)

285

As a writer how do you balance your marriage as you write your epic story? I'm trying my best and maybe I'm fu××ing up but I'm not trying to burn every bridge I cross... I just want to write the best book I know I'm capable of!

Nothing hurts more than when those closest to you don't take your writing/work serious... As a writer/aspiring writers what challenges have you had to face with trying to convince others that your writing is serious, and truly hard work?

Do you drink and write or no? I find my thoughts open up when I have a buzz but not drunk...

Are you a more character oriented writer or a more action oriented writer?

Do you ever feel like quitting as a writer?

Seriously how many characters do you have in your current WIP? Main Characters and Side Characters? I have almost 60 Characters, but many die, and some are on the chopping block! How about you?

In your novel or novels, who is your favorite character you enjoyed writing for the most?

How do you feel about swearing in books, and does your book have a shit load of swearing?

What is the problem with using adverbs? I would really like to understand more about it, because I see a lot of advice telling me to avoid them?

What is your most hated storyline/Character Arcs? Mines is seeing a character go through a psychiatric meltdown and thrown into a facility for telling their paranoid truth only to find out later that said character was right...That ticks me off everytime!!!

In your opinion, what country has the best sci-fi writing? U.S.A, The U.K, etc...

What are your top 5 favorite words? Mine are: Detritus, Gelid, Morose, Assimilation, and Egregious!

What form of currency do you use in your book? Credits, Light Shards, Gil, Yen, etc....

How many words is your first chapter? Mine's Unedited so far is 2,130 words... and I'm still writing it!

To damsel in distress, or not to damsel in distress? If/if not, then why?

Do you ever write about subjects you don't know well? I'm writing a gambling scene but know nothing past pulling down slots! I know a little poker but I'm not an expert! I'm freewriting the scene cause it's on my mind. I'll update it later...

Do you ever write by hand first and type it later? I've been doing that from the start and it's starting to pay off because I can see the errors as I'm typing up a scene or chapter, and can make the additional corrections as needed!

I love Sci-fi, but what attracted you to it? For me it was when my grandmother brought me the revised edition of Star Wars on vhs. I feel in love with it at the age of 8 or 9. Henceforth a nerd was born and I'd rather be a nerd over a jock anyday!!!

Do you all use one space to separate your paragraphs or two spaces? Or is their a special format for books to be typed in that I don't know about?

Do you use words like, "Ergh" and "Uggh" to show description of a grunt or in pain?

What are the most evil names for a God you can think of that isn't cliché? I kinda like Mordaath Silichus, or just Silichus... like or not?

Do you have any easter eggs in your book that only true nerds could put 2 and 2 together? Mines isn't really an easter egg, but I do have a laboratory called, "Laboratory 66," an ode to "Order 66!"

So I've been practicing my dialogue lately because I have not been impressed with what I've produced, but have you ever been disappointed at your scenes of dialogue? If so why? If not why? And what have you done to fix it?

When writing your prose do you ever reread your work and say, "This doesn't sound like it belongs in a book," or, "This doesn't sound like what I want my book to sound like?" If so what is your solution?

So my book is a Sci-fi/High Fantasy book and I have a character who is a God of darkness and I'm open to name changes. I have already changed the names of numerous characters, but I need the most evilest name you can think of to help me out. The characters name is "Mordaath" and as much as I like it to me it sounds too much like "Mordor." What are your opinions, and have you ever had an issue trying to find the right name while trying to be original in some aspect?

When writing do you ever speak your words out loud as you are writing them?

Are you a sadist when it comes to writing? I am. I want to put my characters in as much conflict as I can and watch them fight through the endless struggle of their joyrney.

What is your biggest "Pet Peeve," when it comes to writing? Mines is when I look up a word in the dictionary and then have to look up another word in order to find out what my original word means...Lol don't use a bigger word to explain what a smaller word means!!!

Do you write an individual synopsis for each of your VP characters? If so why? I do because it keeps me motivated and is a way to practice my synopsis writing, and how to integrate them into the story that makes them relevant and exciting!

How do you feel about putting the pronunciation of your character names in the beginning of your book? I feel I may have to because I have some pretty distinct names...

How do you prepare for an action scene? I like to draw a rough map of how and where the action will be taking place, and then write from after I complete the scene's outline.

I've been outlining my story for a while now and noticed that I do not have any female leads out of a possible 7 VP characters. Idk what to do because I think I need to put in a strong female VP. I'm not sexist but I wonder if I should include a female VP instead of numerous female supporting characters. What should I do? And have any of you experienced this situation, if so how did you deal with it?

When outlining do you practice sentence structure or do you just quickly scribble down what's on your mind? So what I'm doing is I scribble down quick notes and then when I go to outline them I take the time to practice sentence structure since I'm still a developing writer. Have any of you done that?

When writing an action scene do you ever notice how fast you begin to type? Lol I'm zooming through this scene and I didn't even know I could type this fast!

How many sub-plots do you have in your WIP? I have "2," that are only seen for a short period of time until book 2 comes around to flesh out the stories that will be part of the central plot.

How many scenes do you normally write for a chapter, and in what way do you go about ordering them? For me I'm just getting used to a Word Editor/Management Program called Ywriter, which is the poor mans Scrivener. (but free and amazing as well). So I save each scene individually and can swap them in and out with ease. I'm still learner though!

Would you ever consider being a co-author to a book? If so why or why not?

How bad was your first draft?

How much does religion play in your novel? Not necessarily having a sub-plot, but personally, how does it apply to your writing style?

How do you treat race, sexual orientation, and homophobic themes in your novel? Idk how I feel! As I was freewriting a moment ago the theme came up... help... How would you deal with it?

What are your feelings on writing/having a "Forward or Preface" In your novel or the novels you have read?

If there was one author you could emulate who would it be, and why? For me Steven Erickson writer of "The Malazan Series." Why, because I love the complex style he writes in. Yeah it could be hard because you have to check the dictionary a lot, but it's challenging and enjoyable for me because I'm learning new words while reading a rich story with a vibrant and beautifully descriptive world. It's up there with George RR. Martin and at times surpassing him if you read the entire series.

Authors' Bios

Drew A. Avera

Websites: https://www.drewavera.com
https://www.facebook.com/pg/authordrewavera

Bio: Drew is an active duty Navy veteran and science fiction writer. His best-selling series, *The Alorian Wars*, have sold thousands of copies worldwide.

Book: The Alorian Wars

We have an evil empire, a spaceship with a ragtag crew, and the lives of trillions in the balance as an intergalactic war spreads across the galaxy. Oh yeah, and we have space pirates!

Buy Link: http://smarturl.it/AlorianWars

Lloyd A. Behm II

Bio: Born and raised in Texas, he's done a bit of everything - civilian contractor in Iraq, volunteer fireman, warehouseman, mortician's assistant, newspaper opinion columnist, tech support, logistics coordination, poet, and even driven a bus for a while. A two time graduate of Southwest Texas State University, he spends his days writing Sci-Fi and Fantasy, painting miniatures, and watching his cats perform parkour.

Sean P. Chatterton

Website: http://www.seanpchatterton.co.uk

Bio: Sean has been a reader of Science Fiction and Fantasy since he could read. Being introduced at a young age to Tolkien's middle earth, E. E. "Doc" Smith's Lensman series, and Asimov's robots, amongst countless others, gave Sean an active imagination and a yearning for something more.

Now, as an adult, he works on internet marketing. Which pays the bills, but isn't what you can call world changing. The death of his older sister from cervical cancer a few years ago made him realise that his childhood ambition of being a writer would slip him by if he did not make serious efforts to make that dream come true.

It took him just one year to get his first short story published, and like the world famous grandfather of modern SF, Arthur C. Clarke, his first published short story was of a teleporter accident. This was sheer coincidence but one that Sean is very proud of. He now produces short stories on a regular basis and has had over twenty published stories to his credit. The first full length novel is on its way...

J. J. Clayborn

I don't necessarily believe the premise of the story I submitted for this anthology. But it always fun to try to think deeply about "the other side" of any position or idea. What would this be like? How would it really work? Why do I think what I think? I like to use my writing to explore those types of thoughts. And that's what I miss the most about Andre. He would ask the kinds of questions that really got you thinking; the kinds of questions that your brain would gnaw on for a while. My story in his memory attempts to honor that part of him. I hope that I've done him justice. You are greatly missed, my friend.

Websites:
https://www.facebook.com/jjclaybornauthor
www.jjclayborn.com

Bio: Johnathan J. Clayborn is an American author from Arizona. He has worked as a freelance writer producing magazine and web content. He runs Clayborn Press, a small publisher that publishes fiction and non-fiction electronically and in print. He writes non-fiction books on a variety of topics. Mostly these pertain to interests in learning or teaching people, or psychology. He holds a Master's of Science in Psychology and works in behavioral health. He also writes Science Fiction & Fantasy and Crime Fiction under the name J. J. Clayborn to differentiate from his non-fiction works.

Books:
Starsong Chronicles: Exodus
Damarien Tierney hasn't always had luck on his side. He was abandoned by his family, and just when things were starting to look up for him, his adoptive father was brutally murdered. He is forced to flee - to leave Earth completely before he suffers the same fate.

He finds an opportunity to save himself in the Exodus Project - a secret colonization effort that will take him farther from home than any human being has ever been. Soon he is exiled on an alien world with no way home and no idea what he's doing. Only his wits and his newfound friends can save him from dangers that he could never imagine, and old threats long-forgotten.

Buy Link:
https://www.amazon.com/dp/B01NBRDVE9

Skin Deep
Forest Ranger James Hutchinson likes things peaceful and quiet in his woods. But a small

asteroid impact has disturbed that peace. People around him have started acting strangely and James must investigate to uncover the truth, before it's too late.

This mystery-scifi-horror book will have you on the edge of your seat. It's a thrilling adventure that has been described as "Great, creepy fun".

Buy Link:

https://www.amazon.com/dp/B074HL51DX

Question of the Day
Cheryce Clayton

Websites:
https://sixpointpress.wordpress.com
https://www.facebook.com/TacomaZombieHunter/
https://www.facebook.com/cheryceclayton/
https://www. amazon.com/author/cheryceclayton

Bio: I was raised on the move; new schools, strange faces, swap meets, and skipping town before the bills came due.

My dad worked construction, always had a new plan, a new company, a new dream to be relayed until he convinced my mom to try again. He shared his Omni magazines with me and we snuck away to watch the latest movies together; he told me my heritage in off-hand comments and misplaced references.

Home was the places I recognized when we returned. Home was great grandpa's garden in the spring, and grandma's house in time for canning the garden; home was stories and barbecues at Ocean Shores, and camping by the Yakima River so the men could go hunting.

Recently, I was asked to be a part of a panel on indigenous creation stories and myths at the world science fiction convention, I agreed thinking that I love creation mythos and study them for pleasure.

So, I'm sitting on this panel with one other woman, she's an experienced and locally-loved storyteller. She opens up telling a beautiful and insightful story about how basket weaving came to man.

And I had the realization that the audience now expects me to tell them a story or two and not to discuss said stories. The microphone comes to me and I scan the room before saying: "Hi. I write literary zombie porn."

The truth is a deflection, it pushes away the need to say "I do not hold my family stories except in fragments gleaned as a child. My creation story is three parts forgotten and two parts yet unwritten. I'll know it when it finds me; I'll tell it when I'm whole."

http://zombpocalypse.cartoonistsleague.org/

I can be found on Facebook as cheryceclayton and my webcomic page is:
 TalesfromtheZombieApocalypse

Nathanial W. Cook

Website: https://poohsnickety.blogspot.com/

Bio: Nathanial W. Cook is a writer and cartoonist based in Salem, Massachusetts. There, he lives with his wife, author E.C. Hanlon, stepsons, and pets.

Book: His self-published novel, *Falling Into Fate*, is available from Amazon, and his flash fiction story, *"Invasive Species,"* was recently published by Allegory (http://www.allegoryezine.com). He enjoys things weird, obscure, and, often, super-cheesy.

Chad Dickhaut

Website:
https://www.facebook.com/groups/588947597942080/

Bio: A native of southern Illinois, Chad Dickhaut has been writing creatively since he entered a young authors contest in grade school (a time travel adventure which, alas, lost to a story about bunnies or something banal like that. Not that he's bitter about it, mind you). He has long been prone to visions of a grand multiverse, and has written a wide variety of science fiction and fantasy short stories and roleplaying game materials on an amateur basis in an attempt to make sense off it all. He took second place in the prestigious Facebook Space Opera: Writers group Fall 2016 flash fiction contest and has participated in nearly every other contest the group has sponsored. He currently lives in northern Indiana with his wife and three children.

Book: I am currently writing a space opera novel titled One Thing Leads to Another, a modern take on such genre classics as E.E. "Doc" Smith's Triplanetary and Isaac Asimov's Foundation. When Dunvan "Deuce" Piper, a Judicor for the

Triumvirate of Stellar Polities, accepted a contract to secure a person of interest and his contraband package, he had no idea he would find himself embroiled in Triumvarite political squabbles, fending off Martekk assassins, and crawling through Okd Empire ruins to find the information they need to circumvent a catastrophe of galactic proportions. But to be forced to do that alongside the irascible Jehera, another Judicor? That's adding insult to injury.

T. L. Evans

Bio: Tom was born in Vancouver B.C. Canada in 1966 to an American mother and a British father. He has a Doctorate in archaeology from the University of Oxford and for the better part of thirty years has lived and worked as an archaeologist throughout Europe, the US and bits of Latin America, specializing in concepts of spatial analysis, gender and identity. Most of his research has been focused on the peoples of Iron Age Europe, but his love of knowledge has led him to study a wide range of cultures from around the globe. In addition to his numerous (and boring) academic publications, Tom began writing science fiction, mysteries and espionage thrillers in 2006, and has both been writing his own work and ghost writing full time since 2009. He now lives with his wife and son in rural Connecticut.

Book: You can read get his first novel, *Strings on a Shadow Puppet*, at Amazon, Barns & Noble, and fine bookstores everywhere. His second novel, *The Traitor's Gambit* is nearing completion and will be available in books stores soon. "*Those Who Control the Question*" uses the same setting as these novels, but neither the characters nor the story line are directly connected.

Thomas A. Farmer

Andre was a person who always engaged our little community. Even more than his "QOTD" was his ability to look at something and say, "what next?" That always prompted me to look deeper into ideas and characters I was working with. This story is, in some ways, dedicated to that: it's part of a much larger tale about people who could not stop asking, "what next?"

Websites:

https://www.facebook.com/tafarmerauthor/
https://www.amazon.com/Thomas-A-Farmer/e/B01A436HFO/

Bio: Born to geeky parents and raised on a diet of Star Trek and Babylon 5, Thomas started writing at an early age, managing to keep the hobby alive long enough to make something of it. His favorite genre to read and write is Space Opera, though he's been known to dabble in other things here and there. When he isn't writing, Thomas also teaches fencing and HEMA.

Books:

I have a short story anthology coming up which should be the first in a series of shared-multiverse stories. Set in an impossible place known only as "*The Inn Between Worlds*," these stories weave together characters from all manner of places as each author puts his or her individual spin on things.

Bryan S. Glosemeyer

My contribution to this anthology is based loosely on my friend Andre's unfinished story. Andre always provided encouragement and unrivaled enthusiasm in times of doubt. His friendship will be deeply missed.

Website:
https://www.facebook.com/BryanSGlosemeyer/

Bio: Bryan S. Glosemeyer lives with his wife in San Francisco, CA, where he works in tech support and drinks too much coffee. "An Ending for Cole" in this anthology is his first published story. He is currently seeking representation for his debut novel, *Before the Shattered Gates of Heaven*, a space opera adventure.

Authors' Bios
Josh Hayes

Website:
https://www.joshhayeswriter.com/
https://www.keystrokemedium.com

Bio:
Hi, there! I hope you liked my little story "Salvation".

In addition to writing and having a full-time job, I also run a live interview show and podcast with fellow authors Scott Moon and Ralph Kern, Keystroke Medium. We talk with authors of all sorts, finding out what makes them tick, what excites them about their stories and connecting them with new readers. Please check us out at www.keystrokemedium.com.

I live in Kansas, with my beautiful wife Jamie, who supports my crazy ideas and ridiculous ambitions. When I'm not driving her crazy, I'm chasing my four children around the house. You can check out my website for more on my books and writing at: www.joshhayeswriter.com

Cheryl S. Mackey

Websites:
twitter: @CSMACKEY_AUTHOR
www.facebook.com/writezalot
Instagram: csmackey_author
www.cherylsmackey-author.com

Bio: Cheryl lives in Southern California with her adorable hubby and 2 sons. She works as a Document Specialist with a mortgage company during the day and a writer during the night!

She has a MFA in Creative Writing and enjoy games, reading and, of course, writing. She grows tall bearded irises and avidly listen to trailer music by groups like Audiomachine, Two Steps from Hell, and Future World Music. She currently has a flash fiction story published online at The Prompt Magazine as well as 3 fantasy books published.

Her favorite genre to write and read is YA Fantasy closely followed by Science Fiction and Space Opera.

R. A. McCandless

Andre Polk was the kind of writer that every author should try to find. He was kind and patient and genuinely curious. His Question of the Day (QOTD) posts always made you stop, think, and consider—exactly the kind that prompt lengthy discussions, pushing for deeper thought and consideration. There was not one single QOTD from Andre that prompted the following story— several of them came together, along with the various discussions, to culminate in the tale of Oss and his tech implants. The highest praise any author can give to another is to thank them for the inspiration to create. Thank you, Andre Polk. Thank you.

Websites:
http://www.highlandrogue.blogspot.com/
Twitter: https://twitter.com/RobRoyMcCandles
https://www.facebook.com/RobroyMccandless
http://robroymccandless.wix.com/ramccandless

Bio: R.A. McCandless has been a writer both professionally and creatively for over two decades. He was born under a wandering star that led to a degree in Communication and English with a focus on creative writing. He's the author of the urban fantasy *Tears of Heaven,* winner of the 2014 Best Science Fiction and Fantasy Preditors & Editors Reader's Poll and a 2015 EPIC eBook finalist, and *Hell Becomes Her*. His shorts have appeared in *In Shambles* (with Kevin J. Anderson), *Nine Heroes*, and *Gears, Gadgets, and Steam*. He continues to research and write historical and genre fiction, battle sprinklers, and play with his three boys.

Book: Tears of Heaven

A child of angels and humans, Del is a sarcastic, fast-talking, dangerous, and unpredictable demon hunter. She and her partner Marrin take their orders directly from the angel Ahadiel. They obey, or they'll be destroyed. It's not the job Del wants, but it's the job she has.

Buy Link:

https://www.amazon.com/dp/B073Y9V9M6/

Scott McGlasson

Websites:
https://www.facebook.com/authorscottmcglasson/
Twitter: https://twitter.com/Scott__M
https://plus.google.com/u/0/b/1059848152319298
42080/
www.scottmcglasson.net

Bio: Scott McGlasson is the author of *Nock* – the winning entry in the Infected Books *Year of the Zombie* Pitch and Page competition - and *Minimum Safe Distance* from the *Explorations: War* anthology.

He is a veteran of both the US Air Force and rock radio, somehow ending up with a career in logistics. Scott currently lives in St Louis, Missouri USA with his wife, Monica, and has two sons, Nicholas and Trip, and two daughters, Evelyn and Emily.

Sales links:
Nock - A post-apocalyptic zombie short story.
https://www.amazon.com/dp/B01M1A740S

Explorations: War - Minimum Safe Distance - a thrilling mil-sci story in an anthology.
https://www.amazon.com/dp/1974126080

B. J. Muntain

Website: www.bjmuntain.com

Bio: BJ Muntain likes to write fun, adventurous stories with some mystery – because what is life without mystery?

G. Michael Rapp

Website:
https://www.facebook.com/gregoryrappauthor/

Bio: Gregory Rapp was born in Grand Forks, North Dakota, but he was raised in and around the San Juan Mountains of southern Colorado. He loves to write fiction and nonfiction, focusing on technology, politics, and cultural change. Greg has been featured in Space Opera: Writers contest anthologies and has won several awards for his stories featured in ENMU's official literary journal, El Portal.

Greg Rapp is currently working on a novel tentatively titled *Rat Box*, which focuses on politics, race, economics, material culture, and a multi-causal apocalypse.

R. T. Romero

Website: https://www.facebook.com/RTRpub/

Bio: Richard Romero was born in California, raised just east of Sacramento, and is now living in Philadelphia. Richard is a graduate of Saint Mary's College of California, with graduate coursework at Western Carolina University and Villanova. He is retired from Federal Service (United States), and is currently engaged in writing the third and final novel in the Modulus series.

Richard is father to three adults, and is a proud grandfather. When not writing, he paints in oils, composes music, and he loves to cook.

Books:
Modulus, Vol 1 of the Modulus series (Science Fiction)
Far Modulus, Vol 2 of the Modulus series (Science Fiction)
Barefoot in the Temple (Poetry)
Volume 3 of the Modulus series, tentatively titled *Moduli Beyond* should be in print in December, 2017.

M. D. Thalmann

Websites:

https://www.facebook.com/mdthalmann/

https://mdthalmann.com/

Bio: M.D. (Michael Dirk) Thalmann, a novelist and freelance journalist specializing in satire and science fiction, lives in Phoenix, Arizona with his wife, children, and ornery cats, reads too much and sleeps too little. He has a couple dogs, too, but doesn't like to mention them due to the slippers one of them ate in 2009, which neither has yet fessed up to. He is originally from Little Rock, Arkansas and has been living in the desert since 2004 when he took the novel Fear and Loathing in Las Vegas entirely too serious and moved on a lark. He has been into journalism in one fashion or another and writing fiction and so on since he was ten years old or so and has gotten at least 20% better since that time. Today M.D. writes freelance and does columns for a few magazines here and there while working on his various novels and cursing his cats.

M.D. Thalmann is influenced by Kurt Vonnegut Jr., Philip K. Dick, Carl Hiaasen, and (obviously) Hunter S. Thompson. His novels, *The 13 Lives of a Television Repair Man*, and, *Static-Redux*, are currently available. Find more of his work at www.mdthalmann.com

Books:

The 13 Lives of a Television Repairman:
https://www.amazon.com/dp/B00UZFKAVY/

Static: https://t.co/d9aVg1qEYX

Dimly, Through Glass:
https://www.amazon.com/dp/B00FK28FE6/

Jeffrey Yorio

Bio: I live in Spencerport, NY, outside of Rochester. I'm 57 years old and have been writing for about 4 years. My educational background has in it a BS in Education and an MS in Operations Management. I am married with three children and a pomeranian that was there one night when I got home.

Book: I am currently working on a vampire book; *Sunndowners: Vampires are only Human.*

Zeprhin Ivano is a vampire hunter, track down and kill those that go ferral. To protect their secret and one of the very best at his job. Unfortunatley, his next job is to track his grandmother down.

Question of the Day
Jo Zebedee

Website: www.jozebedee.com

Bio: Jo writes science fiction and fantasy either in her space opera world of Abendau or on the streets of her native Northern Ireland. Her work is characterised by fast pace and diverse, rich, characters.

She can be followed on twitter @jozebwrites and on her website.

She is bribable with cake and fizzy wine.

Book: *Inish Carraig: An Alien Invasion Novel*
The alien invasion is over. Humanity lost.

In Belfast, John Dray protects his younger siblings by working for the local hard man. Set up, he's sent to the formidable alien prison, Inish Carraig, a fate Henry Carter, the policeman assigned to John, can't stop.

Once there, John discovers a plot which threatens Earth and everyone he loves. To reveal it, he has to get out and there is only one person who can help.

Authors' Bios

A bestseller in Alien Invasion, Inish Carraig is an original science fiction novel 'blessed with an entirely novel storyline' -Alexander Stevenson

'A thoughtful and intelligent writer' - Allen Stroud, British Science Fiction Association reviewer

An exceptional novel. The pace is incredible with hard hitting characters and a powerful plot.' - Sffchronices.com

'Tight and dramatic throughout.' -Sfbook.com

'Onto my pile of best novels of the year.' -JLDobias, author of the Cripple Mode series.

https://www.amazon.co.uk/dp/B012782E0G/

Other Books by Clayborn Press

Science Fiction:
Starsong Chronicles: Exodus – JJ Clayborn
Lost & Stranded – Dave Henry (Coming in 2018)
Starsong Chronicles: Planetside (Coming in 2018)

Crime Fiction:
The Fall – JJ Clayborn (Winter 2017)

Horror/Thriller:
Skin Deep – JJ Clayborn

Follow us on Facebook!
Facebook.com/ClaybornPressBooks

Made in the USA
Lexington, KY
06 October 2017